Escape to
EVERLY MANOR

OTHER BOOKS AND AUDIOBOOKS
BY CHALON LINTON:

An Inconvenient Romance

"Christmas Grace" in *Christmas Grace*

A Tangled Inheritance

"A Christmas Courting" in *A Christmas Courting*

Escape to
EVERLY MANOR

A Regency Romance by
CHALON LINTON

Covenant Communications, Inc.

Cover image: *Woman Wearing Cloak in Forest* © Susan Fox / Trevillion Images

Cover design copyright © 2019 by Covenant Communications, Inc.

Published by Covenant Communications, Inc.
American Fork, Utah

Printed in the United States of America
First Printing: February 2019

25 24 23 22 21 20 19   10 9 8 7 6 5 4 3 2

ISBN 978-1-52440-837-4

To siblings everywhere, but especially mine. And to Mom and Dad, who took me on adventures where I could dream of life in an abandoned cabin.

Acknowledgments

THE LAST THREE YEARS HAVE been the best sort of adventure. Writing has become my escape, and I am forever grateful for the team that helps polish and beautify the words I type. Each story begins with a single idea, and this one is owed to Gertrude Chandler Warner for allowing the Alden children to find an abandoned boxcar.

Kami Hancock is fabulous! She patiently explains grammar dos and don'ts again and again and helps me focus on telling a story the best way possible. She can also make me laugh via email on a regular basis. Stephanie Lacy works her magic in marketing to share my stories with readers, and knowing she does this for so many authors constantly amazes me. Jackie Langlois and Michelle Fryer created this beautiful cover, altering details to fit my story and make me happy. To the entire Covenant team—thank you for your talents, your support, and your faith in me.

Before my manuscript ever reaches my publisher, four lovely ladies beta read my work. Thank you, Melissa, Jen, Kodie, and Laura. You are unique, you are honest, and each of you is a true friend.

Thank you to my readers, who beyond the team above, make this journey possible.

And of course, I am forever in love with my forever family; they love me, support me, and vacuum the floors and make dinners so I can meet my deadlines. Hugs to each of my four children and an extra-large smooch to my husband. He will always be my right-hand man, my champion, and my best friend.

Chapter 1

England, 1813

ELIZABETH STAFFORD WOULD NOT QUIT. Her fortitude was vital if she had any hope of keeping her brother, Thomas, from being shipped off to Ipswich to join the crew of the merchant vessel the *Vendetta*. Lizzy had heard stories of the unjust beatings, the perilous jobs given to young boys, and the despicable conditions that existed on such a ship. Beyond that, Thomas would have difficulty surviving the demands associated with life at sea. He was, after all, but nine years old.

Thomas was Lizzy's half-brother and junior by ten years. Her own mother had passed away when she was eight. Her father mourned for two years before Miss Esther Gale had captured his attention and they'd married. Lizzy's stepmother had treated her kindly, and theirs had been a close-knit family. Memories of sleigh rides, laughter, and joy cycled through Lizzy's mind. Those memories and Thomas were all she had now.

Lizzy wondered, for the hundredth time, why her father and stepmother had ventured from Town that fateful day four months ago. Why did they not let the storm pass and the roads clear before attempting to return home? Surely Thomas would have understood their delay of a day or two in celebrating his birthday. Any child would agree that having one's parents arrive a day late was preferable to having them arrive in a coffin.

Lizzy decided to tell Thomas of his situation when she met him in the nursery for lessons. Rather than review Latin vocabulary, Lizzy suggested they go for a walk. After wandering through the herb garden, she led Thomas on the path to the orchard, far enough into the copse of trees to be hidden from the house. She knelt down and took Thomas's hands in her own.

"I've something very important to tell you," Lizzy said. Thomas scrunched his brow but remained quiet. "You know things have been different since Uncle Cline has arrived at Downey Place."

"You mean it's grown colder?" Thomas asked.

"Yes, it has." Lizzy rubbed her hands up and down Thomas's arms. "I'm afraid that's not bound to change soon." Thomas stood like a statue, waiting for his sister to say more. "Uncle has decided to send you away." Thomas's shoulders sagged. "Don't worry. I have a plan," Lizzy said.

"A plan?"

"Yes." Lizzy hoped her smile conveyed more confidence than she felt.

"What is it?" Thomas asked.

"I can't tell you."

"Why not, Lizzy? That's not fair."

Lizzy squeezed Thomas's hand in her own. "Listen to me, Thomas. Uncle is going to tell you all of the arrangements tonight. He wants you to work on a merchant ship and help the captain and the sailors."

Thomas's brow pinched together. "I don't want to work on a ship."

"I understand, but you must play along. You must make Uncle believe you are agreeable to the idea, and then you must trust me to take care of the rest."

"How?"

"I'm still working out the details. Just know I plan to ride in the carriage with you to Ipswich, and I will not allow you to set foot on that ship."

Thomas blinked and hung his head. "I don't want to be a sailor."

Lizzy placed her fingers under his chin and lifted his face to hers. "I know. But can you pretend for a few days? Imagine you are going to become a pirate, like we read about in your storybook. Can you do that?"

Thomas shrugged.

"Thomas." Lizzy fixed him with a stern glare. "You must play along. I won't let you board that ship, but I can't do this alone. I need you to be brave."

Thomas stared at his sister for a long moment. "I can do it, Lizzy. I'll be brave."

Lizzy realized Thomas had grown to look like a miniature version of their father. Thomas's blue eyes matched his father's and Uncle Cline's and punctuated the soft lines of his face. His trusting countenance lacked the strength their father had possessed, but Lizzy loved his naivety. Her own eyes were almost golden, ringed in black and flecked with darker brown. She had inherited her eyes from her mother, and Lizzy considered them her best feature. Her light-brown hair matched Thomas's, and she had a handful of freckles scattered across the bridge of her nose.

Lizzy pulled her brother into her arms, inhaling the sweaty warmth of Thomas's hair. "There's a good boy. Now, you must convince Uncle you are excited to go to sea."

Thomas's lips pulled sideways. "Like a pirate?"

"That's right." Lizzy reached over and mussed his hair. "Like a pirate."

That night at dinner Lizzy retained her mask of compunction and granted her uncle ideal responses. She hoped to ask Uncle if she might escort Thomas to the docks at Ipswich. Thomas was to leave in two days' time. Lizzy planned for her and Thomas to run away along the route. The more miles between Downey Place and their escape, the better.

Lizzy had witnessed Uncle's temper. She would never forget the burning red fury in Uncle's eyes when he had backhanded her. Mr. Palmer, her father's longtime solicitor, had left shortly after Uncle's arrival, and Uncle Cline had hired a new man of business, Mr. Monroe. The night Mr. Monroe read the will, Uncle had demanded Lizzy turn over her mother's sapphires. She had refused to tell him where she'd hidden them—Father had promised the gemstones would one day belong to her. Aside from a handful of memories, they were the only connection Lizzy had to her birthmother—but the will stated otherwise. The document gave Uncle Cline everything: guardianship of herself and Thomas and ownership of the estate, including the sapphires.

When the new solicitor left, Uncle had demanded the jewels. Lizzy had protested, insisting there was some mistake—Father had promised—and then Uncle lost his temper. He'd grabbed Lizzy by the shoulders, shaking her fiercely as her teeth knocked together, before his hand connected with her cheek. Lizzy's vision had turned from grey to black. Through the darkness she'd heard her butler, Mr. Clarke's, voice. She did not remember his words—only that Uncle had tossed her onto the couch and stormed from the room. Lizzy had clamped her eyes closed, retreating to a dark corner of her consciousness until she could awaken from the awful dream.

Mr. Clarke had cleared his throat and laid a warm hand upon Lizzy's back. Marlow, her maid, had then appeared, whispering soothing refrains, and with Mr. Clarke's assistance, the two had carried Lizzy to her room and tucked her into bed. The next morning Lizzy had discovered the jewels were no longer in their hiding place beneath her wardrobe, and the events of that night were never discussed again.

Lizzy pushed the vile memory from her mind and forced a wide smile. She sat on the sofa in the drawing room and turned to Uncle Cline's mistress. "Have you ever seen the sea, Miss Masterson?"

The redhead harrumphed. "Of course."

"I've only been once, many years ago," Lizzy said.

Miss Masterson looked at her askance and moved her eyes in the direction of the door. Lizzy knew her presence was not wanted; Marlow had related the rumors from the servants in regards to Miss Masterson and Uncle Cline. But tonight Lizzy was on a mission.

She sat straight-backed and clasped her hands in her lap. "Uncle? Would you consider allowing me to escort Thomas to his ship?"

Uncle lowered the paper he was reading. His eyes narrowed. "Why would you want to ride in a carriage for three days, just to turn around and come back home?"

"Well, it's highly likely Thomas will fall in love with the ocean and never wish to return to Downey Place. Or I could very well be wed by the time Thomas completes his service, and circumstances may not allow me to travel to see him." Lizzy clasped her hands against her chest. "I had hoped to spend just a little more time with him."

Miss Masterson snickered. "Wed? You?"

Instead of the glare Lizzy wanted to give, she fluttered her eyelashes and offered a dreamy sigh. "I won't be out of mourning until my twentieth birthday. Would it be conceivable to have a Season at that time?" Lizzy turned to Miss Masterson. "You've experienced a Season, Miss Masterson. What is your opinion?"

Miss Masterson looked over Lizzy's personage. "You might be able to snag a fortune hunter or an old bachelor seeking an heir." Miss Masterson's lips twisted in amusement.

"Well . . . that is something, I suppose." Lizzy's hands fell to her lap.

Uncle folded his paper in half and set it aside. "Not to worry, niece. I have a solution." Miss Masterson adjusted her posture like a cat poised to pounce on its prey, and Uncle Cline continued. "I've recently met with Mr. Simpkin, and he has agreed to accept your hand."

Lizzy's blood turned to ice. Mr. Rudyard Simpkin was the last person on earth she could ever marry. He was boorish, demanding, full of his own self-importance, and Lizzy's senior by at least twenty-five years. She would rather become a cabin boy herself than become affianced to such a man. But, first and foremost, Lizzy needed to take care of Thomas.

Lizzy's lungs seared in pain as she swallowed past the bile in her throat and struggled to maintain her smile. "Are you certain he will have me?"

"Quite." A feral grimace smeared Uncle's otherwise handsome features. "As executor of your dowry and the one who must consent to your marriage, I've met with Simpkin and he is agreeable to my terms."

"It does sound like an ideal arrangement." Lizzy's stomach hurt.

"Indeed." Uncle Cline smirked.

Lizzy mustered every theatrical talent within her. She had to convince her uncle to send her to Ipswich. She clapped her hands. "It's Providence! I can escort Thomas to sea and get a glimpse of the *Vendetta*. And when"— she held up a single finger—"or if, he returns, I will be a married woman, mistress of my own household." She tipped her head sideways and fluttered her eyelashes some more. "May I please go to Ipswich, Uncle Cline?"

With a grunt Uncle answered, "There's no harm in it, I suppose. I'll talk to Simpkin and arrange for you to be wed upon your return."

"Splendid." Lizzy clasped her hands together tightly. "It's so many changes. I can hardly wait."

Chapter 2

The following morning Lizzy wandered through the kitchen and pocketed two warm rolls.

"Miss Stafford, may I be of assistance?" Clarke stood behind Lizzy with his hands clasped behind his back.

Of all the servants, Clarke knew the comings and goings of Downey Place the best. "Actually you can." Lizzy raised her chin a notch.

"Yes?" Clarke tried to push down his smile.

"Is there somewhere private we may speak?" Lizzy asked.

Clarke's smile fell. "Of course." He led Lizzy through the kitchen into the room that served as Clarke's office. "Miss Stafford," Clarke began, but Lizzy held up a hand to stop him.

"Does Uncle still keep my mother's jewels locked in a trunk beneath his bed?" Lizzy asked.

Clarke's eyes narrowed. "Yes."

"Is this where you keep your keys?" Lizzy asked casually as she looked around the small quarters.

Clarke stood, unblinking, and this time did not answer her question. Lizzy glanced at the open door then walked over and pushed it closed.

"Perhaps after dinner you could leave your keys here in your desk drawer." Lizzy hoped Clarke's loyalty to her father would extend to her as well. He had been the Stafford family butler for as long as Lizzy could remember. Lizzy considered him to be fair and level-headed, and she would forever be indebted to him for rescuing her the night Uncle had struck her.

"Miss Stafford?" The concern in his eyes melted Lizzy's resolve.

She ran forward and grabbed his hands in her own. "Please don't ask me anymore, Clarke. You know enough to realize the change at hand. I don't want to jeopardize your position. All I ask is that you leave the keys in the drawer, and when you return in the morning, they will be in precisely the same location."

Clarke's head fell forward the slightest bit. It was all the confirmation Lizzy needed. She squeezed his hands. "Thank you," she said and slipped out the door.

Lizzy spent the rest of the day planning. She rolled and rerolled her clothes, along with a shirt and a pair of trousers for Thomas. While she planned to take her mother's jewels, Lizzy hoped she would not become desperate enough to have to sell them. Her father had been generous with her allowance. Lizzy had never been a spendthrift and had accumulated a good amount of pin money, but her knowledge of economics was limited to the price of ribbon. She had no idea how much it would cost for her and Thomas to survive on their own.

Her preparations exhausted her, but after dinner she lingered a little longer than normal to express excitement for Thomas's adventure and gratitude for Uncle's generosity. She kept her comments slightly subdued, lest Uncle detect her ruse.

After her second theatrical yawn, Lizzy declared she could not decide whether or not she would be able to sleep a wink. Uncle Cline rolled his eyes. "It's all so exciting, is it not?" With her faux smile, Lizzy curtsied to the room in general and swept upstairs.

Once Marlow completed her ministrations Lizzy dismissed her and waited near the bedroom door, pressing her ear against the wood. After counting to one hundred, she deftly turned the handle and opened the door to listen again. Lizzy's heart beat wildly in her chest, but she could not turn back now. Uncle had scheduled their departure on the earliest coach the next morning. Lizzy had to retrieve her mother's jewelry tonight.

On tiptoes she moved soundlessly down the servants' staircase, pausing again at the bottom to listen for movement. A light snore sounded from near the fireplace, and Lizzy peeked around the corner to see one of the kitchen boys curled up near the hearth. She turned the corner and pushed open the door to Clarke's office. Lizzy quickly slipped inside, drawing a breath of relief.

She hoped Miss Masterson would distract her uncle long enough for her to complete her filching, for she could scarce imagine what punishment Uncle Cline would inflict for what she was about to do. With another steeling breath, Lizzy moved to Clarke's desk and opened the drawer, intending to retrieve the key to the trunk hiding the sapphires. However, when she pulled the drawer wide, her heart stopped beating altogether. Sitting there, in a swath of blue velvet, were her mother's jewels.

How had Clarke known? Lizzy didn't want to involve anyone else. Would her uncle suspect the butler? Lizzy had planned to remove the key to the trunk from Clarke's set so Uncle could not accuse the man.

A shuffling sounded outside the office door. Lizzy's gut clenched. She scooped up the sapphires, tucking them into the reticule she'd brought along to transport the jewels back to her room. Lizzy let the arm holding the bag fall to her side, pressing it into the folds of her robe, and left the office without bothering to close the desk drawer. When she rounded the corner of the hallway, she collided with Clarke's broad chest.

"Oh, Clarke." Lizzy's heartbeat sped. "I . . . I wasn't expecting you."

Clarke stood silently for a long while. Lizzy's every limb quaked, though she tried valiantly to control the tremors. "Did you find everything you needed, Miss Stafford?" Clarke asked.

"Yes, but . . ." Lizzy halted her words, wishing to avoid any incrimination in word or deed. "Yes, thank you."

Clarke's face remained stoic. "Do you require any further assistance?"

"No." Lizzy allowed herself a small smile. Amid the turmoil churning through her, the thought of an ally brought immense comfort. "I believe things are properly settled for Thomas and me to depart in the morning."

"It's been a pleasure, Miss Stafford." Clarke bowed his head. "I wish you safe travels."

Lizzy hurried up the back staircase to her bedchamber. She knew she would not sleep, so she lay in bed concocting multiple outlandish escape plans, including a scenario in which the coachman neglected to stop and change horses, so her and Thomas were forced to leap from the moving carriage. Morning could not arrive soon enough.

When trickles of sunlight lit the sky, Marlow appeared to help Lizzy dress. Lizzy sent her to clean an imagined stain from her underskirt and, in Marlow's absence, tucked the precious sapphires into her stays and slipped on a different underskirt. She then donned her dark-grey traveling dress and turned every direction in the mirror to determine if the hidden treasure could be detected. When Marlow finally reappeared and commented only that Lizzy should have waited for her, Lizzy simply smiled and explained she was anxious to get on with the day. Marlow tended her hair, topped her tresses with a plain bonnet, and then wrapped Lizzy in a dark-blue cloak. Instead of calling for a servant to fetch her bag, Lizzy carried it herself, careful not to knock the corners where she'd stashed her pilfered food.

As they settled into the carriage, Thomas's eyes continuously darted towards his sister. He managed a halfhearted show of excitement for Uncle Cline's sake. While Uncle appeared only half dressed to see them off, Lizzy considered it a rather magnanimous gesture on his part that he chose to appear at all. His presence did add a level of trepidation to her actions. It wasn't until the carriage pulled onto the main road that Lizzy dared inhale a full breath.

Thomas, too, seemed lighter, happier, once they reached the open road. "So, tell me, Lizzy, what is your plan?"

Lizzy shook her head and pressed a finger to her lips. *Not yet!* she mouthed to her brother before striking up another topic. "We will get to have an adventure before you even reach the *Vendetta*. Won't that be fun?"

Thomas frowned. A footman rode with the coachman on the bench, and while it was unlikely they could hear the conversation, Lizzy refused to risk any mistakes when freedom loomed near.

Uncle had granted use of Father's carriage only to transport the siblings to the Greendale Inn, where they were scheduled to catch the coach to Ipswich. There the footman opened the door, let down the step, and then assisted Lizzy from the carriage.

"Safe journey," the coachman called from his seat, and Lizzy reciprocated with a wave and a smile. Then she watched the footman unload not only Thomas's trunk from the box but another bag as well.

"What is that?" Lizzy asked the footman.

"'Tis my items, miss," he answered.

"Your items?"

"Yes, miss." The man shifted awkwardly on his feet. The reins whipped across the horses' backs, and the carriage moved to return to Downey Place.

"Wait!" Lizzy cried. She looked frantically at the black-haired footman. "You're going to be left behind."

The footman gave a lopsided grin. "'Tis only a four-mile walk from Tolford to Downey Place, but my instructions are to stay here with you."

"To make sure we meet up with the coach?" Lizzy asked.

"No, miss. Mr. Stafford has instructed me to escort Master Thomas to the *Vendetta* and then return to Downey Place with you." The footman straightened as if proud to be tasked with such responsibility.

Lizzy's temper rose. "Did he now?"

"Yes, miss." The footman sputtered his confused reply.

"Very well," Lizzy spat as she grabbed Thomas's hand and walked towards a set of benches outside the inn.

"May I carry your bag, Miss Stafford?" the footman asked.

"No, you may not."

Thomas's eyes swept over his sister's face, and his lips pressed together as she pulled him to sit beside her on the worn wood. Lizzy could not help but be cross with the footman. With his presence muddling her plans and the discomfort of the jewels pressed into her flesh, she was in a sour mood.

Thankfully they did not have to wait long for the coach to arrive. The footman secured the trunk, and Lizzy touched his arm. "I apologize for my behavior earlier. I was not told you would be traveling with us and realize you are only doing your duty. However, I must wonder why Uncle did not tell me you would be coming."

"I can't rightly say, miss. I didn't know myself 'til yesterday. Mr. Clarke told me Mr. Stafford asked who was the most trustworthy of the footmen 'cause he had a special task for him. Mr. Clarke was kind enough to refer me." The young man raised his chin a notch. "Then Mr. Stafford asked me himself if I'd be inclined to come along. O' course, I'd be a fool to turn down Mr. Stafford, and now I get a chance to see the ocean."

Lizzy's heart lifted knowing that while the young footman believed Mr. Stafford had selected him, the reality was that Clarke had chosen him for the task.

"What is your name?" she asked the footman.

"Henry Buford, miss."

"It will be a pleasure to have you along," Lizzy fibbed.

Lizzy helped Thomas into the carriage, and then Henry assisted her before hopping up to ride on the box with the coachman. For the first hour Lizzy and Thomas enjoyed the comfort of an entire bench to themselves. After two more stops, however, Lizzy held both her bag and Thomas on her lap. She'd removed her cloak, but the heat and smell of sweat, combined with the discomfort of the jewels pressing against her bosom, made time pass unbearably slowly.

The siblings alighted from the carriage only once, when the coach changed horses. Lizzy ordered a quick meal at the inn and pushed Thomas to eat quickly to ensure they could leave when the coach was ready.

They continued on, squeezing close on the cramped bench as dusk settled over the horizon. Once the sky was completely black, the coachman stopped at a brightly lit inn. The majority of occupants exited the carriage, content to enjoy a meal, pay for a bed, and continue their journey in the morning. The coachman informed those who remained that there would be two more stops that evening. Lizzy told Thomas they would remain in the carriage until the next inn, having overheard the other passenger state he would continue for the duration, as his grandfather was gravely ill and he hoped to reach his destination as soon as possible.

They stopped at an inn named the Featherbrained Fowl, but when Lizzy met with the proprietor, he immediately proved to be a kind and competent man. Lizzy secured a meal for her party and two rooms, one for Henry and one for her and Thomas to share. A willowy woman brought them warm stew and corn muffins, and as she poured their drinks, Lizzy asked her the name of the village.

"This here's Hodgly Briar. A right fine place," she said with a genuine smile.

"Is that so?" Lizzy asked.

"I swear it, miss." The woman held the pitcher against her hip. "Will you be needin' anything else?"

"No, thank you," Lizzy said. Thomas lifted pleading eyes from his bowl and stared at his sister. Lizzy laughed. "Perhaps some more stew. It seems your cooking has convinced my brother that Hodgly Briar is heaven itself."

The woman laughed. "Just wait until morning. My pancakes are famous for miles around."

It wasn't until Lizzy locked the door of the room she shared with Thomas that she confided her plan. "Do you think we could be happy in a place like Hodgly Briar?" she asked and patted the bed next to where she sat.

"Really?" Thomas walked over. "You mean I don't have to be a cabin boy?"

Lizzy pulled Thomas into her chest, and his thin arms wrapped around her middle. "No. No. I would never allow it."

Thomas pulled back with a grin. "I know, but when we got in the carriage, I got scared."

Lizzy stroked his hair. "I'm sorry, Thomas. I couldn't tell you before, but I can tell you now."

Thomas eagerly listened to Lizzy's explanation. Then she made him repeat everything back to ensure there would be no confusion in the morning. Lizzy grabbed a few extra items from Thomas's trunk and stashed them in her bag before she tucked him in. Before long his breathing evened, and Lizzy envied his sleep. She lay in the bed, staring at the ceiling and waiting for the rooster to crow.

Chapter 3

DESPITE HER DETERMINATION TO ALLOW Thomas a fitful sleep, Lizzy tossed and turned for hours. Giving in, she finally rose and loosened her stays to retrieve the sapphires. Her skin was numb and marked from the jewels, and Lizzy was more than happy to relocate them to her reticule.

When the first whispers of light floated through the window, Lizzy shook Thomas awake and made him tell her the plan again. They dressed and repacked, and Lizzy sent Thomas to ensure Henry was awake.

The thin, happy woman who had served them the previous evening greeted them with a plentiful serving of scrumptious pancakes. As Lizzy, Thomas, and Henry finished their meal, a carriage sounded outside. Thomas glanced at Lizzy, and she gave a small nod.

"Henry, would you please retrieve Thomas's trunk from our room?" Lizzy asked.

Henry took a final bite, licked his lips, and left to comply with the request. As soon as he disappeared up the stairs, Lizzy grabbed her prepared bag; pulled on her cloak, bonnet, and gloves; and rushed outside with Thomas. The coachman, a burly man who introduced himself as Mr. Grumpkin, responded kindly as Lizzy presented the traveling papers for the group. There were only three other passengers on this leg of the journey. Mr. Grumpkin agreed to help Henry secure the trunk, and then they would be off.

Lizzy bent down and buttoned Thomas's jacket, turning up his collar to offer a bit more protection from the crisp morning. She stood and placed a hand on her brother's back then in a loud voice said, "Go get situated in the carriage, Thomas. I'll be along shortly."

Thomas's eyes grew wide, and he began to shake his head in earnest.

"Go," Lizzy whispered softly.

Thomas stepped away from Mr. Grumpkin as Lizzy turned to address the man again. While his sister feigned a question about the route and timeline of their journey, Thomas walked past the door of the carriage and hurried around the side of the inn.

Within seconds Henry appeared with the trunk, and with the help of the coachman, he secured it to the rear of the carriage.

"Why don't you keep track of our papers since you will be riding alongside the coachman." Lizzy passed the traveling papers to Henry.

"You sure, miss?" Henry asked.

Lizzy waved away his question. "It's best if you take care of it; you are our escort." While she hated setting Henry up for failure, it had to be done. "And here's some food for the journey. It's all we have, so don't open it for several hours. That should be four stops; is that right, Mr. Grumpkin?"

The man gave a single nod. Beyond the food Lizzy had included a letter apologizing to Henry for abandoning him to Uncle's wrath. She did not want Henry to be held accountable and wrote the sad truth, that he would soon find himself unemployed. She asked him to delay reporting their absence to Uncle Cline for as long as possible. As additional recompense, she included a letter of recommendation and five pounds, which she hated to part with, but in good conscience she could not give Henry any less.

Lizzy climbed inside the carriage and nodded a greeting to the other passengers before beginning her performance. She slowly counted to five in her head then touched her hands to her stomach. After another count of five, she moaned as if in pain and shared a look of concern with the woman seated across from her. The carriage shifted as someone climbed atop the box. Time was limited.

"I'm afraid breakfast did not settle well. Perhaps I'll await the next carriage," she proclaimed to the group at large, and without waiting for an offer of assistance, Lizzy opened the carriage door and jumped down from the opening with her bag in hand. She hurried around the rear of the carriage, hoping if anyone watched they would assume she was nauseous and searching for a place to vomit.

Once she rounded the corner of the inn, Lizzy pressed her back against the weatherworn wood. Her heartbeat sounded in her ears, and she held her breath, waiting for some sign the carriage had continued its journey. Birdcall rang from the trees, and muffled voices sounded through the wall.

What was taking so long? Did someone inform the coachman she'd left? Did Henry remove himself from the carriage? Were they looking for her, even now?

Lizzy pressed her eyes closed and began a slow count to ten. When the number seven sounded in her mind, she heard the decisive crack of reins and breathed a sigh of relief as the noise of horses and lumbering wheels drifted farther and farther away.

Lizzy knew Thomas would be feeling the same trepidation, and as he'd been hiding for a longer period of time, he was probably near frantic. She ran around the back of the inn to their designated meeting spot.

Glancing both ways and assuring herself no one was near, Lizzy knocked on the door of the privy. "Thomas?" she called in a loud whisper. "Thomas, it's Lizzy. Are you in there?"

The door cracked open, and Thomas greeted her with a huge grin. "Did we do it, Lizzy?" he asked. "Did our plan work?"

Love for her brother overwhelmed her. Lizzy dropped her bag to the dirt, bent over, and scooped him into her arms. "Yes, Thomas, so far everything has gone according to plan." Lizzy released him and mussed his hair. "But we must hurry. Are you ready to walk for a bit? We need to get away from the road and create some distance between us and this place."

Thomas nodded. Lizzy picked up her bag with one hand, and with the other she held Thomas's small fingers. Without another word the siblings walked into the forest.

Chapter 4

"It was cruel enough for Uncle to send you away; why did he decide to do it during the coldest week of the year?" Lizzy meant her comments to be light and humorous, but her teeth chattered so violently her words had the opposite effect.

Thomas shivered again beside her, and Lizzy wondered for the fiftieth time that day if her plan had indeed been a wise one. Lizzy had tied her wool scarf around Thomas's head. His hands were shoved into his jacket pockets, and he shuffled along without a single complaint. It warmed Lizzy's heart that her brother could be so brave, but his strength depended on her. Now she led him through the shadowy woods with sparse provisions as the sunlight quickly faded.

Lizzy's questions to Mr. Grumpkin had not been in vain. Not only had he told her of the town ahead but he had also informed her of the town farther north, from where he'd departed that morning. Lizzy assumed she and Thomas could parallel the road and cover the four miles before nightfall. She planned to stay the night at the inn then purchase transport for her and Thomas to one of the southern counties. She hoped to either let a small cottage or offer her services as a governess with the provision that Thomas be allowed to remain with her. The prospect was perhaps a bit daunting, but Lizzy had felt hopeful, happy, and ready to conquer the odds.

That was before she realized she'd lost track of the road and only succeeded in getting them hopelessly lost. With the convoluted assurance that no copse of trees could go on forever, Lizzy convinced Thomas, or more accurately herself, that they should walk in as straight a line as possible and eventually they would come upon a farm or a home or some form of civilization. Darkness quickly encroached, and they had yet to discover another human being or any manmade structure.

Lizzy tripped over a protruding root. Thomas's arms reached out to try to keep her from tumbling. "Thank you," Lizzy said as she stabilized her footing. "I think we should stop for the night."

"Here?" Thomas asked.

Lizzy tried to put on a happy smile. "We can eat some biscuits and cheese . . ." An owl sounded nearby and Lizzy jumped.

"It's only a hoot owl, Lizzy." Thomas laughed.

She pulled off her gloves and pressed his hands between her fingers. "You're freezing cold." Lizzy's eyes filled with moisture. Did she save her brother from a life at sea only to condemn him to a bitter death in the middle of an unknown and seemingly eternal forest?

Thomas's brows pushed together. "Don't cry, Lizzy. I'm excited to sleep here. I've always wanted to have an adventure. It will be fun to sleep on the ground, and we can use our extra clothes to make a bed."

"You're a good sort, Thomas." Lizzy gave his fingers a final squeeze and opened her bag to determine what they should eat for dinner.

Between the shadows and the setting of the sun, very little light remained as they consumed the last scraps of food. Lizzy folded over one of her black gowns and motioned for Thomas to sit next to her on the crepe dress she laid near the base of a tree. Thomas sat beside her, and she adjusted the wool scarf around his head, crossing the ends beneath his chin and tucking them down into his jacket. She'd stripped off her bonnet long ago, tying the ribbons to her bag, not caring that it was currently squashed against her side. She preferred the hood of her blue cloak to keep her warm. Lizzy pulled Thomas close against her body, wrapping him in the flow of fabric from her cloak. Sharing warmth was vital.

Lizzy hummed a song while she pressed her cheek against the wool scarf draped on Thomas's head. "Try to get some sleep."

Thomas snuggled against her, his breathing a slow, even rhythm. Exhaustion seeped into her bones. She closed her eyes and was startled by Thomas's small voice. "Thank you, Lizzy. I didn't want to go to sea."

The tears streamed down Lizzy's cheeks. She wrapped her arms tighter around her brother, determined to hold him close and never let him go.

A bright flash woke Lizzy. She opened her eyes to see the sighs of dawn trying to push through the dark clouds that rolled overhead. A sudden clap of thunder cracked nearby.

Thomas woke and jumped to his feet. "What was that?"

"A thunderstorm, I'm afraid." Lizzy's muscles cramped as she shifted to stand. "Help me gather our things." Lizzy held her bag wide while Thomas crudely rolled the extra clothes and stuffed them inside.

"I'm hungry." Thomas pressed both hands to his belly right before a giant raindrop splashed onto his cheek.

"We'll have to eat later." Lizzy grabbed his hand. "Come on."

The canopy of trees provided some protection, but the raindrops found a way to snake through the needles, leaves, and branches. Lizzy was certain some angry cloud sought her out, determined to pelt her with every bit of moisture it contained. Within minutes both she and Thomas were soaked through.

"Lizzy!" Thomas called as the lightning and thunder simultaneously collided overhead. "I'm scared!"

Lizzy stopped running and looked at her brother. The saturated scarf lay limply on his head, and tracks of water ran down his cheeks. Helplessness engulfed Lizzy, choking her spirit and dousing her determination.

She stood in the middle of the forest. Lost. Her garments were wet through to her skin. If she'd only been fool enough to thrust her inadequacies upon herself, she might find the entire situation humorous, but when Thomas stood staring at her, baring his soul through his wide blue eyes, Lizzy acknowledged she had failed him. She should have appealed to the vicar or asked Clarke for help. Why had she thought she could save Thomas on her own? She, a genteel lady who'd been spoiled her entire life, could not simply act a silly scheme to extricate them from the violent storm thrashing overhead.

Another burst of light shot through the sky.

"Lizzy!" Thomas shook the hand she held and pointed into the trees. "Lizzy, look!"

Lizzy peered through the shadows, seeing only darkness. She wiped a hand across her face to clear away the rain. When the sky flashed again she spied what Thomas had seen—a building.

"Come on!" Together they stumbled towards the unknown structure.

It didn't matter what the building was, as long as it provided some shelter from the torrent of rain. Lizzy feared the image might be an illusion, but as they neared, the outline of a cabin took definitive form. Thomas ran ahead and circled the side of the building, leading Lizzy to the front. He pushed against the door, but it didn't budge until Lizzy leaned all of her weight against the warped wood. They stepped inside the space, and Lizzy waited for her eyes to adjust.

Thomas jumped up and down. "We did it, Lizzy! We found shelter."

"You found shelter." A shiver ran through her body. "And not a moment too soon."

The cabin was small and dusty. Lizzy's eyes quickly found the fireplace on the opposite wall. "Let's see if we can start a fire."

While Lizzy pulled off her gloves and searched the mantel for a tinderbox, Thomas pulled back the grate.

"It's all wet in here," he said.

"The flue was probably left open." Lizzy's hand finally fell upon the tinderbox, and she squealed in delight when she realized it contained a handful of sulfur matches. "We have matches; now what about wood?"

Thomas circled the room. "There's only two pieces in the box, but I saw more outside."

"Anything outside will be soaking wet. Two is better than nothing. We'll make the most of it," Lizzy said.

"What about this?" Thomas held up a broken stool. "It's no good with only two legs." Thomas pulled something else from the corner. "Here's the other leg and an old broom handle too."

"Bring them over." Lizzy used the fireplace tools to push aside the wet ashes. She laid the first piece of wood on the cold stone and looked for something she could use for tinder. "Thomas, grab some ticking from the pallet on the floor."

Thomas carried over a handful of dry straw, and Lizzy tucked it under and around the log then lit one of the matches. The flame crackled and caught on the straw. Thomas and Lizzy knelt on the ground and extended their hands. Thomas rubbed his fingers together. The flame of their little fire grew, but the single piece of wood would not provide enough heat to warm the siblings.

Lizzy carefully placed the second piece of firewood on the burning log. "You stay here and get warm. I'm going to look around."

The firelight illuminated the single-room cabin. Several wet spots on the floor marked leaks in the roof. Lizzy stepped around them, grateful to be out of the deluge pouring down outside the cabin. A fireplace hanger and kettle sat on one side of the mantel, and farther to the right, nestled under a window, was a small table with two stools similar to the broken one Thomas had discovered. A tall chest situated near the entrance held another single pot, some mismatched utensils, a sharp knife, two mugs, and four plates. Lizzy noticed a trunk pushed next to the pallet in the corner. She lifted the lid and pulled out a thick, dry blanket.

"Thomas, come change out of your wet clothes."

Lizzy continued digging through the trunk while Thomas shed his dripping garments. "Here, put this on." Lizzy tossed a long shirt behind her.

After Thomas dressed and wrapped himself in the blanket, he said, "What about you, Lizzy? You're wet too."

"I can wear these." Lizzy held up a pair of wool trousers and a white shirt with a brown stain running down the left sleeve.

"Boy clothes?" Thomas asked.

"They're dry. That's what matters. Now, go sit by the fire." Lizzy motioned him away. She pulled off her dress and petticoat then untied the laces of her stays and changed into the musty-smelling clothing.

She laid the wet clothing out near the fire and noticed the flame was already diminishing. "We'll have to burn the stool, and I will compensate the owner."

The solution proved ideal. The three legs matched the diameter of Lizzy's arms, and the rounded seat was easily five inches thick. They were made of oak and would take longer to burn and thus provide more warmth. Lizzy sat cross-legged near Thomas and pulled her drenched bag beside her. Slowly she removed each item and spread them out on the open floor. The last bit of bread had disintegrated to a mushy pile, and a layer of wet slime covered the cheese. Lizzy retrieved the knife she'd seen and cut away the outer section of cheese before offering a slice to Thomas, along with a boiled egg.

As Lizzy chewed on the pathetic fare, she removed her reticule from the bag. Thomas watched with curiosity as coins jingled within, but counting coins was not Lizzy's purpose. She pulled the swath of wet velvet from the reticule and set it aside. Brushing her fingers on her course trousers, Lizzy reverently unfolded the tucked corners and lay the fabric flat to reveal the shiny sapphires.

A smile spread across Lizzy's face as memories of her mother and her stepmother wearing the jewels skipped through her mind.

Thomas dropped his hands into his lap, and his eyes grew wide with surprise. "Mother's jewels? Uncle gave them to you?"

Lizzy touched the tip of Thomas's nose. "No, silly. I reclaimed them."
Thomas yawned.

"You've been very brave, Thomas. I'm proud of you."

"You said we were going to have an adventure. Adventurers have to be brave." Thomas rubbed his eyes.

Lizzy scooted closer, and Thomas offered her a section of blanket. "Yes, they do." She yawned too. "This adventurer is very tired. How about we both close our eyes for a bit?"

Thomas nodded, and Lizzy pulled the blanket over his shoulders. She considered moving to the pallet but could not bring herself to leave the warmth of the fire, so together they lay down on the hard floor. Lizzy placed a kiss on Thomas's temple and whispered, "Our adventure has only begun." Then she closed her eyes and drifted off to sleep.

Chapter 5

SEVERAL HOURS LATER LIZZY WOKE feeling sore but rested. Her feet were not used to hiking long distances, and her shoulders were more accustomed to balancing a parasol than an overstuffed bag. But she and Thomas were dry and, for the time being, safe.

Lizzy stood, and Thomas rolled over to look at her. "Do I have to get up?" he asked.

"No, dear boy, sleep on." Lizzy laughed and walked to the table to look out the single window of the cottage. "But the rain has stopped. Perhaps we can find some food."

"You want to walk more?" Thomas asked.

"Definitely not! I think we shall stay here for the night, but we could use more wood, and I'm hungry." Thomas's stomach rumbled on cue, and Lizzy laughed. "From the sound of it, you are too."

Thomas grinned and began to remove the blanket before he remembered he wore only a shirt. "Oh . . . uh, Lizzy, I need my trousers."

The oak round from the stool still smoldered with a small red flame. The cabin had warmed considerably, but away from the fireplace a chill hung in the air. Lizzy checked the various items of clothes spread across the floor, turning and adjusting them so they could continue to dry. She was grateful she'd draped Thomas's trousers over one of the intact stools and pushed it close to the hearth. The cuffs were still damp, but the legs of the garment were warm and dry.

"Here you are." Lizzy tossed the trousers to Thomas. "Just tuck that shirt in best you can."

The outer clothes were still wet, so Thomas gathered the blanket around his shoulders, and Lizzy wore a tattered vest she'd found in the trunk over the top of her shirt. "We'll make our exploration quick," Lizzy said.

They stepped outside the cabin, and Lizzy pointed to an overgrown path leading away from the front door and into the woods. "I bet that will lead us out of the forest."

"Are you sure?" Thomas eyed the brambles and sticks spread along the trail.

"No, but look, here are blackberries!" Lizzy's hunger trumped the cold, and she ran to the neglected bushes at the head of the pathway.

She stood beside Thomas, plucking the thick berries from the vine and popping them straight into her mouth. Lizzy moaned in delight.

"I never knew blackberries could taste so good." Thomas ate another berry.

Lizzy ate three more. "I'll get the bowls from the house, and we can pick some for later."

The siblings spent the next forty minutes clearing berries from the unkempt bushes. Due to the lateness of the season, some of the berries squished between their fingers. Others were withered and hardened, but there were ample berries to fill their bowls while leaving plenty on the bushes for the following morning.

Thomas carried the bowls inside while Lizzy surveyed the exterior of the cabin. Near the corner of the building she found a sturdy bucket, now filled with rainwater. She skimmed away the leaves floating on top and drank from her cupped hand. Around the side of the cabin stood a chopping block, and an ax leaned against the wall, protected from the rain by the pile of wood next to it.

Together the siblings removed the top layers from the woodpile, working lower until they reached the pieces the rain had not. They each carried multiple armloads of wood into the cabin, filling the woodbox and making another stack beside it.

Circling the remaining perimeter, Lizzy discovered several small animal traps, a neglected herb garden, and some additional tools. The sun set quickly, and the duo was content to return to the shelter of the cabin for the night. Lizzy carried the water bucket inside and filled two plates with sliced cheese and berries while Thomas built up the fire.

"Do you think someone lives here, Lizzy?" Thomas asked.

"Someone did once." Lizzy eyed their footprints scattered through the layer of dust on the floor. "But I don't think anyone's been here for a very long time." Lizzy carried the plates to the table, and Thomas joined her.

"Can it be ours?" Thomas asked with wide eyes.

Lizzy pushed the fuller of the two plates towards him. "It doesn't belong to us."

"But if no one else wants it?"

Lizzy reached across the small table and mussed Thomas's hair. "That doesn't mean we can claim it. Besides, how do you know they didn't want it? Perhaps this cabin belonged to a fairy who lived here with a princess so they could hide from the wicked queen. Maybe the fairy will want it back."

Thomas frowned. "That's a silly story from one of your books."

Lizzy smiled. "Then, who do you think lived here?"

Thomas narrowed his eyes and leaned forward. In a low voice he said, "I think the cabin belongs to a bandit hiding from the constable."

"Oh!" Lizzy feigned shock. "What was his crime?"

"He took money from rich men and gave it to the servants."

Lizzy laughed. "I think I've heard that story before, too."

Lizzy and Thomas continued to swap tales, passing away the evening hours as the moon shone down through the trees. After adding another log to the fire, Lizzy joined Thomas on the small pallet, where they both fell into a contented sleep.

Lizzy planned to stay at the cottage for only one night. But when the rain returned the next morning and the morning after that, she found it difficult to abandon the small sanctuary they'd found and wander out into the unknown.

After the third day, hunger drove Lizzy to explore a little farther into the woods. The siblings followed the trail from the cabin and discovered it led to a clearing hosting a small stream and two other cottages, both of which were inhabited and properly tended. Before returning to the borrowed cabin, they helped themselves to eggs from the chicken coop, four small apples from a lone apple tree, and several handfuls of grain from the barrel outside one of the cottages.

Lizzy began to feel like an outlaw herself. Her parents would be appalled at the example she was setting for Thomas, but she justified her actions because she was protecting him. Surely Uncle knew they were missing, along with the sapphires. He was probably searching for them even now. But she and Thomas did not see another human being beyond the families who lived in the nearby cottages, and after observing them for several days, Lizzy determined they took no interest in the abandoned cabin. Lizzy decided to lay low for a few weeks before continuing with her original plan.

Thomas was a naturally curious boy and had watched the groundskeeper set traps to catch the rodents in the gardens at Downey Place. He remembered the basic process, and between the two of them, they were able to manipulate the mechanisms and lay two traps in the woods beyond the cabin.

After only a day, they were delighted to find a rabbit in one of the traps, but only until they realized the animal needed to be skinned and prepared to cook. Thomas offered to help, but Lizzy set him to another task. She knew what needed to be done, but she stared at the lifeless creature for a full twenty minutes before she dared touch the soft pelt. Lizzy held her breath as she lifted the rabbit's fur and pierced it with the knife. Then she promptly vomited the meager contents of her stomach into a nearby bush.

While Lizzy had touted adventure, she was not keen to skin and slaughter her dinner. She apologized to the dead rabbit, and instead of meat she placed a bowl of stolen grain soaked in water in front of Thomas for dinner. Lizzy was grateful he did not complain. After he choked down the pathetic offering, Lizzy heaved a sigh. "Thomas, I think tomorrow I should try to find a way to town."

"Why?"

"We can't stay here."

"But I like it here."

Lizzy picked up the empty bowls and walked them over to the hutch. "We're safe, but we need more food, soap, and linens. The blackberry bushes are picked clean."

"Can I go with you?"

"I don't think that would be wise. If Uncle's been asking questions, they'll be looking for us together. It would be best if I went alone."

Thomas's eyes fell to the floor. Lizzy walked over and put her hands on his shoulders. "You need to tend to the chores while I'm gone. I'll leave early and be home before noon."

"What if you don't come back?" Thomas could not mask the fear in his voice.

"Of course I'll come back."

"That's what mother said. She kissed me goodbye and said she'd been home in a week, but she never came back." Thomas cried, and Lizzy pulled him to her bosom. She whispered reassurances into his hair.

"What if you get lost? Or hurt?" he mumbled against her.

"If I don't return by the time the sun dips below the trees, I want you to go to the cabin down the path, the one with the chicken coop. I've seen a little girl running around who's almost as old as you. Take the rest of the money, and tell them your name is Reginald—"

"Like father?"

"Yes, like father." Lizzy ran a hand down Thomas's cheek. "Tell them you will work hard. You can do chores and help with their farm if they allow you to stay."

"But—"

"Shhh." Lizzy laid a finger over his lips. "I will return, Thomas. I told you I would keep you safe, and I intend to keep my promise."

After Lizzy tucked Thomas into bed, she tore off a piece of her underdress, warmed some water, and cleaned herself off as best she could. How she longed for a proper bath, and she wondered if she would ever be afforded such luxury again. Lizzy shook out her grey dress, hoping the bit of color, drab as it may be, would not alert anyone on the lookout for a girl in mourning clothes. Her once-fine cloak had become stained and tattered, and if she didn't wear her gloves, her now-calloused hands marked her as a servant. But she didn't mind the work or the hunger. Lizzy's sole priority was to keep her brother safe. No matter how dire their current circumstances, Lizzy knew if her uncle located them, Thomas would be carted off to Ipswich, and that was something she could simply not allow.

Chapter 6

LIZZY HOPED TO DEPART BEFORE Thomas awoke, but he stirred as she dressed. He opened his eyes and watched her gather her reticule, bonnet, and cloak.

"Be brave now, Thomas. I'll see you again shortly." Lizzy slipped out the door, afraid if she stayed longer she'd succumb to Thomas's fears and bring him along.

During her last trip to gather water from the river, Lizzy had crept to the edge of the woods, where she'd seen a dirt road leading south. She determined to parallel the road from the safety of the trees and hoped it would lead somewhere beneficial.

Creeping through the woods took longer than Lizzy anticipated, but she dared not step out of the protection offered by the forest. Determination pushed her forward as brambles tugged on her cloak and branches snagged her tattered bonnet. Lizzy followed a long bend in the road and discovered that the line of cottages continued down the lane.

Lizzy misjudged her step and tripped over a gnarled branch. Pain shot through her ankle, and she winced as she rubbed her hand over the place. Pushing herself up, she tested her weight and determined she could still walk; however, it did slow her momentum. She'd passed almost a dozen homes and knew walking on the flat road would speed her journey. So, with her chin held high, Lizzy emerged from the trees to march down the road as if she belonged.

She only hesitated when the dirt road connected with a gravel drive marked with a regal willow tree. The wagon ruts in the road indicated that the majority of travelers turned right, so that was the path Lizzy chose.

Soon the gravel ended, and Lizzy found herself at the junction of a well-worn thoroughfare. She looked right then left, having no idea which direction to turn. Her swollen ankle began to throb. She considered turning back but knew if she did she would have to attempt the same feat another day.

The lazy clomping of hooves turned Lizzy's head. An old white swayback horse pulled a cart down the road. An older gentleman sat atop the cart on a rough-hewn board, holding the animal's reins.

"Hello!" Lizzy pushed up onto her tiptoes and waved, although the man obviously saw her.

The man called his horse to a stop, with a low, mellow voice. He didn't say anything to Lizzy; he simply leaned his elbows on his knees and held the reins loosely in hand while he watched her.

"Are you heading to town?" Lizzy asked.

"Town?" the man repeated, raising his bushy eyebrows.

Lizzy realized her blunder and to cover up decided to play the part of a scatterbrained miss. She pushed one shoulder forward and waved her hand. "You know what I mean. The village, of course."

"What village might that be?"

The mellow-mannered man clearly enjoyed his teasing. Well, Lizzy would play right along. She fixed her hands on her hips. "Oh, I hardly know. I'm visiting my cousin, you see. She's in confinement, and, well, I found myself rather bored today and decided a jaunt to the village might prove entertaining. So here I am." Lizzy waved her arms over the open road.

"But you ain't at the village."

"Precisely." Lizzy shook a finger at him. "Which is where you come in. Are you perchance heading to the village now?"

The man grunted and nodded his head.

"Since I'm not familiar with the area, would you be so kind as to allow me to ride in your cart?"

His bushy eyebrows scrunched close together. "What's your name?"

Lizzy had coached Thomas on this exact scenario just the day before, but she hadn't thought to come up with an alias for herself. Before she could think she answered, "Elizabeth."

"Elizabeth . . . ?" The man led.

Lizzy looked down at her boots and saw the grey hem of her dress hanging below her cloak. "Elizabeth Grey." She lifted her chin once again.

From the look on his face, Lizzy guessed the man did not believe her. He was not as easily fooled by her playacting as Uncle had been. "Well, Miss Grey, I suppose there's no point in ya walkin' when I'm headin' that direction myself."

Lizzy dipped a quick curtsy and smiled wide. "Thank you, sir."

"Name's Murray."

"Then, thank you, Mr. Murray. I'm most obliged," Lizzy walked towards the back of the cart.

"There's also no point in you riding in back. There's plenty o' room here." Mr. Murray jutted his chin towards the bench.

When Lizzy moved to the open side, Mr. Murray extended his hand and hefted her up to the seat. His eyes continued to follow her hands as she adjusted her skirts and then smiled at him again.

With a grunt Mr. Murray clicked at his horse, and the animal clomped forward again. "Let's get to Hillcrest."

Hillcrest. Lizzy could not place the name of the village and took the opportunity to gather her bearings. The road was lined with a variety of trees. The oak and ash trees seemed determined to shed their leaves, while the pine's evergreen boughs stood tall above them. The ground was covered with a variety of bushes, and every so often Lizzy caught a glimpse of a willow standing with its branches dangling towards the ground.

"Who's this cousin yer stayin' with?" Mr. Murray asked.

Lizzy's heart skipped, but she masked her nervousness with a coy smile. "Now, Mr. Murray, you know I can't tell you that. I've already told you the reason for my jaunt to town—I mean, to Hillcrest. As I'm here to help my cousin in her confinement, I wouldn't want her to think I resented coming."

Mr. Murray glanced at Lizzy before turning his eyes back to the road. "When are you expecting the little one to arrive?"

"A month, I believe. Maybe longer." To Lizzy's relief they rounded a bend and Hillcrest came into view. Lizzy did not like deceiving the man. "I think I shall walk from here." Lizzy began to climb down before Mr. Murray pulled the horse to a stop.

"You in a hurry?" Mr. Murray asked.

Lizzy jumped the final distance to the ground, wincing at the pain that shot through her ankle. She quickly masked her expression. "Not at all. I only hoped to enjoy Hillcrest in its entirety, so I shall begin my exploration here. Thank you again, Mr. Murray." Lizzy bobbed a quick curtsy and through sheer grit forced herself to walk without a limp.

A moment later she heard Mr. Murray whistle to his horse, and when they clomped past she offered a small wave.

The morning started out clear, but billowy clouds now chased each other quickly across the sky. Lizzy would have to complete her tasks and return to Thomas before another storm set in. She stopped a young girl walking by and inquired where she could purchase sundries. The girl pointed to the apothecary, located just past an inn named the Hilly Crest. Lizzy laughed at the turn of phrase and watched the villagers tend to their tasks as she made her way to the apothecary shop.

Lizzy purchased soap, tea leaves, and three tins of hard biscuits. She asked the man who tended her to include a stick of candy, as a surprise for Thomas. The man bundled the items in a square of paper and tied them together with a piece of cord. Lizzy claimed her package and thanked him.

She shifted her bundle to open the door, but as she reached for the handle, the door flew open. Before she could react a gentleman barreled through the entrance and collided directly into Lizzy. Her arms flailed wildly as she and her package tumbled to the ground.

The first thing Lizzy realized was that she had screamed a rather unladylike scream. The second was that her bottom now throbbed along with her ankle and the entire shop was deathly silent.

She blinked, hoping to clear her head, and then focused on her assailant, who now stood over her. Vibrant blue eyes framed with long blond lashes filled his linear face. Wisps of hair the color of hay stuck out from beneath his tall hat. He could not be described as broad—long was a more accurate descriptor. A quick glance verified his good health.

His eyes scanned her body from head to toe. "Dear lady, have you hurt anything?"

Lizzy looked over her legs and adjusted her skirt to cover her ankles. While the entire debacle had occurred in a matter of seconds, Lizzy felt certain this gentleman was the guilty party. Her ire rose. "Don't you mean have you hurt anything? I believe that would be the more accurate question."

Several gasps sounded throughout the shop. Lizzy meant to chastise the man and felt rather chagrined when he began to laugh. Her eyes widened at his insolence.

"Yes, that *would* be the more accurate question. If you will allow me to rephrase: My lady, I apologize for my abrupt entrance and unfortunate collision with your person. Have I caused you any pain or injury?" The man's mouth twitched with amusement.

Lizzy huffed. "I suspect I will be rather sore for a day or two, but otherwise I am unharmed."

"I'm glad to hear it. If I may?" The man extended his hand and assisted Lizzy to her feet. The shopkeeper hurried over, gathered Lizzy's parcel, and returned it to her.

Lizzy thanked the shopkeeper, and then the tall, blond-haired man spoke again. "My deepest apologies, madam. And I am even more disgraced to realize you are not from around here. May I ask your name?"

"You are correct. I am not from the area, and I am quite resigned to forget this entire ordeal. Since I am on my way and you have obvious *urgent* business to attend to, there's no need for introductions. I accept your apology, and we shall leave it at that."

Lizzy swept around the man, but before she could escape he grabbed her wrist. The action startled her so completely she stopped.

He kept his voice soft so only she could hear. "If I shall never see you again, there's no harm in knowing your name." When Lizzy did not immediately answer, he continued. "It's not every day a lovely lady has the opportunity to shriek out loud. I think I shall remember that sound for a very long time."

Lizzy knew he meant the comment in jest, and although she wanted to laugh, in the space of a breath the humorous emotion transformed to something solemn. The man did not release her hand. Instead Lizzy thought he might have tightened his grip, and she felt a strange urgency to sever the strange connection between them.

"Miss Grey," she whispered. The man regarded her, sweeping his eyes over her face. She tried to remain unaffected, but she could not pull her eyes away.

When the stranger smiled, Lizzy's head cleared. She pulled her hand free and, this time, successfully exited the shop. She walked down the steps and inhaled deeply. The man had not offered his name. It was probably better she not know. She meant to leave soon, and the fewer connections she made in Hillcrest, the better.

The smell of warm bread and savory meat accosted her senses. Lizzy hadn't realized how the lack of food had affected her. Weakness consumed her. The scant meals and manual labor she'd assumed over the past days had compounded in her fragile body. The long walk and resulting collision had shaken her more than she'd let on.

Lizzy's stomach gurgled, and although she knew she would later regret her indulgence, she marched into the inn and ordered a meal. When the innkeeper brought her food she said, "This is my first time in Hillcrest. Tell me about your little village."

"Hillcrest is the best village in all of Cambridgeshire," the woman said.

"Really?" Lizzy did not mask her surprise.

"I swear it, miss. Everly Manor is just up the road. Mr. Everly's all that's right and good. Like his father, he is." The woman's conviction intrigued Lizzy.

"Mr. Everly, you say?"

"Yes, ma'am. Best sort of gentleman there is. Now, will you be needin' anything else?"

"No, thank you. This smells divine." The woman moved on to another customer, and Lizzy hungrily devoured the lamb stew. She profusely thanked the proprietor when he set a second slice of warm bread on her plate.

"I've never seen a woman make such quick work of her food."

Lizzy recognized the stranger's voice. Embarrassed, she lifted her napkin and wiped her mouth before she turned to look at the man she had only recently escaped.

"Then you'll be disappointed to know the show is over." Lizzy stood from her seat and walked to the bar.

The gentleman's quick steps matched her own. "Miss Grey, are you running away again?"

"I'm running nowhere, sir. I have obligations awaiting me, and I must return." Lizzy waved the proprietor over and asked him to tally the cost of her meal and include a wrapped loaf of bread and cheese.

The stranger raised his hand. "Add it to my tab, Mr. Hunt."

"That's hardly necessary," Lizzy argued. "I'm quite able to pay for my meal."

"I don't doubt that, Miss Grey, but surely you can allow me. Consider it penance for my earlier bumble."

As Mr. Hunt handed Lizzy the food, she shrugged with feigned nonchalance. "Very well. Thank you, sir. And rest assured you owe me nothing more. Good day." She offered a quick curtsy and hurried out the door to begin her long walk back to the cabin in the woods.

Chapter 7

DESPITE THE PAIN IN HER ankle and the awkward bundles in her arms, Lizzy made good progress on her journey—before the rain began. She knew Thomas would grow concerned if she did not return soon, and that knowledge propelled her forward.

The rain did not match the torrential downpour of the previous storm, but Lizzy still secured the rations within her cloak to keep the precious food dry. The distance that seemed short when riding alongside Mr. Murray continued to stretch before her. She could no longer disguise her limp, and the drop in temperature accelerated the stiffness spreading through her limbs from her fall in the apothecary shop.

Lizzy focused on her steps and plodded on. She had not realized a rider approached until the horse's hooves appeared in her line of vision. She stopped abruptly and frowned when she saw the handsome stranger looking down on her once again.

"Miss Grey!" He swung his leg off the horse and stood in front of Lizzy. "Where is your horse? Your coach? Where on earth are you headed?" The man obviously recognized Lizzy was a lady to presume she had such conveniences accessible. She had not masked her upbringing as well as she had hoped.

Water dripped off the stranger's hat, and Lizzy could not hold his penetrating gaze. Instead she looked over at his horse. "Thank you for your concern, but I am able to manage on my own."

From the corner of her eye Lizzy saw the man shake his head. "You lied to me."

"What?" Lizzy whipped her head around and tried to push away the panic mounting in her stomach.

"At the apothecary you told me you were not hurt, but you're limping."

Lizzy's stomach settled a bit. "My ankle is injured from a previous incident, sir."

His blue eyes lit. "You mean to tell me you hurt yourself before our collision in the apothecary?"

Lizzy raised her chin. "I twisted my ankle earlier this morning."

Lizzy could tell he wanted to laugh, but he did a notable job of suppressing his amusement. "And yet you still walked to Hillcrest?"

"I did . . . until Mr. Murray kindly allowed me to ride in his cart."

"Murray, eh?"

"Yes. Now, if you'll excuse me, I need to be on my way."

Lizzy adjusted the bundle in her arms, and the man tsked her. "Miss Grey, you realize that, as a gentleman, I cannot in good conscience leave you to yourself in this situation. My mother would tan my hide if I let you continue on your own. I insist you allow me to help you."

Riding sounded so very enticing, but Lizzy could not allow questions or connections of any kind. "No, thank you."

"At least let me take you to Everly Manor, where you can wait out the storm." The man offered an appeasing smile.

Lizzy looked the man over, wondering if he might be Everly himself. She shook her head. "I have someone expecting me."

"Then allow Brutus to carry you to your destination." The man indicated the horse behind him.

"Brutus?"

"I'd accompany you, too, of course. Now, what do you say, Miss Grey? May I assist you into the saddle and we can be off?"

"I don't make a habit of allowing strangers to escort me anywhere." Lizzy tilted her head and adjusted the hood of her cloak.

"Strangers?"

"Yes. You never told me your name."

The man chuckled. "My friends call me Barton." So he was not the famous Everly the proprietress had spoken of.

The rain continued to fall, and Lizzy knew Thomas would worry. She hoped he would remain at the cottage and not do anything rash. "Very well, Mr. Barton." The man smiled at Lizzy's use of his name. "Now that we have been properly introduced in an entirely improper way, I will admit that I would appreciate your assistance." Mr. Barton's mouth twitched once again. She decided to continue the tale she'd spun to Mr. Murray. It was best if she returned to Thomas as quickly as possible. "However, I'm staying with my cousin, who tends to be quite a gossip. I'd prefer to avoid her censure, so I can't allow you to escort me home. We shall stop a few houses away, and then I shall walk the remaining distance. Are we agreed?"

"Not at all," Mr. Barton replied. "But I will respect your wishes."

"Thank you." Lizzy found Mr. Barton's manner refreshing. He spoke plainly and truthfully, and from the little they had conversed, she surmised he possessed a quick wit.

Mr. Barton lifted Lizzy into the saddle and waited for her to situate her purchases before he climbed up behind her. Brutus was a large enough beast to easily carry their combined weight. Mr. Barton adjusted the reins and positioned himself to be able to control the horse without making Lizzy feel uncomfortable. While the situation could be construed as intimate, Mr. Barton played the part of a perfect gentleman, and Lizzy felt immense gratitude for the man's mother.

Lizzy's ankle pulsed in pain as the horse plodded through the mud. She hoped Thomas was all right, that today he would be brave. She would reach him soon.

Lizzy pointed ahead to the gravel drive. "We will take this turn here."

Brutus's speed increased as his hooves crunched along the road. "Are you sure this is correct?" Mr. Barton asked.

"While I have not been here long, I do know my way home, sir." Lizzy clutched the bundles close to her chest, anxious to sit in front of the fire with Thomas. She spied the large willow tree marking the dirt road. "Now turn left."

"Left, you say?"

Lizzy pinched her lips. "Yes."

"Very well." Mr. Barton pressed his heels into Brutus's sides, and the horse followed the command. "I ride this road often. 'Tis a wonder we haven't met before, Miss Grey."

"As I mentioned, I'm only recently come to visit my cousin. Her confinement has been difficult for her," Lizzy tacked on, remembering the story she had told Mr. Murray.

"Who is your cousin?" Mr. Barton's mouth was very near Lizzy's ear.

She sucked in a quick breath, and while her heartbeat slowed, she counted the cottages she had passed on her journey to Hillcrest, deciding

Mr. Barton could take her to the trio of cottages about halfway down the lane. "I shan't reveal her name, sir, for I've confessed far too much, to both you and Mr. Murray. I'm afraid I'm not quite myself these past few days, for it isn't like me to talk ill of my relations." Lizzy realized her comment was riddled with half-truths, as she could easily talk ill of Uncle Cline, but she rationalized her act by thinking of Thomas, his safety, and her plan to soon leave Hillcrest far behind.

"Are you a direct relation?" Mr. Barton asked. When Lizzy did not immediately reply, he continued. "I don't mean to pry; it's only that this road leads to the tenant cottages, and from your manners I assumed you to be the daughter of a gentleman."

Drat! She had given herself away. "Are the manners you refer to my eating habits at the Hilly Crest?"

Barton chuckled. "Not in particular. It is more the way you speak, the way you carry yourself."

Lizzy chose her response carefully. "My father was a gentleman, sir. But he has recently passed away. I offered to assist my cousin, hoping to ease some of the sorrow I've felt at his loss. If I can be of service to another, perhaps my own pain will lessen."

"I'm sorry for your loss, Miss Grey. Your cousin is lucky to have your support."

Lizzy promptly changed the topic. "You mentioned waiting out the storm at Everly Manor. Does that mean you are acquainted with Mr. Everly himself?"

"Yes, I know him quite well."

"You are a guest of his, I assume?"

Mr. Barton laughed. "One he can't seem to be rid of."

"Oh?"

Lizzy began to wonder if the gentlemen were friends or if Mr. Barton fit the mold of unwelcome houseguest. If so, she pitied Mr. Everly. Her experience with Miss Masterson allowed her to understand the challenge of such an acquaintance. Miss Masterson had arrived at Downey Place almost immediately after her uncle took residence. Lizzy doubted the woman would ever leave as much as she doubted Uncle intended to marry Miss Masterson.

Brutus carried them to the cluster of three houses. Lizzy said, "You may let me off here." When Mr. Barton stopped Brutus, Lizzy spoke her mind. "Then the rumor I heard of Mr. Everly's generosity must be true."

"You believed it only to be rumor?" Mr. Barton dismounted and then assisted Lizzy down.

"Seeing as I've never met the man, I have only the opinion of the proprietress at the inn. She raved about Mr. Everly and his abundance of goodness."

"Is that so?"

The rain had lightened to a drizzle, and Lizzy shook the larger droplets from her cloak. "As I said, that was her opinion."

"Perhaps you should form your own." Mr. Barton kept a hand on Brutus's bridle. "You should call at Everly Manor and meet the owner yourself. I can assure you, you would be most welcome."

Lizzy shrugged the suggestion away. "Thank you for your kindness, Mr. Barton. Impeding houseguest or not, I appreciate your assistance."

Mr. Barton smirked, leaned forward, and touched his hat. "I'm glad to be of service. If you change your mind about calling at Everly Manor, give them my name and you will be welcomed. Good day, Miss Grey."

Lizzy watched Mr. Barton turn Brutus in the road and disappear around the bend before she dared push back into the trees to follow the river to the cottage.

Chapter 8

THE CHILL SETTLED DEEP IN Barton's bones, but as fervently as he longed to return home and call for his valet and a warm bath, he also recognized that he and Miss Grey had much in common—they both had a secret.

When Miss Grey had misunderstood his introduction, Barton did not correct her. He'd given her his name, but only a portion of it, for his calling card read *Harrison Barton Everly of Everly Manor*. His friends truly did call him Barton, and when Miss Grey assumed it to be his surname, he had simply smiled. He did not mind a lovely woman calling him by a familiar name, and Miss Grey was a lovely woman.

Her light-brown hair was nothing significant, no, but her eyes drew Barton in. When he'd burst through the apothecary door, he'd been eager to talk to Mr. Grimes. The man had promised him first pick of his hound's new litter, and Barton was anxious to select his new hunting companion. When he'd toppled Miss Grey to the ground in his haste, she'd glared at him with furious indignation. Barton was immediately captivated by the combination of brown and gold in her eyes and acknowledged the fortitude he saw within. When she promptly pinned blame on him, he wondered if she approached all aspects of her life with such tenacity. Barton found the combination of her blunt humor and fragile features refreshing. Miss Grey had taken no offense when he laughed and did not act the part of distressed debutante, although he did not believe she could be more than nineteen years old.

Barton appreciated a straight answer, and therein lay the problem: he knew Miss Grey had lied, too, for he familiarized himself with every one of his tenants, including those living along the west road, and only Mrs. Pickett was currently expecting a child. As Miss Grey had led him past the Picketts' cabin, the validity of her story had been compromised.

Barton kept Brutus at a trot until he rounded the corner, and then he guided the horse onto a path obscured by the trees, determined to follow Miss Grey to wherever it was she called home.

The dampened ground muffled his movement through the woods, and water continued to percolate from the trees. Barton reached a branch of one of several streams on his property. This segment ran parallel to the road, and he guided Brutus forward, hoping to discover Miss Grey's destination. He searched to the left, watching for movement through the trees, when a sudden flash of blue pulled his head right. Brutus was extremely docile for such a large animal, and as soon as Barton sat back in the saddle, the horse halted.

Barton watched Miss Grey hold her skirts high as she picked her way across the small river. He remained far enough upstream that she took no notice of him. Something was amiss, yet Miss Grey made no effort to cover her tracks. The sound of splattering drops hitting the trees alerted Barton to the fact that the rain had commenced once again, but his need to uncover the truth about Miss Grey was insatiable.

Barton dismounted, turned Brutus towards the road, and with a slap on the animal's hindquarters, urged him to go home.

It didn't take long for Barton to catch up to Miss Grey. He was familiar with his land—the sheep pastures, the farms, and especially the forest. Barton and his brother, Franklin, had spent many hours exploring the woods, filling themselves with berries from the thickets, battling imagined intruders, and listening to the tales of their old gamekeeper, Mr. Doyle. They'd help him oil the traps while he told them of his life in Ireland. Mr. Doyle filled their heads with fanciful notions of an adventurous boy who'd left home and struck out on his own. The stories always ended with the boy finding refuge at Everly Manor, being taken in by a kind family, and living happily ever after. Barton had always known the boy in the stories was Mr. Doyle, but until his studies at university, he didn't understand the dire circumstances Mr. Doyle had survived and the destitution he'd left in Ireland with the hope of finding a better life in England.

Three years ago Barton's father and Mr. Doyle had died within six months of each other. Mr. Doyle's cabin remained untouched, and his position had been filled by one of the tenants. At the age of twenty-four Barton had assumed Everly Manor, and in his effort to maintain the legacies of his father and grandfather, his explorations with Franklin had fallen to the wayside.

Barton hadn't been to the cabin in almost a year, but when Miss Grey stood at her full height and her steps quickened, he knew that was her destination.

He dared not reveal himself by walking on the trail and instead worked his way east, climbing through the brambles and branches. He smelled smoke and, through a clearing in the trees, saw the steady grey stream blend into the sky.

When Barton reached the edge of the clearing, he crouched down in the bushes and watched Miss Grey push against the door until it creaked open. A young boy barreled into her, reminding Barton of their earlier collision. Miss Grey yelped as she steadied herself against the doorframe. The boy's hair matched Miss Grey's, and he was obviously eager to see her. Barton was too far away to hear the conversation, but Miss Grey lifted her injured ankle, and the boy's eyes grew wide. She waved away his concern and handed him the packages she had so carefully guarded, before they both disappeared inside the cabin.

A million questions filled Barton's mind. Was Miss Grey living in the old gamekeeper's cabin? Who was the boy? How long had they been there? Surely they were newly arrived, for he visited Hillcrest often. Between his trips and the constant chatter of servants and villagers, he would have heard if Miss Grey had been around for any length of time.

He remained in the cover of the trees and walked a wide circle around the cabin, emerging on the left side and hiding behind the woodpile. Barton's heartbeat sped with a rush of excitement. It was a silly notion, since he stood on his land outside a cabin he rightfully owned, but he wanted to solve the mystery of Miss Grey, to solve the riddle she'd become.

After a few minutes of silence, Barton left his secluded spot and inched closer to the single window of the cabin, hoping it might allow him a glimpse inside or an opportunity to listen to a bit of conversation. Ducking low, Barton pressed himself against the wall until he'd moved within a foot of the window. He immediately recognized Miss Grey's voice, and after listening for a moment, he could decipher the boy's voice as well. The boy spoke of building up the fire and carrying water from the stream earlier in the day. Then Miss Grey told him about her trip to the village. When she told the boy about Brutus, he squealed. Barton peeked through the glass to see Miss Grey's hand raised above her head when she described Brutus's height. She told the boy about going to the apothecary and being knocked on her backside.

"Who was it, Lizzy?" the boy asked.

"A gentleman named Mr. Barton," she said.

"Is he like Uncle?" the boy asked.

Barton ducked back down, but he dared not move. He wanted to hear Miss Grey's answer.

"Not at all. Mr. Barton is much younger than Uncle. He apologized for knocking me over and offered to buy my meal at the inn. When he found me walking home in the rain, he stopped and let me ride Brutus," Miss Grey said.

"Did you ask him to help us?"

Barton heard more footsteps and couldn't resist peeking through the window again. Miss Grey stood in front of the small table, holding the boy in a hug. She whispered something in his ear as she stroked his hair. The boy nodded then returned to the table, where he zealously consumed his meal.

Barton snuck back around to the woodpile, reviewing the information in his mind.

The boy had referenced an uncle and the need for help. Miss Grey's lies insinuated she had something to hide. The boy must be Miss Grey's brother, and Barton didn't miss the fact that he'd called her Lizzy. *Miss Elizabeth Grey.* The name rolled through Barton's thoughts as he walked through the woods back to Everly Manor. He wondered how to convince Miss Grey to confide in him so he could be the one to help her.

The waitress at the inn had been kind in her words about him, and Barton had had to bite his tongue to contain his laughter when Miss Grey had called him an obtrusive houseguest. The highest compliment Barton could receive was that he took after his father.

Barton's late father had taught him the importance of every individual. Though society divided men by rank and class, Mr. Everly saw mothers, fathers, and children, striving to get through the trials of life with the means they possessed. While the Everly family had been bountifully blessed in their means, Barton's father had used his wealth for the benefit of all, and his generosity had been noted.

Barton's mother oft praised his father's kindness, claiming her son would rightly carry on her late husband's legacy. Barton's older sister, Bethany, thought he behaved too munificently for his own good. Her protectiveness humbled Barton, but he could not change something so ingrained in his soul.

Beyond wealth, the Everly posterity had been blessed with intelligence. On the rare occasion someone did attempt to swindle his late father, the ruse had been detected and the offender confronted. Most often the guilty party left town with his tail between his legs. Rumors had spread quickly, and frauds had felt the wrath of a town bound to their philanthropist.

So while Bethany's fears played in the forefront of Barton's mind, his gut told him Miss Grey had not deceived him for profit, for she did not know his true identity. So, the question remained—what were the siblings hiding, and how could he convince Miss Grey to let him in on the secret?

Chapter 9

After three days, Lizzy was pleased to discover the pain in her ankle had substantially diminished. She opened the cabin door to discover half a dozen biscuits wrapped in an oilcloth and two game hens sitting in a pan, cleaned and ready to be cooked. Her heart dropped to her boots, and she searched the trees for whomever was responsible. Although the gift was generous, it meant someone knew she and Thomas were residing in the cabin. They also knew of their dire circumstances.

Lizzy had scrimped together enough money to prevent them from being desperate. Yet, food disappeared quickly. Now that Lizzy knew the way to town, it would not be so difficult to purchase necessities; however, returning them to the cabin unnoticed was an entirely different matter, a matter which no longer signified, as they'd been discovered. She and Thomas would have to leave. Soon.

Lizzy did not see anyone lurking in the shadows of the trees. She determined to depart the next morning and set the pot with the hens inside on the table. She ought not waste a perfectly good meal.

After a breakfast of biscuits and cheese, the siblings completed their morning ritual. Thomas carried in several armloads of wood, while Lizzy used the last of the water to wash the dishes. Instead of walking alone to the creek, she suggested Thomas walk with her. Lizzy had made a promise that nothing would happen to them, and she could only keep an eye on Thomas if they remained together.

She carried the brunt of the weight from the full bucket. Thomas tried to assist by holding on to one side of the rope handle, but his efforts only managed to tilt the bucket off balance and splash cold water on Lizzy's boots.

She opened her mouth to tell him she could manage, but when she looked up and saw Mr. Barton standing outside the cabin door, her mouth went dry. Thomas did not notice the man, nor did he notice that Lizzy had stopped moving. He continued forward while Lizzy stood stock-still, causing the remaining water to slosh out of the bucket and soak Thomas's trousers.

"Lizzy!" he griped. Thomas looked up at Lizzy and followed her gaze to the cabin, where he spied Mr. Barton. He clamped his mouth shut, dropped his hand from the bucket, and quickly moved to stand beside his sister.

Lizzy lowered the bucket to the ground and took Thomas's hand in her own. While she knew it would be foolish to try to outrun Mr. Barton, she could think of no other alternative.

Before she could dash into the trees, Mr. Barton bowed his head and addressed her. "Miss Grey, lovely to see you again."

Thomas turned his wide eyes to his sister. Lizzy blinked a few times then dipped in an awkward curtsy. Meeting an acquaintance on a dirt road among the overgrown woods had not been covered in the etiquette lessons her stepmother had given her.

"Mr. Barton," she said simply.

The man inclined his head and then motioned to the now nearly empty bucket at her feet. "May I help you with that?"

Lizzy looked between him and the bucket, uncertain how to proceed. She merely nodded. Mr. Barton smiled, walked over, and retrieved the bucket before heading to the river to refill it.

Thomas's hand remained clasped in Lizzy's, and she could not think clearly.

Mr. Barton returned with the water and walked to the doorway. "Would you like this inside, or shall I leave it here?"

"Just inside the door would be fine." It became difficult to maneuver words around her hazy thoughts.

Thomas released his grip and quickly ran ahead of Mr. Barton to push the door wide. Mr. Barton set down his load and stepped back outside.

He squatted down to Thomas's eye level. "And what's your name?"

Thomas glanced at Lizzy. The fear in his eyes cleared the fog from her brain. She moved behind him and laid a hand on his shoulder. Mr. Barton did not rise. He proceeded to look between the two of them and waited for an answer.

"This is Thomas, my brother."

Mr. Barton extended his hand. "How do you do, Thomas? I'm Barton."

Thomas looked to Lizzy again, and when she nodded, he shook Mr. Barton's hand. "Hello, sir." His head tilted and he continued. "Are you the man who gave Lizzy a ride home?"

"Yes, although Brutus actually did most of the work." Mr. Barton gave Thomas a quick wink and then stood.

"Brutus. That's your horse. Did you bring him?" Thomas eagerly looked around the clearing, and Mr. Barton chuckled.

"Brutus carried me most of the way, but I thought if I brought him to the cabin, he might scare you off. I tied him up near the road."

"Can I see him?" Thomas asked, rocking back and forth on his toes. "Lizzy said he was a giant."

"Did she?" Mr. Barton grinned, and reality hit Lizzy squarely in the chest.

"You followed me," Lizzy said curtly. "I asked you to allow me my privacy—"

"Those were not your exact words," Mr. Barton cut in. "You requested I allow you to walk alone to your *cousin's* house. I never promised not to follow and assure your safe arrival."

Lizzy suppressed her sudden desire to throw something. Instead she crossed her arms. "Did you leave the food as well?" Lizzy asked.

Mr. Barton lazily lifted his shoulders. "I figured you would appreciate the gesture."

"Obviously I do not." Lizzy pinned him with a glare.

"Obviously." Mr. Barton's lips twitched.

Lizzy spoke her fears aloud. "No doubt you told Mr. Everly we were here." She and Thomas would have to leave tonight. Perhaps they could stay at the Hilly Crest for one night and then catch the coach at first light.

"I've told no one," Mr. Barton said.

Lizzy pressed her eyes closed for a moment, offering a silent prayer of gratitude. "Thank you, sir." She could not risk her name or description being shared with such an influential member of society. Despite his inordinate charity, Mr. Everly would be bound to reveal her and Thomas's whereabouts to her uncle. "The truth is, Thomas and I were caught in an awful storm. We ventured into the woods seeking shelter, and that's when we came upon the cabin. We did not intend to remain, but I'll admit it's an ideal situation for us at this time."

The humor disappeared from Mr. Barton's face. "How long have you been here?" he asked.

Lizzy straightened her shoulders in an attempt to appear unruffled. "Ten days."

Mr. Barton did not hide his shock. "Ten days! Miss Grey, why did you not seek shelter at Everly Manor? Surely you would have been offered a room, which would be decidedly more comfortable than your current accommodations."

"You are wrong, sir." Lizzy waved a dismissive hand. "Thomas and I are most content here. The cabin appeared to be abandoned, so I didn't think it would cause any harm for us to remain. However, I realize we've overstayed our welcome. We shall be on our way in the morning."

Mr. Barton took several full breaths before he spoke again. "And where will you go?"

Lizzy tried to fake nonchalance, but her shrug was stiff and her smile pinched.

Mr. Barton's eyes narrowed. "Have you no family? No relations to provide for you?"

Lizzy's mouth drew tight. "We are not paupers, Mr. Barton. As I've explained, we simply got lost in the woods, and Thomas enjoyed the adventure, so I let the charade continue. Now that I know my way to Hillcrest, we shall be on our way. While you owe me nothing, I would ask that you do not reveal our existence to Mr. Everly until after our departure. I've heard he is a sensible and kind man, but I do not know him myself and therefore cannot trust his discretion in this matter."

Mr. Barton's brow creased. "Miss Grey, what are you running from?"

Lizzy clasped her hands in front of her bosom. She could not sort through the combination of emotions Mr. Barton caused. She was flustered by his appearance, yet touched at his consideration. "Please don't concern yourself with our affairs. I've things well in hand, and it's nothing nefarious, I promise. Two days will be ample time."

"Two days?"

"Yes, and then you may reveal to Mr. Everly our encroachment on his property. I will leave compensation for his kindness." Lizzy's chin inched up a notch as she feigned a confidence she did not feel. "Will you promise your silence?" Lizzy could only hope she'd convinced him to not reveal her and Thomas's presence at the cabin. She'd asked for two days' time, but she now planned to be gone by nightfall.

Mr. Barton turned and evaluated Thomas before he answered. "I will not tell anyone you are here, on one condition." Lizzy's eyebrows shot up. "You must allow Thomas to meet Brutus."

Mr. Barton's stipulation caught Lizzy off guard. His smile appeared to be sincere, and a visit with Brutus would lift Thomas's spirits. Showing Thomas a horse seemed a simple thing. She schooled her shocked expression and looked to her brother. "Would you like that, Thomas?" Her brother nodded eagerly. "Very well, Mr. Barton. Lead the way."

Barton led the siblings down the path, occasionally glancing over his shoulder to make sure Miss Grey and her brother followed. While he engaged Thomas in menial conversation about his horse, Barton considered his options. The siblings appeared to be faring well, but he could not in good conscience allow them to remain in the dilapidated cabin.

He'd seen Miss Grey's poorly masked fear when he'd questioned their circumstance. Her speckled eyes reflected both pride and apprehension. If she had means, why was she squatting in a cottage in the woods?

He had no intention of leaving them to themselves and had only suggested meeting Brutus to buy time. As they neared the river, Barton stepped off the path and walked upstream a short distance to where Brutus stood, tied to a tree.

"He is a giant!" Thomas declared.

Barton laughed and untied the reins. "Come over here, so I can properly introduce you."

Thomas walked forward with wide eyes. Barton tugged the reins so the horse would dip his head down to the boy's level. Introductions were made, and Barton showed Thomas a spot above Brutus's eyes where he enjoyed being rubbed.

While Thomas busied himself talking to the horse and rubbing his hands over Brutus's large head, Barton watched Miss Grey. She constantly scanned their surroundings, and she stood stiffly, as if she were afraid any movement would sound an alarm.

Barton stepped near and whispered, "What are you looking for, Miss Grey?"

She yelped and jumped nearly a foot. Color flooded her cheeks, and her hand flew to her chest. "You startled me, Mr. Barton."

"That much was obvious. And while I find it delightful to hear you squeal again, I must admit you baffle me. You are obviously distressed, yet you refuse to tell me why." As Barton spoke he saw Miss Grey restore her composure and erect her walls.

"Do you have any siblings, Mr. Barton?"

While the change in topic was unexpected, Barton hoped the conversation would provide further insight about the woman standing before him. "Yes, I do."

"Are you close?"

"My elder sister has always seen herself as a second mother. Since my mother doted on me, my sister inserted herself into the role of critic and protector. Thankfully, she is now married, and her husband is the recipient of her attentions. We are amiable, but I am closer to my younger brother."

Miss Grey's eyes softened as she watched Thomas.

Barton turned back to the boy. "Would you like to sit on Brutus's back?"

Thomas looked to his sister for approval, and when it was granted, a wide grin spread across his face.

"Step onto my knee, and then swing your leg over Brutus's back." Barton patted his thigh, and Thomas followed his instruction.

Once Thomas was in the saddle, Barton tossed him the end of the reins while keeping hold of the horse's bridle. "I like this part of our adventure, Lizzy. Now I feel like a giant."

Miss Grey laughed with her brother and then spoke so only Barton would hear. "Would you do anything for your brother, Mr. Barton?"

Barton hoped if he kept the tone light, Miss Grey would continue talking. "Other than give him my share of dessert, yes, I would."

"Thomas is my half-brother, but I love him beyond all else. I would do anything for him. As he said, we are on a grand adventure. There is no need for concern."

"So, you refuse my help?"

"Not true." Miss Grey motioned to her brother. "I accepted your food, I've ridden your horse, and I've met your conditions. Please inform your mother and your sister that you've completed your gentlemanly duties, for which Thomas and I are grateful." Miss Grey stepped beside Brutus and extended her arms. "Come down now, Thomas."

Once Thomas was safely on the ground, Miss Grey held his hand in hers.

"Thank you, Mr. Barton," the boy said.

"You're very welcome. Perhaps next time, you can go for a real ride on Brutus's back."

"Really?" Thomas asked, but before Barton could offer any assurance, Miss Grey cut in.

"Thank you for your time, Mr. Barton. And please remember you gave your word not to disclose our trespass for two days."

Barton inclined his head but said nothing more. He clenched his fists as the duo walked away. Barton was a man of his word, thus his only option was to mount Brutus and return to Everly Manor.

Chapter 10

BARTON EYED THE ANGLE OF the cue and struck the ball. It fell into the corner pocket with precision, and he walked around the table to line up his next shot. However, before he could shoot, his mother and sister swept into the room.

"You missed tea." Bethany had never been one to beat about the bush.

Barton sighed. "Yes, I did." He stood at his full height and held his cue at his side. "I trust Henderson informed you I was unavailable."

"Of course." Bethany pulled off her gloves. "But he used the word *indisposed.*" Bethany removed a cue from the rack and picked up where Barton had left off. After missing her shot, she harrumphed and twisted her lips into a frown.

"It's a tricky game." Barton offered an unrepentant smile.

"Where were you, Harrison?" Barton's mother always called her children by their Christian names. Since she had not been consulted on the gender of her children, nor was she able to choose their surname, she claimed their names were the one thing she got to have an opinion about and she meant to make the most of it.

"I was here, Mother."

"You missed tea for a game of billiards?" His mother looked positively shocked.

Barton laid his cue aside and moved to take his mother's hand. He placed a kiss on her fingers. "My apologies. I'm a bit out of sorts today."

Barton's mother placed her hand on his cheek. "Are you unwell?"

"No. I'm trying to figure out how to help someone who refuses my assistance." Barton stepped away from his mother and walked to the window. He chuckled, despite the confusion churning within. "That's the irony, isn't it? Wanting to do something but knowing your hands are tied?"

"Anything I can help with?" His mother's voice was tinged with curiosity.

Barton shook his head and turned his back to the window.

"Are you speaking of a tenant?" Bethany asked.

"I've promised her I won't reveal any details."

"It's a woman?" Bethany asked and gave her mother a conspiratorial grin.

"Bethany, remind me again when the renovations on your kitchen will be complete." Barton raised a single eyebrow and smirked at his sister.

"Oh, come now, Barton. I will be gone in a matter of weeks, and you will miss me immensely." Bethany aimed again, this time pocketing the billiard ball. She stood straight, with a triumphant smile. "Now, tell us. Who is this woman?"

Barton ignored the question. "Please excuse me. I owe Murray a visit." He gave a quick nod to his mother and headed to the stables to saddle Brutus.

When Barton arrived at Murray's cottage, he was greeted with Murray's familiar grunt. Barton tipped his hat and walked to the fence surrounding the corral where the man stood haltering his old swayback horse, Rose.

Murray worked in silence, and Barton observed likewise. The old man secured the halter and then walked the animal through the open gate. "It's gonna storm later," he said.

Barton looked upwards and squinted his eyes. "The sky looks clear now."

Murray scoffed. "Suit yerself."

Barton followed Murray to the small stable. He knew better than to be offended by the old man's gruffness. Murray had served his family for more than fifty years and had only recently agreed to concede his position as stable master. Barton had promised to bring any new foals to Murray for training before his old friend would agree to move to the cottage Barton had had built for him. The cottage was not large, but Murray did not need space inside. He needed space outside. Barton had assisted in the construction of a small paddock and helped fence the grazing pasture that extended behind the cottage down to the trees.

The day the servants had moved Murray's belongings to the cottage, he'd complained the entire time. Barton worried that perhaps he had been too rash. But that first day, when they'd set Rose loose in the pasture, Barton saw the moisture pool in Murray's eyes, and Barton knew he'd done the right thing.

Murray secured the lock on Rose's stall and turned to face Barton.

"What can you tell me about Miss Grey?" Barton asked. "You gave her a ride to the village a few days ago."

"I remember." Murray walked past Barton and said nothing more until he'd settled into a chair outside his front door. "Pretty lass."

"Yes, she is." Barton disappeared into the cottage and then returned with a second seat in hand. "Can you tell me anything about her?" Barton sat down.

"She talked a lot at first, but it was all a yarn. Some story about her cousin having a baby." Murray rubbed a hand down the side of his face. "Didn't seem to know her way around either."

"She told me a similar tale." Silence settled between them, and Barton watched the breeze play with the leaves of the linden trees. "She has a brother, and I think they might be in trouble."

Murray frowned and nodded his head in agreement. "She's too skinny."

Barton had noticed. "Anything else?"

Murray didn't say anything more. Barton stayed, meditating in the silence, until he saw the angry storm rolling westward over the trees.

"Good night, Murray." Barton touched his hat, mounted Brutus, and rode back to Everly Manor.

Chapter 11

Lizzy could only hope Mr. Barton would leave them be for two days' time. When they returned to the cabin, Lizzy made tea, and then, not knowing how exactly to prepare them, she boiled the hens. She and Thomas would eat one before they left and take the other with them, in case, heaven forbid, they found themselves unable to spend the night at the inn.

For the next hour Lizzy instructed Thomas as they tidied the cabin, returning everything to the place they'd discovered it—well, everything except the stool they'd used as firewood. Lizzy pulled two crowns from her bag and set them on the mantel.

"Can't we stay a few more days?" Thomas asked. "Mr. Barton was nice, and he said I could ride Brutus."

Lizzy would not admit to her brother that Mr. Barton's offer was one of the many reasons it was necessary to leave that evening. "I think you're trying to get out of walking again. Aren't you up for more adventure?"

"Riding Brutus would be an adventure." Thomas crossed his arms and kicked at an imaginary rock.

Lizzy moved to kneel before him. "Riding Brutus would be an adventure. And I'm sorry you will miss it, but you know we can't let Uncle find us, or he will escort you to the *Vendetta* himself. Mr. Barton was kind today, but we can't trust anyone yet. We'll leave tonight and tomorrow travel south, where we can let a cabin of our own. No sneaking around, no feeling hungry—"

"And no Brutus," Thomas finished with a pout.

Lizzy sighed. "Where's my brave brother?" Thomas looked up through his lashes, and Lizzy reached over to muss his hair. "Come on, now, help me finish packing our clothes."

Thomas sulked for another full minute until Lizzy tossed him his extra clothing and asked him to roll it up. She placed the sapphires in her reticule and loaded their meager belongings into her bag. Then she served Thomas a generous portion of meat, and they ate a silent meal.

One hour later the siblings stepped out from the trees and turned to follow the road to Hillcrest.

Thirty minutes after that, it began to rain. Torrentially.

Chapter 12

DESPITE THE FACT THAT COOK had prepared one of Barton's favorite meals, he had no appetite. The sleet hitting the windows was a prickling reminder of his foolish promise to Miss Grey. The gamekeeper's cottage was adequate shelter in an average storm, but the winds howling outside and the intermittent hail pelting the windowpanes was anything but average.

Barton ignored the conversation at the table and tensed every time the sleet crackled against the glass. Why had he given his word? Would the derelict cabin be able to weather the storm? Did the siblings have enough wood? Enough blankets? Enough food?

When Bethany shouted his name, he dropped his fork to his plate. "Have you heard a word I've said?" she asked.

Barton glanced at his mother and brother, who both granted him a look of pity. "My apologies, Bethany. My mind is elsewhere."

"Are you thinking about that girl?" she asked.

"What girl?" Franklin asked, leaning forward.

"The mystery girl Barton met but can't tell us about." Bethany lifted her chin and folded her hands in her lap.

"That's enough." The matron eyed each of her children.

"I can't do it." Barton pushed out of his seat. "I have to make sure they're safe."

"What are you talking about?" Franklin raised his hands in frustration.

"They?" Bethany asked. "It's not just the girl?"

"What girl?" Franklin's voice rose.

"The one he can't tell us about," Bethany offered. "Although now it sounds like there's more than the girl."

"Harrison, where are you going?" Barton's mother asked as she motioned for the footman to pull back her chair. Barton's siblings also stood, and the trio followed him to the front hall. Barton called for his greatcoat, a lantern, and for Brutus to be saddled.

Mrs. Everly's eyes grew wide as she watched Henderson, the butler, secure Barton's greatcoat. "It's horrendous outside. You cannot go out in this weather," she protested. Barton ignored his mother while he pulled on his gloves and arranged his hat. "Harrison! Where do you think you're going?" she demanded.

"To Mr. Doyle's cottage." He accepted a lantern from Henderson.

"Why?" his mother asked. "The place has been empty for years. There have been no repairs, and it could easily crumble to bits in this storm."

"Exactly." Barton leaned forward and kissed his mother's cheek. "Please have an extra room prepared. I'll return soon."

Chapter 13

LIZZY WOULD READILY ADMIT SHE had deplorable timing. While she could mentally justify every decision she made, fate seemed determined to test her resolve. Once again Mother Nature decided to release her fury on Cambridgeshire. Lizzy began to wonder if Thomas's fate aboard the *Vendetta* would be preferable to death by hailstorm.

Thomas yelped in pain. "It hurts, Lizzy!"

"Try to keep your head down," she called over the noise of the storm.

A violent gust winged across the open road, sending needles of sleet cutting into Lizzy's exposed skin.

"Run to the willow tree." Lizzy pointed to the large tree off the side of the road.

Thomas covered his head with his hands and ran straight through the thrashing boughs. As Lizzy followed him, a branch whipped across her face, but she ignored the sting on her cheek and pushed forward until she sat huddled with Thomas near the trunk of the tree. The hail continued to fall, but the multitude of branches helped deflect some of the onslaught.

"I'm sorry, Thomas. I'm so sorry." Lizzy pulled him into her arms and let her tears mix with the moisture running down her face.

"I'm scared, Lizzy," Thomas said. "Can't we go back to the cabin?"

Lizzy pressed a kiss to the top of Thomas's head. "All will be well. It has to be." The words were meant to reassure her as much as they were meant to comfort her brother. But even as Lizzy said them, she doubted their veracity.

The large tree creaked and groaned as the violent wind pulled and pushed it in conflicting directions. Lizzy chanced an upward glance and realized the shelter they'd sought was riddled with half-dead branches and limbs. Fear clenched her gut, and she pulled on Thomas's arm.

"We have to move," Lizzy yelled.

"No!" Thomas yanked away from Lizzy's grip. He wrapped his arms around his legs and tucked his head low. With a muffled voice he yelled, "I'm not leaving."

Lizzy pushed her bag back on her shoulder and stuck her hands under her brother's arms. "Thomas, it's dangerous. We have to go, now!"

The sweeping wind snaked through the low-hanging boughs, and the deadened wood groaned from the pressure.

"Don't you hear that? The tree is going to fall!" Lizzy diligently pulled Thomas upwards, but he shifted and shrugged and broke her hold.

With the next gust of wind, several large limbs broke free and crashed down through the higher branches. Lizzy screamed and threw her body over Thomas. She waited for the limbs to strike her back, but fortunately she remained unscathed. Shivers of cold and fear quivered through her body as she stared at the large branch that had landed only a foot away. Thomas looked up, too, and his wide eyes turned to his sister. His breathing quickened, and his face scrunched in a combination of guilt and fear. Lizzy reached for Thomas's hand, and he pushed up to his feet.

Then they ran.

Lizzy meant to head for the road and shielded her eyes with her free hand to gain her bearings. The wind tore at her clothing, tangling her cloak and skirt around her ankles. She pressed on, spying the narrow span of dirt where the trees lined the thoroughfare. She was determined to run all the way to town. Moving was paramount to survival. Movement occupied her body and mind. Stillness meant fear. Stillness meant danger.

When they were only ten feet from the road, a violent gust thrashed overhead. Lizzy heard the crack, the splitting of wood, but it was too late. An entire tree was torn from the earth. Thomas's feet simply stopped. His hand slipped from Lizzy's as the tree fell towards him. He closed his eyes to brace for the impact, but in the next moment Lizzy shoved him—hard.

She turned. The crack of splintered wood echoed with her scream as the tree knocked her to the ground, and her vision went dark.

Chapter 14

BARTON SPOKE LOW, URGING BRUTUS forward on the overgrown path. Thankfully, his horse remained undaunted by the onslaught of hail and the merciless wind. Barton held a lantern close to his body, hoping to protect the flame from the wind. The shadow of Mr. Doyle's cabin came into view, and Barton took a deep breath. Soon Miss Grey and Thomas would be in the saddle, and he could lead them back to the safety of Everly Manor.

With a command from his master, Brutus came to a stop, and Barton jumped down. The door had swollen from the rain and stuck when he tried to open it. With a fierce shove of his shoulder, he wretched it free, but the darkness inside the cottage pulled a curse from his lips.

The siblings were gone. The hearth lay cold, the room absent of any personal effects, yet Barton's mind could not comprehend that they would depart in the storm. Miss Grey had asked for two days. He never considered they would leave that very day.

Miss Grey was a stubborn, misguided fool. How were she and Thomas going to navigate this storm? They had no horse, no transportation beyond their own feet, and there would be no one on the road to offer them assistance. Certainly Miss Grey would come to her senses and stop at one of the tenant farms to wait out the tempest.

He should return home and do the same himself, except as he stood in the cold, empty cabin, Barton considered the events of the day. In leaving during the storm, Miss Grey may have played the part of a fool, but she was not daft. She'd left because she felt she had no other choice. Barton didn't know whom she was running from, but revealing himself earlier had scared her off.

He should have waited longer before approaching the siblings or tried to discover the reason for Miss Grey's secrecy. If he had not appeared today, she and Thomas would be huddled in the relative safety of Mr. Doyle's cabin. Although he justified his visit as charity, providing the pair with food, his real reason had been curiosity about the cautious, witty woman with golden eyes. Guilt churned through him. Miss Grey and her brother had left because of his interference.

A large crash overhead pulled Barton from his thoughts. The violent wind knocked through the trees, scattering branches on the roof of the cabin. Barton stepped back into the storm as Brutus shifted his hooves, anxious to be away from the falling debris.

"Come on." Barton swung into the saddle and turned Brutus back to the path. "We can't go home quite yet."

Barton moved down the west road, inquiring at each cottage along the way. Every stop plummeted his hopes further. No one had seen Miss Grey or her brother.

Several of the men opted to join in the search, and soon a party of seven riders spread across the road, waving their lanterns and calling out for the missing siblings. Barton had left Miss Grey shortly after two o'clock. The storm had started just before dinner, and while Barton hoped Miss Grey and her brother had covered the distance to Hillcrest in that time, he knew it was impossible.

Barton assumed Miss Grey's destination to be the village, but because he knew so little of her situation, the group decided to split up at the main road. Two men headed west, and another rider was sent to Everly Manor to inform Mrs. Everly that Barton was well and inquire if perhaps the siblings had wandered to the safety of the estate. Barton and three more men turned east, towards Hillcrest.

The moisture converted the dirt road to a strip of mud. The sludge, combined with the darkness and a maze of debris, slowed the search. Barton's breeches were soaked through, but his greatcoat protected his shoulders and chest and held back the biting cold. He maneuvered Brutus around a mass of twisted branches and stopped as a gust of wind pelted his face with razor-edged sleet. Brutus whinnied and tossed his head away from the onslaught of hail. The burst of wind died away, and Barton pressed his heels to Brutus's side as a cry sounded through the air.

"Whoa!" he called, and when the other Hillcrest-bound riders looked to him, he lifted the lantern to illuminate his face. He held up his hand for silence. His ears strained to hear the call again.

The faint sound carried across the breeze, and Barton recognized the cry for help. The other men heard it, too, and without a word the group split apart and searched the edges of the road. Barton's heart flapped wildly in his chest as his eyes scanned the shadowed rocks and trees.

"Hello?" he called into the night. "Hello there!"

"Help!" The voice rang closer.

"Keep calling out, so I can hear you!" Barton shouted to the darkness and held his lamp even with his hat.

"Please, help!" came the reply.

As he neared, Barton discerned that the voice belonged to a child, a child he recognized. "Thomas?" he called but no reply came. "Thomas!" he shouted again. "Is that you? Brutus and I can't see you."

"Mr. Barton?" came the shaky reply.

"Yes." Barton whistled for the other members of his search party. "Can you see my light?"

"Yes."

"Walk towards me, Thomas." Barton slid out of his saddle.

"I can't," Thomas's voice sounded through the trees.

Blast the darkness! Barton could not see a thing. "Yes, you can. Just walk slowly, and I'll wait right here."

Barton held the lantern higher, straining both his ears and his eyes for any sign of the child. The other men approached, and he called for silence.

"Thomas?" he called again.

"I can't leave Lizzy," came the reply.

Barton's heart stopped altogether. The next moments passed in a blur as he organized the men into a line and then moved them forward as a unified front to find the siblings. A shout from the far left sent Barton running in that direction.

His light fell upon Thomas. The boy was soaked through, his skin tinged blue as he shivered violently. One of the men reached forward to heft him from the branches, despite his cries of protest. Thomas flailed against his rescuer, determined to keep hold of something on the ground. Barton called out reassurance as he waded through the branches to reach the boy.

Thomas's hold finally broke, and he was thrust into Barton's arms.

"She's dead!" he sobbed against Barton's shoulder. "She's dead, and it's all my fault."

Barton did not need to ask about whom Thomas referred. He shifted Thomas to his side and peered down into the hollow of the tree branches where the boy had sat. One of the men lowered his lantern, and the sight made Barton's heart ache. Miss Grey's face was covered with a mixture of blood and dirt, and her body lay pinned beneath the large tree.

Barton's longtime tenant Mr. Willard leaned low and peered at Miss Grey's form. "She ain't dead. She's breathing, sir."

Relief flooded Barton's heart.

"It's slight, but I see it." Willard pointed in excitement.

Without a second thought, Barton ignored Thomas's cries and tossed him into the arms of a man standing clear of the felled tree. "Get the boy to Everly Manor, and send someone for the doctor. And send a rider to notify the other men that Miss Grey has been found." Then Barton spoke quickly to Thomas. "Go with Mr. Lancaster. Now I must help your sister."

Barton did not watch the man leave; instead he kicked aside the loose limbs of the tree and climbed to where he could reach Miss Grey. Willard held a lantern aloft.

"Miss Grey," Barton called, placing his hand on her face. "Elizabeth, can you hear me?" He moved his hands across her shoulders and down her arms, searching for injury. Beyond the gashes on her forehead and cheek, he found nothing obvious. Nevertheless, his heart continued its frantic pace. She was near frozen and had most likely suffered various internal injuries.

"Set the lamps aside; we must lift the tree and pull her out." Barton moved to where he could easily access the large tree trunk, and the other two men joined him. "Willard, you pull her free while we lift." Each man nodded. "One. Two. Three." Barton and his companion grunted with the effort.

"A little more," Willard called, looping his hands under Miss Grey's arms.

Gravity worked against the men. The weighted wood and awkward angle forced them to cradle the bulky trunk in their arms. Barton was not the most robust of men, but his muscles were firm from working beside his tenants. Those muscles seared with pain as he pushed upwards with his legs and arms.

"That's it," Willard called, and he slowly dragged Miss Grey to an area free of debris.

Once Barton ensured Miss Grey was clear of any danger, he counted off again, and in unison the men dropped their heavy load. He took no consideration for the tears in his greatcoat, nor did he think on the dull throbbing in his arms. Instead Barton moved directly to Miss Grey.

He looked over her person again, his heart swelling in his chest. The confident, witty woman he'd met had been stripped to a shell of fragile humanity. Willard removed the bag hanging over Miss Grey's arm. Barton shed his greatcoat, and with the assistance of his tenants, wrapped the thick garment around Miss Grey's frame. Then he motioned for Willard to follow as he made his way to Brutus. It took the combined efforts of Willard and his companion to lift Miss Grey up to Barton after he'd climbed into the saddle. Willard carried Miss Grey's bag, and soon they were settled and on their way to Everly Manor. Barton strengthened his hold and offered a prayer that Miss Grey would survive.

Willard and his companion held the lanterns and flanked Barton on their return to the manor. When they neared the house, Barton saw his brother standing watch at the front window. Franklin called to someone in the house, and an army of servants met their small group.

Franklin rushed out and reached for Miss Grey, and Barton gently handed her over to his brother. "How is she?" Franklin asked.

"Alive. But barely." Barton slid out of the saddle and put a hand on Brutus's head. He turned to the groom holding the reins. "Brush him down until he's dry. Then give him an extra bucket of oats and make sure he's covered for the night."

"Yes, sir." The groom led Brutus away.

Barton bounded up the front stairs and into the foyer behind his brother.

"The boy insisted you would save her," Franklin said over his shoulder.

"She's not in the clear yet. Have a maid change her into dry clothes and build up a fire." Barton watched Franklin carry Miss Grey upstairs before he turned to Henderson. "Please bring the men inside to wait for the rain to let up. They, too, need a blazing fire and something warm to eat and drink."

After Henderson left to do his master's bidding, Barton's mother came rushing down the stairs. "You're going to catch your death." She placed her hands on Barton's arms and looked him over.

Barton took his mother's hands in his own. "I'm well, mother. Has the doctor arrived?"

She bit her bottom lip and shook her head. "You can't expect him to travel in this storm."

Barton refrained from sharing the response that immediately came to mind. He took a deep breath. "I think the worst of the storm has past. How is Thomas?"

"Scared. His hands were cut and scraped raw. When we asked what happened he said he tried to pull the branches off his sister, but there were too many. His wounds have been cleaned and dressed. They'll heal, in time." His mother shook her head and squeezed Barton's hands. "The poor boy. He's lucky you found them, Harrison. Bethany sat with him, singing lullabies. He's sleeping now."

"Where did Franklin take Miss Grey?"

"To the blue room."

"Thank you, Mother." Barton leaned forward and kissed her cheek. "I shall change and join you there shortly."

Barton made quick work of changing into dry clothes and then went directly to Miss Grey. He found his housekeeper, Mrs. Brown, wiping Miss Grey's forehead with a damp cloth. "How is she?" he said.

"It's hard to say, sir. The poor thing hasn't yet opened her eyes." Mrs. Brown pulled the cloth back and stood up straight. "Might have a broken rib or two, though we won't know until she wakes or the doctor comes."

Barton thanked his housekeeper for her ministrations. "I'll sit with her for a bit while you check on the boy."

Barton pulled a chair beside Miss Grey's bed and evaluated her condition. Her hair had been plaited into a loose braid, and she looked peaceful in sleep. Barton reached for her hand, and once he confirmed her body had warmed, he felt for her pulse in her wrist. It took him several attempts to find the rhythm, but he finally located the steady thrum. Barton watched her breathe while he rubbed his thumb over the soft skin on her wrist.

"Harrison." His mother bustled into the room, and Barton nearly tossed Miss Grey's hand onto the bed as he jumped backwards. "Thank goodness you're dry. I shall have a tray brought up."

Mrs. Everly made her request, and while they waited for the refreshment to arrive, Barton recounted the events of the evening. His mother remained quiet until after the tea arrived and she'd poured out. "This is the woman you spoke of earlier?"

"Yes," Barton replied.

"What do you know of her?"

"Very little." Barton glanced at Miss Grey's unconscious form. "And I've given my word not to reveal the little I know."

"Hmm." His mother pursed her lips.

Barton rubbed a hand across his face.

"Harrison. The entire situation sounds like trouble."

Barton turned back to his mother. "Are you suggesting I should have left her alone?"

"Not at all." Barton's mother touched his arm. "I would expect nothing less than for you to help. It's in your blood. Look at her." His mother waved her hand towards Miss Grey. "There's been trouble already. If the poor thing lasts the night, I suspect it may be only the beginning."

A knock on the door announced the arrival of the doctor. Barton excused himself from the room to allow the doctor to perform a thorough examination, and after assuring himself Thomas still slept, Barton thought on his mother's words.

The trouble had not begun when Barton approached Miss Grey at the cabin. He'd sensed trouble the moment he looked into her mesmerizing eyes as she sat on the floor of the apothecary shop. Now he had to figure out what to do about it.

Chapter 15

THE DOCTOR DIAGNOSED LIZZY WITH at least three broken ribs and predicted her injuries would produce deep, colorful bruises. Thankfully, he did not believe she would suffer any permanent injury and emphasized how fortunate Lizzy was to only have suffered a mild concussion along with the scrapes on her head and face and the injury to her ribs.

A young blonde maid related these details, as well as Thomas's situation, to Lizzy when she woke in the middle of the night. "I've been left with instructions to wake Mr. Everly, ma'am."

"Please don't." Lizzy held up her hand in protest and then cried out as pain radiated through her body. She fell back against her pillows with a moan. "I'm going to fall back asleep now. There's no need to wake him, as we can sort it all out in the morning."

The maid reluctantly agreed, and Lizzy closed her eyes, but she could not sleep. Her entire body ached, and her head throbbed. She could not reconcile how she came to Everly Manor. The last thing she remembered was clutching her bag as she ran through the storm with Thomas.

Her bag! Her mother's jewels. Dread filled Lizzy's chest, and she forced her breathing to remain even. As much as she wanted to open her eyes and search for her belongings, the maid sat quietly in a corner of the room, and Lizzy did not want the young girl to wake Mr. Everly. She needed time to evaluate her situation and come up with a new plan.

As her mind circled through the options, Lizzy became acutely aware of the pain pulsing through her body. She concentrated on pushing it away, determined to win the battle. But the hurt continued to spread until Lizzy's body surrendered and she passed out again.

Consciousness returned slowly. Lizzy's body felt heavy, and her mind filled with a heavy fog. Lizzy's eyes remained closed, but her ears tuned in to the conversation floating around her.

"What about internal bleeding?" a definite masculine and somewhat familiar voice asked.

"We won't know for sure for a day or two. The best indicator will be the patient herself. If she is able to eat regular meals and move around on her own, we will know her body is healing." This voice was not familiar at all. "You've done all you can, Mr. Everly. Miss Grey is lucky you found her."

"Thank you, doctor," the first man, Mr. Everly, replied. Then Lizzy heard the door open and close.

She counted to one hundred, straining to catch the sound of movement or a breath, and when she heard nothing, she slowly opened her eyes. Lizzy discovered she was not alone. A man, most likely Mr. Everly, stood no more than five feet away, but he did not notice her consciousness, because he was staring out the window.

A fire crackled in the fireplace directly across from the bed. Blue cotton curtains framed both the window where the man stood on the right and another window farther along the wall. To the left side of the bed a wardrobe was situated in the corner and a chair sat near the bed, although it looked out of place. A beautiful quilt, dyed a regal shade of blue, covered the bed Lizzy lay in.

She evaluated the man standing in her room. His even frame stood just over six feet tall, and as Lizzy noted how well his dark-brown coat fit across his shoulders a vague familiarity trickled over her. Various shades of yellow trailed through the loose waves of his hair, and a sudden warmth flooded Lizzy's senses. In her effort to evaluate him further, she shifted and cried out in pain, alerting the man to her consciousness.

The figure turned from the window. "Mr. Barton," Lizzy said, surprised she had not recognized him earlier.

Mr. Barton smiled and tipped his head. "Good morning, Miss Grey. I'm sorry if I disturbed you."

"Not at all, I . . . well, I did not expect to see you is all." Lizzy's hands fluttered around until she stilled them in her lap.

With quick strides Mr. Barton moved to the bell pull. "I'm sure you would like some refreshment."

Lizzy was parched. She nodded her agreement.

A servant arrived, and Mr. Barton made the request. He then turned back to Lizzy. "I also sent for Thomas. He's been worried about you."

"Oh!" Lizzy covered her mouth with her hands. "I'm ashamed I did not ask for him sooner."

Mr. Barton stood at the foot of her bed. "You've nothing to be ashamed of, Miss Grey. You've endured a rather harrowing accident. My sister, Bethany, has taken Thomas under her wing. I'm confident you will find him well."

"I did not realize your sister was in residence at Everly Manor."

Mr. Barton's lips twitched, and his eyebrows rose. "Did you not?"

Lizzy's head throbbed. "Do you know if my belongings were recovered? My bag contained several personal effects."

Mr. Barton waved a hand towards the bureau. "You'll find your belongings there."

"Thank you. And thank you to Mr. Everly. Perhaps when he has a free moment he would be willing to relate the story of my . . . rescue?" Her cheeks warmed, and Lizzy looked down at her hands.

Mr. Barton laughed lightly. "I'm sure Everly would be happy to indulge your request. In fact—"

Mr. Barton's words were cut short when the blonde-haired servant girl arrived with Thomas in hand.

Lizzy's heart warmed as she noted the bandages wrapped around Thomas's palms. "Hello, Thomas."

Tears welled in Thomas's eyes. "Mrs. Bethany told me you needed lots of sleep to get better. Are you better now?"

"Yes, dear boy. I'm a bit sore and I am tired, but I will recover." Lizzy reached a hand forward and wiggled her fingers. "Come here." Thomas moved near, and she placed her hand on the side of his cheek. "Thank you for being brave."

Thomas grinned and held up his hands. "I hope I get some scars so I can tell a good story."

Lizzy wanted to laugh with him, but a smile was all she could manage. Exhaustion consumed her.

"Shall we let your sister rest?" Mr. Barton asked. He sent Thomas with the servant girl, with a promise that Thomas could visit more with Lizzy that afternoon.

The moment Mr. Barton turned back towards Lizzy a middle-aged woman swept into the room as if she were right at home.

The woman looked between Mr. Barton and Lizzy. "Good. You're awake."

Mr. Barton held a hand towards the matron. "Miss Grey, may I present Mrs. Everly?"

"How do you do?" Lizzy felt woefully inadequate, unable to give the woman the proper courtesies while sitting in bed. Mr. Barton introduced the woman as Mrs. Everly, but surely she was not the current mistress of the household. The streaks of grey in her hair and the soft wrinkles around her eyes led Lizzy to believe this woman was Mr. Everly's mother.

"It's nice to finally be properly introduced, Miss Grey. How are you feeling?" Mrs. Everly looked at Lizzy while she straightened the corner of the blanket.

"Honestly I feel like I've been trampled by a horse." Lizzy tried to sit up straighter but winced as pain splintered through her body.

"That's not surprising, considering a tree fell on you." Mrs. Everly walked to the window, and after a quick glance outside, she turned back around. "Harrison, have you called for a tray?"

Lizzy looked at Mr. Barton—*Harrison Barton*. Lizzy liked the sound of his name.

He shifted his weight and then cleared his throat. "It should arrive shortly."

"Good. Good." Mrs. Everly adjusted the folds of the drapes then turned around and clasped her hands in front of her. "I will send Drew, my maid, up to sit with you. You get some rest so you can heal." She smiled at Lizzy, but it was stilted. After she blinked a few times, she turned to Mr. Barton. "Harrison, you're needed downstairs."

"Of course," Mr. Barton replied.

Mrs. Everly swept from the room, leaving the door open wide behind her. Mr. Barton walked to Lizzy's side and reached for her hand. "Your body needs time to heal, but I promise you will have your explanation soon." He bent forward and kissed her fingers.

Lizzy stared at the back of her hand and wondered how such a simple kiss could warm her entire person.

Chapter 16

"Harrison, what are your intentions?" His mother did not beat about the bush.

Barton choked on his tea. "Excuse me?"

Barton's mother rolled her eyes and waved away his shocked expression. "Don't play daft. You like the girl. Now." She settled back in her chair. "Tell me your intentions."

"With all due respect, Mother, my intentions are not your concern."

"Not true." She wagged her finger at her son. "Your selection of a spouse concerns us all, Miss Grey in particular."

"A spouse?" Barton repeated with a teasing grin. "Are you her protector, then?"

Without hesitation, his mother countered, "Do I need to be?"

Barton chuckled.

"I don't enjoy reopening old wounds—" his mother began.

Barton sobered. "Mother," he said with a warning.

"Well, someone has to be the voice of reason. You are besotted with this girl you hardly know anything about. She is secretive, perhaps manipulative. You know so very little."

Barton pushed out of his seat and paced across the room. He turned back to his mother. "It will be fine."

His mother's blue eyes peered over her teacup. "That's exactly what you said about Miss Newhall."

Barton scoffed. "Miss Grey is nothing like Miss Newhall."

"Are you certain?" The teacup clinked as his mother returned it to the tray.

"Yes." Barton's concise reply was met with a look of skepticism. He continued. "Miss Newhall had an elaborate scheme from the beginning. She played coy and sweet—"

"And stole your heart," his mother finished.

Barton growled and ran a hand through his hair. "Manipulation was her goal from the start, and I was simply too naïve and trusting to see it. I've learned my lesson."

Only sixteen months ago Barton had confessed his love for the ebony-haired beauty. She'd arrived in Hillcrest right after Christmas. Her mother was a recent widower and sought the quiet of the small town. At least, that was the story the duo had propagated. Miss Newhall had charmed her way into the hearts of the townsfolk. Words flowed easily for her, and her practiced smile had seemed sincere. Barton had fallen along with the others, enjoying her laugh and beautiful face. She was indeed a handsome woman, cultured in grace and civility and, Barton learned, duplicity as well.

Thankfully, while Barton had confessed his love, he'd had yet to propose. He'd wanted to surprise Miss Newhall with a specially commissioned pendent of amethysts, for they were her favorite. When he'd gone to town to collect the piece, everyone kept turning away, offering only the briefest waves of acknowledgement. Barton had soon found out why. With the jewelry tucked into his pocket, he stopped by the Hilly Crest for nuncheon. Margaret, a young, chatty girl who usually waited on him, had acted skittish and tongue-tied. Moments after she'd deposited Barton's meal, a familiar tinkling laugh rang out. Barton had turned to the doorway of the private dining room and watched a brown-haired bloke shower the back of Miss Newhall's hand with kisses. She stood there, chittering and giggling, placing a hand over her heart and looking at the stranger with adoration. Barton had seen that look many times. As it turned out, Mr. Honeybourne's income surpassed Barton's by nearly five thousand pounds. Miss Newhall had left on his arm, sparing Barton only a smug lift of her shoulder.

Barton knew it was for the best, but it had taken ten months before he could speak of Miss Newhall without clenching his fists.

He sighed. "Miss Grey is different."

"I hope so," his mother said softly. "But either way, you cannot loiter in Miss Grey's room without a chaperone. You know it is highly improper, and as I know nothing of the girl or her relations, I can't say how she could twist the present situation to her advantage."

Barton rubbed a hand over his upper lip. "To be honest, I do have concerns, but not about her." Barton sat back down.

He watched his mother's curiosity swell. With a sigh of frustration she finally asked, "If not her, then what?"

Barton shook his head. "I don't know. She refused to reveal the whole of her story, but I can't think it's good. What sort of desperation drives a young lady into a storm or to take refuge in an abandoned cabin?"

"Perhaps it's time to confront her again."

"I don't think that approach will work. Miss Grey is obviously stubborn and living in fear, and she's desperate to protect herself and her brother. In this case a more subtle approach is called for." Barton mulled through the facts he knew. "I only want to help her," he said on a whisper.

"Your fatal flaw." Barton's mother leaned forward and touched his knee. "You're very much like your father. And Miss Grey fits the part of damsel in distress to perfection. Keep your wits about you. Secrets can be dangerous."

Barton met his mother's eyes. "That is a truth I'm not likely to forget."

Chapter 17

Mrs. Everly's maid sat near the bureau, mending in hand. The food settled comfortably in Lizzy's stomach, yet no matter how shattered Lizzy's body felt, her eyes would not drift closed. Her mind jumbled with too many questions, too many concerns for her to fall into even a restless sleep.

How long would it take for her to heal? Would Mr. Everly demand answers and reveal her location to her uncle? Would Mr. Barton keep her secret?

As soon as Lizzy thought of Mr. Barton, her mind wandered to the image of him standing near the window. He'd watched over her and Thomas. Mr. Barton's blue eyes were sincere when he'd asked after her needs. She'd thought about confessing everything to him. Her circumstance would be much more bearable with an ally by her side, but could she count on him to be her accomplice? Would Mr. Barton allow her and Thomas to complete their escape? He had no reason to risk his name, his character. Nor did he have any obligation to devote his time and energy to aid her and Thomas, but after the way he'd looked at her . . . Lizzy wondered if maybe he would.

She was getting carried away in her thoughts and needed to reassess her situation. "Drew?" Lizzy asked. "Might I see my brother?"

The woman set her work aside. "Of course, ma'am. I'll go find him."

Drew left the room, and Lizzy longed to get out of her bed, to do something. If only she could move to the window or even sit on the side of the mattress. She lifted her back from the pillows, gritting her teeth as dizziness swept in with the pain. Her breaths quickened, and a cry of frustration rang from her lips as she fell back and punched the mattress.

A knock sounded on the door, followed by Mr. Barton's entrance. "Miss Grey, are you all right?" He glanced around the empty room.

Lizzy's hands shook with frustration and anger, but she hid them in her lap and squeezed them tightly. "Yes." The single word was all she could manage.

Mr. Barton stepped farther into the room, leaving the door ajar. "I was hoping I might have a moment to speak with you."

He searched her face, and Lizzy wondered what caused the uncertainty flashing through his eyes. Had he learned of her situation? Lizzy's dizziness returned.

Mr. Barton motioned to the chair next to the bed. "May I?" he asked.

Lizzy responded with only a nod and then pressed her eyes closed for a moment.

When she opened them again, Mr. Barton stood watching her closely. He eventually sat down. "How are you feeling?"

Lizzy inhaled deeply, attempting to push away the pain, before she answered. "As well as can be expected."

Mr. Barton leaned forward, evaluating her. "Why did you leave the cabin?" he asked.

Lizzy's discomfort, her uncertainty . . . it was all too much. Lizzy's voice shook. "I . . . well . . ."

Mr. Barton gave a disheartened chuckle. "Have I still not earned your trust?"

Lizzy pressed her eyes closed again and took another steeling breath. After a long moment she opened them and replied, "Mr. Barton, you and Mr. Everly have been very kind. I am indebted to both of you. I cannot imagine what would have happened to Thomas if Mr. Everly had not found us. I don't know how I can repay him."

"About that . . ." Mr. Barton sat up in his chair and brushed his hair away from his eyes. "There is something I need to clarify."

"Lizzy!" Thomas burst through the door and jumped up on the bed while Drew called for him to stop.

Lizzy cried out in agony when Thomas landed beside her. Thomas's bright eyes shot wide as she grasped at her ribs, struggling to draw a breath. Tears escaped down her cheeks.

In an instant Mr. Barton stood, latched an arm around Thomas's waist, and lifted him from the mattress. Moisture filled Thomas's eyes as Mr. Barton set him on the ground. "I'm sorry, Lizzy. I'm sorry." Thomas held his hands out to his sister.

Lizzy sucked in a series of quick breaths.

"Give her a moment," Mr. Barton said.

"My apologies, sir." Drew stood twisting her apron. "He was so excited. I should have warned him, settled him down or something."

"It's no one's fault, Drew. Just a mistake." Mr. Barton grasped Thomas's shoulder and looked back at Lizzy. "Perhaps you would like a cold compress? Or a salve?"

Lizzy barely moved her head, but Mr. Barton understood her meaning. "Drew, will you please ask Mrs. Brown to prepare a salve and bring up some cool, damp cloths?"

"Yes, Mr. Everly." Drew dipped a curtsy and left the room.

Lizzy swept the tears from her eyes, but she could not speak. *Mr. Everly?* What did Drew mean? Lizzy looked up and knew the answer. Mr. Barton's, no—Mr. Everly's mouth turned down, and his eyes held a hope she could not reconcile with the disappointment churning inside her. How she'd wanted to believe the man when he'd said she could trust him. And now, he'd trampled her hopes.

"Miss Grey . . ." he began.

And with those words, Lizzy remembered she had lied too. Her hands began to shake, and then the tremors moved throughout her body. Physical pain seared every inch of her being, and a different sort of pain splintered her soul. Could she trust no one? Would she forever be hiding, friendless, and fearful?

"May I explain?" Mr. Everly asked.

"I'd like to be alone," Lizzy managed to whisper.

Mr. Everly evaluated her in silence for a very long time. "Very well." He bowed. "Come, Thomas, let your sister rest. We'll check in on her later."

Lizzy watched them leave the room. Crying hurt. It hurt her heart. It hurt her wounds. So, Lizzy held back the tears, forced her eyes closed, and waited anxiously for sleep to arrive and put her out of her misery.

Chapter 18

BARTON HAD KNOWN IT WOULD happen. He should have told his staff; he should have told Miss Grey. He'd wanted to. His intentions were nothing nefarious, but what must she think of him now? Barton had tiptoed around the issue, hoping to gain her trust, but he'd watched Miss Grey's eyes shift from golden-flecked to dark brown, and he knew the bridge he'd worked so hard to build had just collapsed beneath him.

"Shall we go visit Brutus?" Barton asked Thomas. He figured the animal would provide entertainment for the boy and allow himself time to think.

Thomas eagerly agreed, and they walked to the stables. Several grooms glanced up at their entrance and then continued their chores. Barton's presence in the stables was not uncommon. He removed his coat and grabbed two combs, handing one to Thomas.

"Slip the strap over your bandages. There." Barton assisted Thomas. "Do you know how to brush a horse?" Barton asked.

"I've seen it done," Thomas said.

Barton moved to Brutus's stall and secured the horse before beckoning Thomas to join him. "Be mindful of your feet, and make sure you don't move behind him."

Thomas looked down at his boots then upward. Brutus was easily twice his height. Barton laughed and then moved near Thomas to show him which direction to pull the brush across Brutus's shoulders and side. "There you are. Nice even strokes." Barton stepped away and watched the boy work.

"I can't reach his back." Thomas stood on his tiptoes, reaching his arm as high as he could.

"Concentrate on the parts you can reach, and I'll get the rest." Barton admired the boy's enthusiasm and wished his own worries could so easily be brushed away. "Thomas, do you attend school?"

"Lizzy tutors me," he said. "Father hired Mr. Mercer to teach me, but Uncle dismissed him. I like Lizzy better anyway."

"Tell me about your father."

Thomas did not turn around, but his brushstrokes slowed. "He died, sir."

Miss Grey had told Barton as much, but something remained amiss. "How?"

"The carriage turned over in a storm."

No wonder the boy had been reluctant to be separated from his sister in the woods. "And your mother?"

"She was with Father in the carriage. She died as well." Thomas stopped moving.

Barton stepped forward to brush the high places Thomas could not reach. Soon the boy continued the routine. Barton's movements were mindless as he considered the information. Miss Grey and her brother were orphans, and it seemed at one time they lived with their uncle. How did they end up in Cambridgeshire, alone, without a carriage, and seemingly on the run?

Barton's inherent goodness had led to his downfall with Miss Newhall. She'd appeared to be sad and alone. He'd wanted to help and admired her for moving with her mother to the country. She'd volunteered on the parish welfare council and donated several dresses to a family who had lost their belongings in a fire. He'd been drawn to Miss Newhall because of her seemingly charitable heart, but in the end her actions had only been a charade and Barton had been played for a fool. His mother was right to worry about Miss Grey. It was in Barton's nature to want to fix, to assist, and while Barton knew Miss Grey would be furious with him for posing the questions to Thomas, it could not be helped.

Normally when he endeavored to help someone the obstacle to overcome was simple—a new henhouse or the payment of a small debt. He'd donated funds to expand the church and provided work for those in need. Miss Grey's dilemma was not so easy to catalog. She needed help, Barton was sure of it. What he didn't know was the how or why, and Thomas might be able to shed some light on the situation.

"Thomas, why were you and your sister in Doyle's cottage?"

Thomas stopped brushing and looked at Barton with a grin spread across his face. "Because it was raining. Lizzy said it could be part of our adventure."

"You like adventure, then?"

"Yes, sir." Thomas's eyes narrowed. "Except when Lizzy got hurt. I didn't like that part, but I'm glad we're here now." Thomas's expression lightened once again, and he moved to Brutus's other side and continued brushing.

After ten minutes Barton declared Brutus beautiful, and Thomas laughed, claiming Brutus couldn't be called beautiful because the horse was a boy.

Barton crouched down to the boy's level. "Would you like to ride him?"

"Really?" Thomas asked. He looked up at the large horse. "He's so big."

"When you sit in the saddle, it feels like you're king of the world." Barton motioned for Thomas to follow him from the stall. They walked to a bench sitting against the barn wall, and Barton sat down. "I'm glad you like it here." He patted the empty spot on the bench, and Thomas joined him. "It will be a while before your sister is better and you are able to go home. That's a long time to go without completing your studies. I think I will ask Franklin to tutor you."

"Your brother?"

"Yes. And if you do well in your lessons, I will have a friend of mine give you riding lessons. How does that sound?"

Thomas cocked his head and looked up at Barton. "Will the lessons be on Brutus?"

"That's up to you."

Thomas pointed to a black horse with a bold white blaze. "I like that one."

"That's Starfly. She's a handsome horse, but she's feisty. Brutus is big, but he's very gentle. You see, you must start out on a gentle horse when you're first learning."

Thomas leaned back against the wall and sat quietly.

Barton wondered if the boy was upset that he could not ride Starfly. Surely he didn't expect a good sulk would change Barton's mind. A new rider would find disaster on Starfly's back; she needed to be handled by a trained rider. Barton motioned to the multiple stalls in the barn. "As you can see, there's a stable full of horses, so if you don't want to ride Brutus, my friend Mr. Murray will find you another horse to ride."

"My father said he would teach me," Thomas said quietly.

Barton realized he'd misunderstood the lad's sudden somberness. "I'm sure you miss him."

"I do." Thomas wiped at his nose. "I told Uncle I wanted to learn, but he refused to teach me. I guess he knew I couldn't ride a horse on a boat."

Barton's mind exploded with possible explanations about Miss Grey and her brother. He looked down into Thomas's eyes. The answer to his next question suddenly felt as vital as breath. "Why would you be on a boat, Thomas?"

"'Cause that's where Uncle wanted me to go." His thoughtful expression was replaced with a smile. "But Lizzy wouldn't stand for it. She promised I wouldn't have to be a cabin boy, and she promised we'd have our own adventure."

Suddenly Barton understood. Miss Grey's secrets, the hiding, the half-truths, were all to protect her brother. And while Barton wanted to ask more, he knew he'd already pushed the boy for more than was fair. He didn't have all the pieces, yet he knew enough. The next conversation needed to occur with Miss Grey, for while he now knew why she was running, he needed to know what would happen if she got caught.

Chapter 19

Pain shocked Lizzy awake as a pair of hands lifted her back from the pillows she'd been sleeping upon. Morning sunlight filled the room.

"Sorry, ma'am. Doctor Allen needs to check your bandages." Mrs. Brown sat near Lizzy on the bed and leaned her forward.

A man, whom Lizzy presumed to be the doctor, stood on the opposite side. He was young, with dark-brown hair and a long face. "Forgive me, Miss Grey, but I must verify your wrappings are secure."

Lizzy cried out as the doctor tightened one of the lengths of fabric tied around her ribcage. She could not keep her tears from falling.

"Broken ribs are a nasty business." Doctor Allen cinched another knot. "There you are, now."

Lizzy pinched her lips together and whimpered softly.

Mrs. Brown slowly leaned Lizzy back against the pillows. "'Tis all over now, dear. Shall I fetch some laudanum?"

Lizzy shook her head. It would take a long time for her body to heal; time Lizzy could not afford. The sooner she learned to deal with the pain, the better. Despite Mr. Everly's hospitality, Everly Manor was too close to Downey Place, and Lizzy determined she and Thomas would leave as soon as possible.

"Well, then." Mrs. Brown straightened. "I'll bring you some chamomile tea."

Lizzy nodded slightly and only half-listened while the doctor told her to try to take full, deep breaths. "Some people have a full recovery after a month or two, but others suffer discomfort for the rest of their lives," Dr. Allen said.

Another reason Lizzy should learn to suffer through the pain. Hurt, anger, and remorse were already a part of her life. Adding pain to the *mélange* seemed a trifle of a thing.

The doctor left, and Mrs. Brown helped Lizzy apply a salve to her bruises. Between the sticky poultice on her skin and the dirt still caked in her hair, Lizzy longed for a bath, and she said as much to Mrs. Brown.

"The doctor said rest is the thing you need most, Miss Grey." Mrs. Brown rearranged the blankets around Lizzy's midsection.

"I understand that, but as a woman you must understand the desire to clean this filth from my person." Lizzy hoped she could convince the woman to acquiesce.

Mrs. Brown looked at the sheet under her hands, and her lips twisted. "How about you take a nap, and then I'll have some water sent up before suppertime."

A genuine smile filled Lizzy's face. "That sounds delightful." She reached over and covered Mrs. Brown's hand with her own. "Thank you." The woman tsked at the show of affection, but a bit of color touched her cheeks.

Lizzy was able to sleep, although it was hardly restful. Her conscious slipped away only to replace reality with visions of Uncle's face scrunched in anger or Thomas's cries as he was tossed onboard a ship seconds before it pulled anchor and floated out to sea.

She woke covered in beads of sweat and profusely praised Mrs. Brown as an angel when warm water was sent up. The blonde maid, who Lizzy learned was called Bastian, arranged a screen around the tub, and with Bastian and Drew's help, Lizzy slid to the side of the bed, stood, and slowly made her way to the bath.

It was decided that Lizzy's bandages should remain in place while she bathed, and they were quickly forgotten as she slipped into the warm, divine water. Immersion in the steamy bath soothed her body and mind. Ugly bruises marred Lizzy's skin. The majority of the purple, black, and yellow patches were hidden under Lizzy's bandages, but several discolored striations traveled farther down her midsection. Her legs were marred with similar contusions, and Lizzy ran her fingers over her blemished skin.

The warm water washed over her, and she stretched out as much as she was able in the tub. As the kinks in her chest and legs slowly abated, Lizzy's eyes drifted closed and she began to plan.

Uncle Cline did not care about what happened to her or Thomas. Perhaps he would call off his search, in time. But until she was certain, she could not, would not, shirk her duty. Her vow to Thomas was also a promise to herself that she would live the life she wanted, the life her parents intended her to have. Things would have been so different if Uncle had not been named benefactor. Lizzy still wondered why her father had chosen Uncle Cline when he had not previously pursued a relationship with his brother. Perhaps, being that Uncle Cline was Father's only living sibling, the decision was out of his control.

Downey Place could no longer be the backdrop for Lizzy's future, but she still intended to make memories, happy ones, and she knew that was impossible under her uncle's care or as the wife of Mr. Rudyard Simpkin. She shuddered and then winced at the pain the reaction caused. She could not allow her injuries to waylay her for a month.

Lizzy realized she would have to tell Mr. Everly the truth, but not all of it. He obviously knew she was not visiting a cousin. And he knew she and Thomas had been leaving town when they were caught in the storm. But certainly he would understand the need for subterfuge, for he had concealed his true identity as well. He must have had his reasons, and as much as Lizzy wanted to know what they were, she decided it would be best to acknowledge his deception and ask no questions. Perhaps if she let him have his secrets, she could keep her own.

The cleansing bath and accompanying meditation lifted Lizzy's spirits. She now considered her injuries only a minor setback, until she sat in the chair in her room and attempted to read a book Mr. Everly had sent up with Drew. The words melted together, the letters twisting and spinning. Lizzy's head hurt, and she had to set the book aside.

Mrs. Brown arranged for a table to be set with a small dinner for the siblings to share, and Lizzy welcomed Thomas with a smile. Thomas talked nonstop of the entertainments he'd enjoyed at Everly Manor. It seemed Mr. Everly's siblings had been assigned to keep him occupied, and Mr. Franklin and Mrs. Bethany, as Thomas called her, had fulfilled their duties, top-notch.

"And then, today, Mr. Barton took me to the stables." Thomas stuffed a large bite of lemon tart into his mouth. Lizzy could not blame him for indulging in the generous portion. Mr. Everly's cook was superb, and her sweets equally so.

"Did you get to see Brutus?" she asked her brother.

He nodded vigorously, and Lizzy watched him until he swallowed. "Mr. Barton let me brush him, and—oh, I almost forgot. Mr. Barton said if I did my lessons with Mr. Franklin, he would have someone teach me to ride."

"A horse?"

"Yes!" Thomas grinned and shoved another bite of lemon tart into his mouth.

It seemed Mr. Barton—no, she must remember that was not his name—Mr. Everly had taken a genuine interest in Thomas. Was his kindness a charade? Mr. Everly employed a host of servants. Any one of them could be tasked with Thomas's care, but Mr. Everly had asked his siblings to assist, and he himself had taken Thomas under his wing.

"Does he mind you calling him Mr. Barton?" Lizzy asked her brother.

His eyebrows scrunched together. "What do you mean?"

Lizzy pressed her lips tight then shook her head. "Never mind."

A knock sounded on the door, and Lizzy assumed the visitor would be Bastian or Mrs. Brown. Instead, when the door pushed open, she saw a beautiful blonde-haired, blue-eyed woman whom she knew in an instant was Mr. Everly's sister, Bethany. Now that Lizzy knew his true name, the connections of his mother, brother, and sister made far more sense.

"Pardon my interruption," the woman said and turned to Thomas. "Are you finished with your dinner, Thomas? It's time to head to the nursery."

Lizzy's mouth dropped open as Thomas stood from his chair and slipped his hand into the woman's offered grasp. Getting Thomas to bed had always been a chore. Lizzy couldn't help but feel a bit chagrinned at the ease with which Thomas complied with the request. The woman smiled down at Thomas with undeniable adoration, and Lizzy didn't know whether to feel jealous or grateful.

Mr. Everly then entered the room and evaluated the situation. "Bethany, I'm glad to see you've made Miss Grey's acquaintance."

She turned her attention to her brother, and her cheeks flushed. "Actually I've . . ." She glanced at Lizzy then turned back to Mr. Everly.

"We've not yet been properly introduced. Perhaps you would do the honor?" Lizzy interjected. There was no reason for Lizzy to step in and defend the woman's poor manners, but seeing her face light when she spoke to Thomas had softened Lizzy's heart. Thomas needed someone he could rely on, someone he knew cared about him.

"Very well. Miss Elizabeth Grey, may I introduce you to my sister, Mrs. Bethany Haskins?" He inclined his head towards his sister. "Bethany, Miss Grey, our guest and Thomas's elder sister."

Keeping hold of Thomas's hand, Mrs. Haskins executed a precise curtsy. "It's a pleasure to meet you, Miss Grey. Please forgive me for not introducing myself earlier."

"Not at all." Lizzy moved her arms to her chair, determined to stand.

"No, no, no!" Mrs. Haskins waved her free hand at Lizzy. "Don't get up on my account. Please, you must rest."

Lizzy relaxed back in the chair. "Thank you."

"Now that we've been properly introduced, I shall visit another time and we shall get to know each other. I'll introduce you to my husband as well, when he returns from his business in London next week. My brother has been very tight-lipped about . . . well, everything." A mischievous smile lit Mrs. Haskins's eyes.

"Bethany . . ." Mr. Everly warned.

"Regardless"—Mrs. Haskins shot him a look of indifference—"I should like to hear about your adventures in the storm. Thank goodness Barton knew to seek you out. I can't imagine being trapped beneath a tree."

Mr. Everly cleared his throat and angled his head towards Thomas, who stood near Mrs. Haskins's side looking frightened.

"My apologies." Mrs. Haskins shook Thomas's hand that remained clasped in her own and then stooped down to look in his eyes. "Shall we read a story tonight, or would you like me to tell you one of my own?"

"Will you read the one about the bear?" Thomas asked.

"Certainly. Now, give your sister a kiss." Mrs. Haskins led Thomas to where Lizzy sat, and he lifted up onto his toes to press a kiss to her cheek.

Lizzy ruffled Thomas's hair. "Sweet dreams." She watched the duo walk from the room, keeping her eyes fixed on the open door so she would not have to acknowledge Mr. Everly.

But his eyes were fixed on Lizzy. She could feel it. Could he not leave her be? Mr. Everly proved to have an exorbitant amount of patience. He chuckled. "It seems my family has a distinct lack of tact when it comes to introducing ourselves to you."

"Your mother did just fine."

Mr. Everly smirked. "Yes, my mother's manners are above reproach. The same cannot be said for her children. I'm afraid we put a blight on her pristine record."

"The difference in her manners involved only being truthful about her identity, sir." A pain simmered in Lizzy's chest, and she knew it had nothing to do with her injured ribs.

Mr. Everly's smile fell. He moved to the chair Thomas had previously occupied, and without receiving an invitation he sat himself down. "I apologize for the misunderstanding, Miss Grey, but to be fair, I did not lie to you. My friends do indeed call me Barton, as do my siblings." He shrugged a single shoulder. "I simply did not correct your assumption that it was my surname."

"Your friends call you Barton, your mother calls you Harrison, and the villagers call you Everly?"

"You can see how one might be confused." Mr. Everly fought to restrain his grin, and despite her frustration with the man, Lizzy wanted to smile with him. Mr. Everly reached across the table, placed his hand over Lizzy's, and squeezed gently. "Will you forgive me, Miss Grey? I was wrong to not clarify my identity, but sometimes it's nice to allow others to form opinions without any preconceived notions."

Lizzy stared at her fingers resting below Mr. Everly's solid grasp. His sincerity touched her heart. She knew he was sorry and realized she was quite eager to do as he asked. That thought scared her. Lizzy blinked and pulled her hand from his.

"Very well," she said. "There was no harm done, and you have been very attentive and kind to Thomas and me." Exhaustion washed over Lizzy, but she knew she needed to express her feelings. "I want to extend my deepest gratitude, Mr. Everly. If you had not sought us out in the storm . . ." Relief swept through Lizzy's chest. "Will you tell me what happened that night? I only remember bits and pieces."

Mr. Everly leaned back in his chair and related the tale of watching the storm worsen and not wanting to leave her and Thomas alone in the cabin. "You asked for two days, so I was shocked to find you had already abandoned the place. I intended to bring you back here, but you'd gone." His blue eyes narrowed, but he paused for only a moment before continuing. "I followed the west road, asking the tenants if they knew your whereabouts. Several men joined me, and we split up at the intersection of the main road. As we worked our way towards town, I heard Thomas's cry for help."

Lizzy pressed a hand to her mouth. "How frightened Thomas must have been."

"He refused to leave you." Mr. Everly explained how he had to pry Thomas away from the tree and force him to go with Mr. Lancaster. Mr. Everly's voice lowered, and something softened in his eyes. "He stopped kicking only once I assured him I meant to help you."

"He's so brave," Lizzy said on a whisper.

"After you were pulled from the tree, I brought you back here." Mr. Everly sat comfortably, his arms resting on his chair and his left foot laying propped across the opposite knee.

"Thank you, Mr. Everly. For everything. I do not mean to intrude, and we will be out of your way as soon as possible." Lizzy chanced a glance at her rescuer, who studied her in return; his eyes were serious and questioning. Her stomach churned with her confession of gratitude. Not because Mr. Everly's gesture was unappreciated, but because she appreciated it more than he would ever understand. "Without your"—Lizzy swallowed—"help, I might have died. And heaven knows where Thomas would have ended up."

Without hesitation, Mr. Everly responded, "At sea, perhaps?"

Lizzy's lungs were robbed of breath. Mr. Everly watched her, unwavering in his attention, waiting for her reply. Fear clustered in her throat, and she could not speak for a full minute. She felt as though her tongue had been smeared with honey. Lizzy did not know how to continue. She'd scolded Mr. Everly for his deceit while she continued her own, and despite wanting to tell him the truth of her situation, she could not. While he had been decent and respectful and everything kind, how could she be certain he would not reveal her to her uncle? It would be his gentlemanly duty to disclose her whereabouts to her relatives. Yet, what did he know, and how did he know it?

When Lizzy could finally inhale fully, she ignored the questions she really wanted to ask and instead said, "Thank you for the book you sent up."

Mr. Everly rubbed a hand over his forehead, and his expression lightened. "Did you enjoy it?"

Lizzy looked down at her lap. "I . . . well, I don't believe my mind is quite recovered from my accident. The words were a bit jumbled."

Mr. Everly reached for the book, and opening the cover, he pressed the first page flat. Then he began to read. The words flowed in silky hues, wrapping around Lizzy like a soothing sunset. Rich and fluid and solid, Mr. Everly's baritone voice tangled through her mind. Unknowingly her eyes drifted closed. The melody swayed her, moved her to a peaceful oasis she hadn't felt for a long time.

Lizzy could not recall when Mr. Everly stopped reading. Nor could she recall the specifics of the story he read. And she only vaguely remembered his arms slipping beneath her to carry her to her bed.

Chapter 20

AFTER A RESTLESS NIGHT BARTON rose early and headed to the stables. He waved the stableboy away and saddled Brutus himself. He mounted without a destination in mind, but as the sun rose higher in the trees, he found himself in front of Doyle's cabin.

Barton recalled his conversations with Miss Grey, and no matter how neutral the topic, he realized she approached every interaction with skeptical caution. He should not have made the comment about Thomas going to sea. He had obviously upset her, and if he'd thought for even a moment before speaking, he would have withheld the words.

Barton wandered inside the cabin and scanned the meager furnishings. The pallet lay in the corner, just as he remembered it. The storm left several notable holes in the roof that would require repair, and the walls needed patching as well. He noticed the woodbox was stocked and sobered to realize it was only filled because Thomas and Miss Grey hadn't planned on leaving—until he'd frightened them away.

Barton pressed his eyes closed, grateful he had been guided to find them in the storm. When he opened them again, his eyes focused on two glinting coins atop the fireplace mantel.

When Miss Grey had insisted she would leave something for Mr. Everly, he'd dismissed the notion, knowing he neither cared for nor needed payment. Yet, Miss Grey had left two crowns, despite her precarious circumstance, and for that simple action, Barton admired her even more. It seemed that, while she had secrets, she was vastly different from Miss Newhall.

He pocketed the coins, and as he exited the cabin, a bird called from a nearby tree. Barton searched the branches for the fowl. It took him several minutes, but he finally located a small yellow-breasted finch perched amid the boughs of an evergreen. Barton whistled to the bird, who cocked its head first one way then the other, admiring the intruder. Barton whistled several more times, waiting patiently while the finch hopped forward and evaluated him. Finally the bird chirped a reply. Barton took a final look at the cabin, mounted, and turned Brutus back towards the road.

He could wait for Miss Grey, just as he'd waited for the bird. She could posture and defer for only so long. He could be—he would be—patient. The lovely Miss Grey obviously needed a friend, a confidant who could help alleviate her fears, whatever they may be, and for some inexplicable reason, Barton hoped he could be that someone.

Instead of returning to Everly Manor, Barton rode to Murray's house.

Murray sat on the ground outside his barn, repairing tack. Barton rode directly to the paddock, dismounted, and secured Brutus inside the gate.

"Broken bit?" Barton asked as he knelt next to Murray.

Murray glanced over his shoulder and glared at Barton before returning to his project.

Barton laughed. "Do you need parts from the manor?"

"If I do, I know where to find them." Murray looked Barton over again. "What can I do for you?"

"I was hoping I could convince you to come to the manor and help me with a project." Barton picked up a metal ring and fumbled it through his fingers.

Murray stopped his work and met Barton's eye. "What kind of project?"

"I need a riding teacher, and you're the best." Barton flicked the metal ring into the air and then caught it in the palm of his hand.

"Who'd I be teachin'?"

Barton cleared his throat. "Remember Miss Grey?" Murray gave a small nod. "She ventured out in that storm we had a few days ago. Found herself in a bit of trouble . . ."

"I told you a storm was coming," Murray said with a smug grin. "I assume you came to her rescue?"

Barton shifted his weight and stood up. "You could say that. A tree was torn from its roots, and Miss Grey found herself caught beneath it. She and her brother, Thomas, will be staying at Everly Manor while she recovers. Thomas is nine and has expressed an interest in learning to ride. I thought it would be a nice diversion for him while his sister recuperates."

Murray made a noise that sounded like a grunt.

"What do you say? He's a good lad, and it would give you something to do," Barton said.

Murray pushed himself up from the ground. "I've got plenty to do, as you can see." He waved a hand over the equipment he'd been tinkering with.

"Well, you can bring your projects along, pass them off to my groom to mend or save them for another day." Barton clapped a hand across Murray's back. "It would mean a lot to me."

"So, she wasn't visiting a cousin?" Murray chuckled softly, and Barton shrugged.

"Seems not."

"You ain't trying to impress the lady, are you?" Murray raised a single eyebrow.

Barton laughed. "I currently live with two women. I'm always trying to impress a lady."

Murray frowned. "Fine. Tell the boy to be ready tomorrow."

Barton suppressed the smile he wanted to share and simply nodded his head. "Thank you, Murray."

"The lad will have to work hard. I ain't goin' easy on him." Murray rubbed the side of his face.

"I'll pass that along."

"You owe me, Barton."

"Yes, sir." Barton offered a halfhearted salute then went to the fence and whistled for Brutus.

Chapter 21

THOMAS'S RIDING LESSONS REMAINED THE dominant topic of conversation for three days straight. Lizzy would try to talk to him about his lessons with Mr. Franklin Everly or his walks with Mrs. Haskins, but Thomas only wanted to discuss how he needed the help of the groom to mount Brutus because even when he stood atop the mounting block, he still could not reach the stirrups. Thomas no longer wore the bandages on his hands, and this made it easier for him to grasp the reins. Thomas told Lizzy that Mr. Murray was impressed with his horsemanship. He talked of learning how to properly feed and brush a horse. He'd learned how to secure a saddle and told Lizzy the importance of taking care of the horse's hooves. Thomas tried to demonstrate how to use a hoof pick, by bending his leg and lifting his foot, but as he reached back to grasp his ankle, he tumbled over onto his side.

Lizzy grasped her ribs, pain radiating with her laughter. "I'm glad you are enjoying yourself, and I hope you are minding your manners."

Thomas sat himself up on the floor, and a very stern expression crossed his face. "Mr. Barton said that Mr. Murray is the best teacher. He told me I have to listen, or Mr. Murray won't teach me anymore."

Lizzy almost corrected Thomas and told him to address Mr. Everly by his proper name. But then she realized Mr. Everly didn't care, and he had counseled Thomas on the importance of showing adequate respect to Mr. Murray. If Mr. Everly remained content with the arrangement, she would not interfere.

"I'm glad you are enjoying yourself," Lizzy said again. She opened her arms, and Thomas climbed off the floor to give her a hug. "Softly," Lizzy whispered as he wrapped his arms around her middle. When he stepped away she smiled. "I needed that."

Soon afterwards Mr. Everly joined Mrs. Haskins when she came to collect Thomas. Lizzy thanked her for her continued attentions. The woman smiled and led Thomas from the room with the promise of a bowl of fruit.

"How are you faring?" Mr. Everly asked.

"I can't rightly say. I . . ." Lizzy closed her eyes and ran her fingers across her temples. "My head still aches when I try to read."

"The doctor said your recovery would take time."

"Yes, but I am not usually so still. I prefer to be . . . moving, active." Being bound to her room tried Lizzy's patience.

Mr. Everly walked near and picked up the book. "Perhaps I could read from where we left off the other day."

Lizzy opened her mouth to object, but before she could form the words, Mr. Everly had taken a seat near the fireplace and thumbed the book open. Lizzy's cheeks warmed as she considered how the last time Mr. Everly read to her, his voice had lulled her to sleep.

The rich, gentle tones of his voice resumed and calmed Lizzy's nerves. When she focused on the rhythm and pitch of the words, all of Lizzy's concerns melted away and she focused only on . . . him.

For the next two days Mr. Everly visited Lizzy in the morning to read another chapter of the novel. Then Mrs. Everly joined Lizzy for tea. Lizzy found their visits broke the monotony of her confinement.

Mrs. Everly's knowing gaze reminded Lizzy of her former governess. Initially the matron's directness had worried Lizzy. She did not want to lie to the woman, and she could not confess her situation. However, Mrs. Everly expertly directed the conversation and avoided any discussion involving Lizzy's family. Instead she asked about Lizzy's interests and her education, and they discussed her relationship with Thomas. Mrs. Everly shared her own history, telling of the pranks she and her brother had played on her two elder sisters. Then she spoke of her late husband, specifically how he'd worked to maintain the favor of his tenants and gain the respect of the villagers. Lizzy's impression of the late Mr. Everly's efforts and determination continued to grow.

"It sounds like he was good to his core," Lizzy said.

A distant memory lit Mrs. Everly's face. "He was. Harrison is very much like him."

Unsure how to respond, Lizzy settled on the truth. "You have raised a very fine son, Mrs. Everly. His attention to my care and Thomas's happiness has been very generous. I don't know how I can ever repay him."

"Bah!" Mrs. Everly waved a dismissive hand. "He doesn't do it because he expects something in return. He is kind because, as you said, it is in his core." Mrs. Everly took a slow sip of her tea. "I must admit, his natural inclination to trust worries me. There are some who would abuse his kindness and exploit his charity . . . or break his heart." Mrs. Everly held Lizzy's gaze. "Harrison has seen enough of dishonesty and the pain it brings. As his mother I cannot allow him to be hurt again. You understand, of course?"

"Of course." Lizzy acknowledged Mrs. Everly's unspoken warning. Lizzy's deception was meant to protect her and Thomas, not to hoodwink Mr. Everly. But Lizzy could relate to Mrs. Everly's fierce determination to protect her son, and she once again determined she and Thomas would leave Everly Manor and its generous, handsome, thoughtful owner as soon as possible.

Lizzy's accommodations were beyond anything she had a right to claim, but she needed a change of scenery. The next morning Bastian helped her change out of the borrowed nightdress. She wore a very loosely tied corset and borrowed one of Bethany's gowns. Bastian dressed her hair in a basic style. The simple act of donning a dress greatly improved Lizzy's spirits.

Lizzy could walk down the hallway with only minimal discomfort, but negotiating the stairs proved to be more difficult. Her breath caught as she moved down the first step, and after three more a cold sweat spread across her brow. She debated turning around, considering she would have to ascend every step she descended, but in that moment even climbing back up the four stairs seemed impossible. Her fortitude quickly fled.

Lizzy should have waited longer or simply paced the hall before she attempted the stairs, but her stubbornness had won out, and she had not considered the ramifications of navigating the steps in her condition.

Mrs. Haskins's voice cut through her self-incrimination. "Miss Grey! What are you doing?" Mrs. Haskins quickly ascended the stairs to where Lizzy stood. "Barton!" Mrs. Haskins hollered.

Lizzy shook her head. "Please, Mrs. Haskins, I'll be fine."

"Hardly. You're pale, and look." Mrs. Haskins pointed to Lizzy's fingers. "You're shaking."

Mr. Everly, along with the butler, appeared at the bottom of the staircase. Henderson looked at his master, and Mr. Everly muttered a muted curse before he bound up the stairs to where Lizzy stood. Embarrassment washed over Lizzy, and her eyes filled with moisture.

Mr. Everly stood before Lizzy, his face drawn tight. "Good morning, Miss Grey."

Lizzy offered a sputtered laugh, and a few tears splashed down her cheeks. Mr. Everly's words were a direct contradiction to the displeasure on his face. What could she say? "I thought—"

"Oh, Barton, stop gabbing and help her." Mrs. Haskins shook her brother's arm.

Mr. Everly looked back and forth between the women before his blue eyes cleared and settled on Lizzy. "May I be of assistance, Miss Grey?"

Lizzy wiped her hand across her face before Mr. Everly withdrew a handkerchief from his pocket. "Thank you." Lizzy accepted the linen and dried her eyes. "I apologize for causing such a ruckus. I only meant to find a quiet place to sit for an hour or two. I didn't consider that walking down the stairs would prove so difficult."

"Is there not a chair in your room?" Mrs. Haskins asked.

"Yes. The room has been lovely."

Mr. Everly spoke again. "But you missed being active?" With his next breath, Mr. Everly's face softened. "My apologies. You told me, and I should have made accommodations."

"Not at all." Lizzy raised a hand. "You've been more than generous. I only hoped for some variety."

"In that case, I can be of assistance." Mr. Everly grinned.

Relief filled Lizzy. "Thank you."

She faced forward, ready to continue down the stairs, assuming Mr. Everly would offer his arm for support. Instead he placed one arm behind her, and the other swept beneath her knees as he lifted Lizzy into his sturdy arms.

"Mr. Everly!" Lizzy exclaimed, ignoring both the pain and pleasure flowing through her.

"Are you comfortable?" Mr. Everly asked with a maddening grin spread across his lips.

Mrs. Haskins placed a hand over her mouth to hide her giggle.

Mr. Everly took slow, even steps. "I'm only doing as you asked, Miss Grey. You didn't specify what type of assistance you would like, and I think this is rather efficient."

Lizzy could not think of a reply and instead turned her head away to hide her blush.

At the bottom of the stairs, Mr. Everly paused. "Perhaps if it warms up later, we can arrange for a chair to be placed outside, but I'm afraid it's too cold now. Would you prefer the drawing room or the library?"

Lizzy chose the library at the same time Mrs. Haskins suggested the drawing room.

"The library it is." Mr. Everly ignored his sister's look of annoyance.

"I can walk on my own now," Lizzy insisted.

"Perhaps. But if you don't oppose, I'll carry you to your destination. It will save me from having to come back later should you find yourself unable to cover the expansive distance to the library."

"You tease me, sir." Lizzy chanced a glance at Mr. Everly.

"Only a little." Mr. Everly kicked the library door wide. Mrs. Haskins walked past and held it open while her brother carried Lizzy through. Mr. Everly delicately lowered Lizzy to a comfortable white couch and whispered near her ear, "Do you mind my teasing, Miss Grey?"

Lizzy's heart hammered in her chest, and she could only manage a small shake of her head. What was wrong with her? She should not be encouraging Mr. Everly's flirtatious behavior, even if she did enjoy the way his teasing made her heart race.

Mr. Everly straightened and looked down at Lizzy with a mischievous smile. His sister bustled over with a pillow in each hand.

"What can I do to make you comfortable, Miss Grey?" Mrs. Haskins asked.

Lizzy leaned forward while Mrs. Haskins tucked one of the pillows behind her back. "I'm well. Please. I did not intend to disrupt your day."

"A book, perhaps?" Mrs. Haskins moved to one of the many shelves and placed a finger across her lips while she evaluated titles. Mrs. Haskins called out a few possibilities, but before Lizzy could respond Mrs. Haskins negated her own selections.

Mr. Everly's eyes remained on Lizzy, and she tried to will her heart back to its regular cadence. "Are you yet able to read?" he asked.

"My mind feels clear. I believe I can manage." Although, Lizzy would have preferred hearing Mr. Everly's masculine voice.

Mr. Everly ran a hand along his chin. "In that case, I think Miss Grey would enjoy a swashbuckling tale of adventure," he said.

"Really?" Mrs. Haskins considered this for a moment then clapped her hands together. "Oh, I know. I'll be right back." Then she dashed out the door before Lizzy could protest.

"Was I close to the mark?" Mr. Everly asked.

"No. Yes. Oh, I don't know." Lizzy was so flustered she could not form a coherent though. She took a breath, determined to speak rationally. "I do find books about history or philosophy to be a bit tedious."

Mr. Everly walked over and sat next to Lizzy on the sofa. She watched his every movement and noted that he sat very close. Her heart rate escalated.

"In my opinion, everyone needs a good bit of adventure every now and again." Mr. Everly lifted one leg and crossed it over the other. He looked far too casual. How could he be so at ease while an anxious thrum rattled Lizzy's entire body?

She realized Mr. Everly awaited her reply. "I think I've had my fair share of adventure for a while."

Mr. Everly took a breath as if he would speak but exhaled without saying another word.

Mrs. Haskins returned with a book in hand. "Here's a rather diverting novel. It's a collection of Captain Cook's explorations." Mrs. Haskins's smile faltered. "You may have read it already, but . . . well . . . Barton mentioned a tale of adventure, and I finished it yesterday."

"It sounds perfect." Lizzy accepted the book and ran her hand over the front cover.

"I'll ask Mrs. Brown to bring tea in an hour. In the meantime, we'll allow you some peace." Mrs. Haskins turned towards her brother and gave him a small but meaningful smile. "Barton."

Mr. Everly stood. "Enjoy your adventure, Miss Grey." He bowed and followed his sister from the room.

Guilt washed over Lizzy as she turned the book over in her hand. The Everlys had proven everything attentive and kind, yet she continued her farce and kept her secrets.

During the past week, Lizzy had verified the contents in her bag numerous times. Her jewels remained safe. Two trinkets and twenty-two pounds represented the extent of her income. Could she find a place for her and Thomas? A place that would be safe and free from her uncle?

Lizzy spread the book open on her lap, but she could not focus on the words. Mr. Everly had alluded to her preference for adventure. Did he hint at something deeper, or was he merely being playful? Or perhaps he shared his mother's distrust of Lizzy and her motives. No matter how diverting the novel may have been, Lizzy could not clear her mind to absorb the words.

As promised, Mrs. Brown arrived an hour later and set out the tea things. "There you are, Miss Grey. Mrs. Everly and Mr. Everly should be joining you shortly."

Lizzy offered her thanks and pushed herself to her feet. She needed to stretch her legs, to walk and move, to feel in control of some aspect of her situation. Lizzy walked to the window in time to see Thomas sitting atop Brutus. Thomas smiled wide as Mr. Murray gave direction and walked along beside them. Since arriving at Everly Manor, Thomas's smile appeared more often, and he laughed freely. His change in countenance was exactly what Lizzy had hoped for when she'd pulled him into the woods behind the inn at Hodgly Briar. She longed to give him the peace that should come with childhood, the innocent escapades of youth, the moments Uncle Cline had marred with ugliness. It lifted her spirits to see Thomas happy, but her own happiness was shrouded with fear she could not provide the same contentment life at Everly Manor offered.

Mrs. Everly's voice startled Lizzy. "Harrison told me your parents have passed away."

Lizzy turned to the matron. "Yes. My father and stepmother were killed in a carriage accident this past June."

Mrs. Everly's lips pursed together. She moved near the tea tray and motioned for Lizzy to join her. "Have you informed your remaining family that you are here, well and safe?"

Lizzy retook her seat on the sofa. Since Mrs. Everly had never pressed for information, Lizzy stiffened and wondered at the cause of her sudden questions. "It's only Thomas and me now."

Mrs. Everly poured the tea, added the sugar she knew Lizzy preferred, and handed the cup and saucer to Lizzy. "Remind me, how did you come to be at the gamekeeper's cabin?"

"Mother." Mr. Everly offered the stern greeting as he entered the room. "You're looking lovely today."

Mrs. Everly twisted her lips before greeting her son. "Harrison."

Mr. Everly walked to the tray and served himself three berry scones. "Mrs. Brown knows these are my favorite." He dramatically settled himself into the chair across from Lizzy. "Did you enjoy your book?" he asked.

"I found it difficult to concentrate." Lizzy looked down at the teacup in her lap.

"Miss Grey, did your father leave you an inheritance?" Mrs. Everly asked. Mr. Everly cleared his throat, and his mother feigned innocence. "I only ask because Franklin told me your brother is excelling in his studies. I hoped he might have an opportunity to attend school. Eton is our family preference, but Harrow would suit as well."

"Mother, I'm sure Miss Grey has things well in hand."

Lizzy watched the silent warning Mr. Everly sent his mother. And while she was grateful, she wanted to defend herself. "I hope Thomas has the opportunity to attend when he comes of age. His mother was my stepmother, and we are both still adjusting to the loss of our parents, but I am confident things will work out." Even as the words left her lips, Lizzy acknowledged the lie, because she didn't feel confident at all. Lizzy wondered if her tired mind exacerbated Mrs. Everly's questions to more than a simple query.

The conversation moved on to gratitude for the reprieve from the rain and the condition of the west fields. Words muted in Lizzy's mind as she thought over her situation again and again.

"I'm afraid I've overexerted myself," she suddenly said.

Mrs. Everly froze mid-sentence and turned to look at her.

"Of course." Mr. Everly set his plate aside and stood. "May I help you to your room?"

Lizzy accepted the arm Mr. Everly offered. She needed his support more than she cared to admit. When they reached the foot of the stairs, Mr. Everly once more swept her into his arms.

"I don't think this is necessary, sir." Lizzy's cheeks warmed.

"I told you I opt for efficiency, Miss Grey. There's no need to risk further injury when I am able to assist."

This time she did not look away. She took advantage of the opportunity to examine Mr. Everly's profile, the waves in his hair, and his vibrant eyes. He easily negotiated the two flights to Lizzy's bedchamber and eased her down onto the mattress.

"Thank you," Lizzy whispered.

Mr. Everly's arms slipped away, but he stood gazing at her, his chest rising and falling from the exertion of his task. He was breathtaking in that moment, and Lizzy wanted to say something more, to somehow express the cluster of emotions burning within, but the words clogged somewhere between her mind and her mouth.

When Drew bustled into the room, ready to take over Lizzy's care, Mr. Everly broke the connection. He stepped aside and made to leave but turned back in the doorway. "I hope you will be able to rest, Miss Grey, and dream about the adventures you and Thomas may have in the future."

Lizzy openly gaped at Mr. Everly as he bowed and departed. She knew his poignant words held truth; he wanted her to be happy. She also knew that this time his words held meaning and that he had chosen them on purpose.

Chapter 22

ALTHOUGH BARTON FEIGNED A SMILE, Bethany was not fooled. "You've hardly touched your food. What's the matter?"

Barton sighed, and Franklin answered on his behalf. "I'd say he's pondering how he can play chivalrous knight to our houseguest."

"Did you not hear about his daring rescue on the stairs? Barton is playing the part quite well." Bethany smiled, and their mother watched them all with a keen eye.

Barton cleared his throat. "As a matter of fact, I was thinking about Miss Grey. I want her to be comfortable here and not feel like she has to flee. I scared her off once, and I think she may be contemplating running again."

His mother set her utensils on her plate. "It sounds as if you plan on having her around for some length of time."

"The doctor said it would take several weeks before Miss Grey had healed enough to travel. Would you have me shoo her along before she's ready?"

"Of course not," came his mother's tart reply.

Barton turned to his sister, and his voice rose. "And what if she leaves too early and is unable to take care of Thomas? The boy's not able to work or take care of his sister. If she were to reinjure herself, he could end up in a workhouse or an orphanage."

Bethany glared at her brother. "There's no need to paint such a grim picture." No matter Bethany's feelings about Miss Grey, Barton knew she'd formed an attachment to Thomas. Bethany had been married for almost eight years and wanted nothing more than to be a mother. "I don't understand why you insist on being so sour."

"Unless your feelings go beyond those of being her rescuer," Franklin added with a grin.

Barton cursed under his breath and tossed his napkin to the table. "I've no appetite for this." Expressions varied from surprise to mirth as Barton pushed back from the table and stood. "No matter your combined theories, Miss Grey has made it veritably clear that she has no desire to stay at Everly Manor. She wishes to be on her way as soon as possible. Excuse me," he said and walked out of the room.

Barton never lost his temper. A dishonest man boiled his blood, and beggars seeking a free handout received a stiff rebuke, but he'd always been able to segregate his emotions and remain calm enough to deal with whatever situation arose. Yet, enduring his family's jibes and pondering on the mystery Miss Grey presented clouded Barton's usually clear head. He needed time to himself.

After a brisk walk through the dark garden, Barton's heart pounded in his chest, and somehow the steady, rapid rhythm grounded him. He inhaled deeply and tipped his head up to the sky. But his eyes never made it to the stars. Instead he focused on the flicker of light coming from Miss Grey's window.

Shadows passed behind the curtains, and finally the candle snuffed out. Barton again inhaled deeply and reached into his pocket. His fingers closed around the two crowns he'd discovered at Doyle's cabin. The coins symbolized Miss Grey's guilelessness. She had planned to never see Barton again, let alone meet Mr. Everly, but she had been true to her word and left recompense for her time at the cabin. She was not desperate, but neither was she wealthy. To Barton, it spoke of her integrity and the goodness she possessed. If only he could know more of what lay within her heart. If only he could convince her to trust him.

Chapter 23

LIZZY SAT ALONE ON HER bed and pulled back the blue-velvet wrappings that held her mother's jewels. The sapphires reflected the sun streaming through the window, casting blue shadows across the back of Lizzy's hand. She'd never worn the jewels before. She'd felt too young and undeserving. But every time she looked at them she thought of her mother. Her stepmother, too, had worn them on occasion, but Lizzy had always believed the sapphires would come to her, and she cherished the connection to the memories of her mother and her own carefree days of youth.

The pads of her fingers brushed over the ornate setting before Lizzy unhitched the clasp and draped the jewels around her neck. The cool gemstones settled on her skin, and she walked across the room to look at her reflection. Lizzy had asked Drew to arrange her hair in a simple knot, and she wore a green muslin gown Mrs. Haskins had loaned her. When Lizzy gazed into the mirror, she gasped. The image staring back was her mother. After her mother's death, Lizzy had spent many hours staring at her portrait hanging in the upstairs hallway at Downey Place. With her light-brown hair pinned back and the jewels hanging over her fair skin, Lizzy looked just like her.

How she wished her mother and father were alive to tell her what to do, to help take care of Thomas, to hold her tightly in the security of their arms. A tear slipped down her cheek, and Lizzy quickly shook her head and wiped it away. Emotions did not solve problems.

After a quick knock on the door, it opened wide. "Miss Grey, I have something I believe belongs to you." Mr. Everly stepped in with a smile.

Lizzy's hands flew to cover the jewels around her neck. Why did she not think to lock the door?

"I'm sorry—" Mr. Everly took a single step backwards before he froze. His eyes moved to Lizzy's hands then to the sapphire earrings and bracelet she'd left on the bed. His mouth pinched closed, and his jaw locked.

"May I explain?" Lizzy asked as her shaky fingers moved to the clasp on the necklace.

"Please do." The muscles in Mr. Everly's jaw remained tight, and he set his hands on his hips.

Lizzy's heart beat so hard and fast the tremors ricocheted through the rest of her body. Her fingers fumbled with the latch, and she could not unfasten the clip.

Mr. Everly dropped his hands and sighed. "Allow me." He walked behind Lizzy, and time seemed to stall. She inhaled, waiting for him to loosen the clasp and demand answers. But when his fingers brushed the skin on her neck, she gasped and a shiver raced down her spine.

Mr. Everly lifted the jewels away, but Lizzy still felt their weight on her chest. She turned and extended an open palm towards Mr. Everly, a silent question. His eyes never left hers, and Lizzy could see the battle he fought within himself. She began to count slowly in her head to distract herself from the sorrow in his eyes. It wasn't until she reached number thirty-eight that Mr. Everly placed her mother's necklace into her hand.

Lizzy pressed her eyes closed in a brief prayer of gratitude before she whispered, "Thank you."

She stepped around Mr. Everly and returned the necklace to the velvet wrappings before tucking the jewels under her pillow. Mr. Everly did not move. She wondered if he even breathed.

Lizzy slowly turned to face him. "I owe you an explanation." The tight line of Mr. Everly's mouth told Lizzy he was not angry; he was disappointed, which made her gut churn worse. He would be even more so after Lizzy finished her tale. She glanced at the door, wishing she could close it but knowing propriety dictated otherwise.

"I didn't steal them." The words burst out before Lizzy thought them through. "They belonged to my mother, and after she passed, Father promised them to me." Lizzy didn't know what more to say. There was more, so much more, but where to begin?

"Why were you in the cabin?" Mr. Everly asked.

It was not the response Lizzy expected, but she answered the question. "Because of the storm."

"But there's more."

"Yes." The answer cracked in Lizzy's throat, and Mr. Everly's stern expression dropped away. "From the beginning?" Lizzy asked.

Mr. Everly walked to where Lizzy stood and took her elbow. He led her to the chair near the window then stood with his back to the mantel. "From the beginning."

Chapter 24

"I can't let Uncle Cline find us," Miss Grey concluded. "Thomas would die at sea."

Barton rubbed a hand across his forehead. "And what was your plan, exactly?"

"I wanted to head south, maybe to Surrey or Kent. Somewhere far away from Uncle. I have a few pounds, and I hoped we could get a cottage or I could find work as a governess." Lizzy looked to where she'd stashed the jewels. "If necessary, I'd sell Mother's sapphires."

"You left money in the cottage," Barton said.

"I have a bit of savings. It seemed right to compensate you for our intrusion." Miss Grey's fingers fumbled in her lap, and she hung her head. "Although I did not realize it was you at the time."

Barton reached into his jacket and pulled out the coins. "I mean to return your payment to you. I don't want your money, Miss Grey." Barton lifted her fingers from the arm of the chair and dropped the coins into her palm.

Lizzy pressed her eyes closed. "Stafford," she said.

"Pardon?" Barton paused.

"My name is not Elizabeth Grey. It's Elizabeth Stafford. My father is, was, Reginald Stafford of Downey Place, Leicestershire." Miss Grey, or Miss Stafford rather, rose quickly to her feet, gritting her teeth from the pain of the movement. While Barton loathed the lie, he admired her strength. "I'm sorry I lied, but you must understand we cannot go back. Please don't tell Uncle we're here. I couldn't tell you the truth, because I didn't know whom I could trust."

Barton wanted to reach forward, to smooth the worry from her brow and run his finger down her cheek. But he feared even the most minute action would send Miss Stafford into further panic. Quietly he asked, "Do you trust me now?"

"Yes." Miss Stafford blinked her eyes clear then placed her hand on his arm. "I've lost everyone else; please don't let him take Thomas from me."

Miss Stafford's plea speared Barton's heart. He'd wanted to know her secret, to unravel her mystery, and now he understood the reason for her lies. Despite the surprise of seeing the jewels around her neck, she'd looked lovely wearing them. She looked lovely now. Barton stared at her, wanting desperately to take her in his arms and tell her he wouldn't let any harm come to her or Thomas.

Then she whispered, "I'll do anything."

Barton immediately took a step away, pulling his arm back from Miss Stafford's touch. As much as he wanted to pull her close, to feel her warm body next to his and whisper words of comfort, he refused to exploit her desperation. Barton's heart hammered a rapid cadence, and he could only speak again after inhaling deeply and turning his thoughts away from Miss Stafford's pleading eyes. "Are you sure your uncle is looking for you?"

"No. He doesn't care where we are as long as we are out of his way. But . . ." Miss Stafford's hand moved to her throat, where the gems had rested only a few moments earlier.

"The sapphires," Barton finished the thought. "They are yours?"

"Yes! I mean, Father always told me the jewels were meant for me. But the will left everything to Uncle Cline, and he said that meant the jewels as well. I know Father wanted to leave them to me. The will was wrong. I don't know why Father didn't specify, but Uncle Cline refused to believe me. He took the sapphires and kept them locked in his room." Miss Stafford dropped her eyes to the floor. "I reclaimed them before we left."

Barton ran a hand through his hair as he paced a small circle around the room. "Do you have a copy of the will?"

Miss Stafford shook her head. "Father's solicitor, Mr. Palmer, resigned after Uncle arrived, and his new man of business hardly acknowledged me. My uncle is cruel in his words and extreme in his expectations. I believe many of the staff would have left also, if it weren't for Thomas and me. I worry about them, even now."

Barton considered his options. "Let me make a few inquiries to discover if your uncle is searching for you."

"Thank you." Miss Stafford held out her hand to return the coins to Barton.

"'Tis your money."

She offered a broken smile and let her arm fall to her side. "But I owe you so much."

"And I know what I want for payment, Miss . . ." Barton paused and furrowed his brow. "What shall we call you?"

Miss Stafford lowered her eyes. "Miss Stafford will do."

Barton straightened to his full height, and he cleared his throat. "Very well, then, Miss Stafford." He gave her a knowing glance. "All I require is your word."

Miss Stafford swallowed. "My word?"

"Promise you won't disappear again. I can't help you solve a problem if I'm always having to run off and rescue you in a rainstorm. You claim to trust me—"

"I do!" Miss Stafford insisted.

"Then trust me to keep Thomas and yourself safe. Trust that Everly Manor is where you need to be right now. And"—Barton raised a single finger—"no more secrets." He then extended his hand, intending to shake on the agreement.

Miss Stafford's lips twisted up into a smile, and she grasped his hand and hung on tightly. "Very well. You have my word, *Mr. Barton*."

Barton laughed at the same time he considered how nicely Miss Stafford's hand fit in his own.

Chapter 25

SHARING HER CONFIDENCE WITH MR. Everly provided Lizzy an unexpected amount of relief. She knew he was fond of Thomas and would not willingly put him in danger. Yet, Uncle Cline's actions remained unknown, and Lizzy could not be too cautious. She still planned to leave as soon as she was able and hoped to feel fit for travel within a fortnight.

The following morning dawned sunny and clear. Thomas had reminded Lizzy on three different occasions that Mr. Murray promised to teach him how to canter, and Lizzy was determined to watch firsthand. Concentrating on the deep breaths the doctor had prescribed, Lizzy slowly made her way down the staircase without assistance. As she walked towards the door, Mr. Franklin Everly appeared.

She'd only seen Mr. Franklin when he'd brought Thomas to her room after lessons and once as she'd walked the hall outside her bedchamber. He had the same blond hair as his brother, but where Mr. Everly had loose, striated waves, Mr. Franklin wore his hair longer around his neck and ears; his eyes were greyer than his brother's, but both men radiated a happy countenance.

"Good day, Miss Gr—excuse me—Stafford." Mr. Franklin bowed and tried to mask his grin.

"And to you, Mr. Franklin." Lizzy dipped into only a shallow curtsy, for that was all the pain she could bear. "It seems I have made quite a mess of things."

"Not at all. Barton did not tell us the particulars, but he said your use of an alias was necessary for your safety, as well as your brother's. He is a determined and willing protector. I'm sure it will all be sorted soon."

"I haven't properly thanked you for the attentions you've paid my brother. He enjoys your instruction."

Mr. Franklin laughed. "Oh, I doubt that. He gives his lessons a good crack, and he's a bright lad, but I think he'd much rather be reading with Bethany or wandering through the stables than reviewing his multiplication tables."

Lizzy smiled. "I believe that's the nature of little boys."

Mr. Franklin nodded agreement.

"I hoped to watch him ride today," Lizzy said. "Do you know if they are to work near the stables?"

"That seems to be Murray's preference. Shall we investigate?" Mr. Franklin stepped beside Lizzy and offered his arm.

She accepted, and together they walked outside. Lizzy inhaled the glorious fresh air.

"It's a lovely day," Mr. Franklin said.

"Indeed." Lizzy raised her face to the sky.

Mr. Franklin led Lizzy to a circular pen behind the barn. "Ah, here they are."

"Hello, Lizzy!" Thomas shouted from atop Brutus. He released one hand from the reins to wave at her, but Mr. Murray barked at him to keep control of the horse, and Thomas's attention turned back to his task.

Mr. Franklin laughed. "Old Murray hasn't changed a bit."

"Now, kick him in the side, and ease into the canter," Mr. Murray told Thomas.

Lizzy beamed with pride as she watched Thomas's determination. He kicked at the horse with all his might, but Brutus ignored him as if he were a pesky fly.

"Kick harder, boy," Mr. Murray said.

Thomas's face scrunched in concentration, and as his boots connected with the horse's flanks, Mr. Murray slapped Brutus on the hindquarters. Brutus jumped a bit, and Thomas yelped and clutched the reins tighter as the horse's legs extended in long, even strides. After only one lap Thomas rocked and swayed with the movements of the horse cantering fluidly around the enclosure.

"Bravo, Thomas!" Lizzy called and waved her free hand.

She saw Mr. Everly applauding Thomas from the opposite side of the barn. He looked rather dashing, wearing a green coat and dark-brown trousers. When his eyes met hers, Lizzy realized she'd been staring, and a blush heated her cheeks.

Mr. Everly walked to where she stood with Mr. Franklin. "Miss Stafford. May I have a chair sent out for you?" he asked.

"No, no. Please. I'm quite content. The sun feels delightful, and I breathe easier when I am standing."

Mr. Franklin turned to Lizzy. "Thank you for the pleasure of your company this morning, Miss Stafford. I'm headed to London for a few days on an errand for my mother, but I leave you to Barton's devoted hospitality." He quirked an eyebrow at his brother then turned back to Lizzy. "I will resume Thomas's studies upon my return."

"Safe travels, sir. And thank you again for your care for Thomas and for your assistance this morning." Lizzy knew her words did not adequately convey her gratitude.

Mr. Franklin granted Lizzy a sincere smile. "Of course. I'm sure my brother will be willing to escort you back to the house when you are ready." Mr. Franklin tilted his head and then departed for the house.

Mr. Everly stepped beside Lizzy. "Thomas is doing well," he said.

She nodded agreement. "I am so proud of him."

Mr. Everly clasped his hands behind his back and cleared his throat. He glanced at her. "Your complexion is improving."

Lizzy raised a hand to her cheek but did not reply.

Mr. Everly cleared his throat again. "I've just come from Hillcrest."

"Oh?" Fear replaced the warmth Lizzy felt only moments ago, and her hand fell away from her face.

Mr. Everly focused on her. "Would you care to take a turn through the gardens?"

Lizzy didn't speak. She couldn't, for the fright chilling her bones. She glanced back at Thomas, who grinned as he bounced on Brutus's back.

Mr. Everly touched her arm. "He'll be all right." Mr. Everly pulled her arm through his own, and Lizzy numbly matched his slow cadence as they walked to the gardens.

Mr. Everly guided Lizzy to a bench on a secluded path, away from the watchful eyes of the household staff.

"I'd prefer to stand." Lizzy clasped her hands in front of her.

"Very well. As long as you don't dash away," Mr. Everly teased, but Lizzy could not bring herself to smile.

"That depends on what news you have to share." Lizzy pressed a hand to her middle and sucked in a breath as her tender bruises gave way to pain.

She preferred the physical pain to the unknown. The bruises and swelling were visible, measurable. The unknown filled every minute with dreaded mystery.

Mr. Everly brushed a wavy lock of hair from his forehead. "A man came through the village a few days ago asking about a lady and a young boy. Thomas was never seen with you, so no one thought to suggest your arrival to the gentleman. He accepted it without question, and he hasn't been seen since."

"What did he look like?" Lizzy asked.

"Well-dressed, portly but handsome, with blue eyes and greying hair. He didn't leave a name."

Lizzy ceased breathing. She clamped her eyes closed and worked hard to force her tears away.

"Miss Stafford," Mr. Everly whispered. "Look at me."

Lizzy shook her head. Reality would arrive far too soon; she needed to remain in blackness a bit longer.

"Elizabeth." Her name sounded like a lullaby, and when Mr. Everly's fingers brushed Lizzy's check, she could not refuse his request. She opened her eyes to see his beautiful face filled with sincere concern. A tear rolled down her cheek, and he brushed it away with his thumb. "Don't cry."

As much as Lizzy wanted to obey, she could not. More tears fell, and Mr. Everly pulled a handkerchief from his pocket to stem the deluge. Lizzy accepted the linen and dabbed at her eyes, but it was no use. She covered her mouth as her body shook. Uncle's anger remained fresh in her mind. She could practically feel his breath hitting her face as he cursed her actions, cursed her existence. Wearing a mask and acting brave had taken a toll. Lizzy could no longer maintain the façade. "He can't find us. He can't . . . He'll take Thomas . . ."

"Shhh," Mr. Everly said, and when his words did not soothe Lizzy's tremors, he pulled her into his arms. "You're safe here. He won't hurt Thomas. He won't hurt you. I won't let him. I will keep you safe, Elizabeth. Both of you. I promise."

Lizzy cried into Mr. Everly's coat, wishing promises were as easy to keep as they were to make.

Chapter 26

ONCE BARTON SETTLED MISS STAFFORD in her room, he went directly to his office. While he had accrued a reputation for being charitable, his deeds applied to simple acts of service: a monetary donation, an offer of employment, the Everly endowment to the girls' school, or his patronage of the local parish. Never had someone's life depended on him, and Barton wasn't entirely sure what to do.

He paced the room, anxious for answers to reveal themselves, his steps stiff and frantic.

"A difficult day?" his mother asked from the doorway.

Barton turned on his heel and faced her. "What is it, Mother?" Her eyes widened. "Sorry." Barton rubbed a hand over his face then collapsed into a chair and propped his elbows on his knees. His mother sat in the chair opposite, and after a moment Barton finally looked up. "It has been a trying day, and it's far from over."

Barton's mother glanced at the clock on the desk, and her brows rose. "Harrison, what are you not telling me?"

Barton exhaled. "Miss Stafford's story is not mine to share."

"You've discovered more of her situation, then?"

Barton rubbed a hand over his face. "Yes."

"And?" When Barton did not answer, his mother huffed in exasperation then rose and walked to the window. She pulled her shoulders taut and drew a slow breath. Finally she turned back to her son. "She's lied to you about her name. How can you be certain she's telling you the truth now?"

Barton quickly steeled himself. "I believe her."

His mother crossed the room and placed a hand on her son's shoulder. "Remember what happened the last time you ventured down such a road.

It almost broke you, and I cannot bear to watch you suffer again. You're finally back, Harrison. Don't let your faith in others blind you to the truth."

Barton reached up and covered his mother's hand with his own. "I want to believe her."

"But wanting does not make it the wisest course. Be careful, son." Barton's mother placed a kiss on the top of his head and walked out of the room.

Once Drew cleared the breakfast tray, Lizzy sat at the desk and compiled a list of the preparations to be completed in order for her and Thomas to depart. Despite Mr. Everly's reassurance, the confirmation that someone—Uncle—had been searching for her had smothered any security she'd felt. Beyond her fears was the matter of Thomas to consider. He had grown comfortable at Everly Manor. The longer they stayed, the more difficult it would be to leave.

Mr. Everly had been cordial and kind, and Lizzy cringed when she thought of her breakdown the previous day. Feeling Mr. Everly hold her close, whispering her name with promises of safety, provided a comfort she hadn't felt since before her father's accident. The months since his passing had been filled with turmoil and confusion; it had been a struggle to come to terms with the hand life had dealt.

Mr. Everly stood strong, soothing, his care constant. Beyond comfort Lizzy felt important as he held her in his arms. She quickly dismissed her quickened heartbeat as a consequence of her anxiety, yet Lizzy wished she could remain in the haven he provided. Alas, she could not. Danger remained. Lizzy and Thomas could not disappear quickly enough.

Lizzy's injuries healed more each day, and while travel would not be comfortable, she was determined to endure it. Somerset would be her destination—the farther away from Downey Place, the better. She would need food for their journey, and she would need to procure a new coat for both her and Thomas, as their garments had been torn beyond repair during the storm.

Remembering her promise, Lizzy felt obliged to inform Mr. Everly of her errand and pending departure. After all, use of his carriage to return to Hillcrest and his advice on routes and inns would be invaluable. Then again, maybe Lizzy should only request transport to the village. It might be best if Mr. Everly remained oblivious of her chosen destination.

A knock sounded on her door, and Lizzy quickly slid a fresh piece of paper atop the list she'd been composing and called for the guest to enter.

Mr. Everly walked in, looking quite dashing. The azure waistcoat he wore brightened his eyes, and his dark-beige jacket accentuated the darker-blond streaks strewn through his hair. With a lazy smile he bid her good morning, and Lizzy knew she would miss his relaxed manners and easy conversation. What startled her was the sorrow that washed over her heart at the realization.

Lizzy blinked free from her musings. "Good morning."

Mr. Everly smiled, and warm feelings of comfort, whispers of home, began to flood Lizzy's senses. "My brother-in-law has returned from Town. Bethany asked if you'd join us for tea."

"Yes, of course." Lizzy stood and followed Mr. Everly to the top of the stairs, where he offered his arm, and they began their descent.

"Your improvement is commendable," Mr. Everly said. "But I must admit I prefer the previous method of assisting you down the stairs."

Lizzy's cheeks warmed. She agreed, although she would never admit such a thing aloud. Rather, she changed the subject. "I hope to be well enough to travel soon."

Mr. Everly stiffened beside her. "Do you think that's wise?"

They reached the main floor, and Lizzy released a breath of relief. "I think the sooner we leave, the better. For all of us."

Mr. Everly searched her face. "I disagree. Please do not make such presumptions on my behalf."

Lizzy spoke before he could say something to shake her resolve. "Thomas and I will both need to purchase new coats for the journey. Do you think I might be able to find something suitable in Hillcrest?"

Mr. Everly looked at her quizzically, and before he could respond, a man unfamiliar to Lizzy greeted him.

"Barton!" The handsome gentleman with black hair and even blacker eyes walked to where they stood. The man stood shorter than Mr. Everly. The stranger's shoulders were broad and sturdy, and joviality stirred the air around him. Mr. Everly dropped Lizzy's arm while the man clapped him on the shoulder.

"Welcome back, Haskins. I trust your business went well?" Mr. Everly asked.

Mr. Haskins's smile faltered for only a moment as his eyes flickered to acknowledge Lizzy at Barton's side. "Everything's been settled, and our renovations should be complete soon. I'm glad to be heading home. Though, now that the estate has a new kitchen, Bethany believes we need to extend the renovation to the dining room. I'm not looking forward to that endeavor, nor the expense."

"May I introduce you to Miss Elizabeth Stafford? Miss Stafford, this is my esteemed brother-in-law, Marcus Haskins." Mr. Everly stepped back to allow the new acquaintances to bow and curtsy in turn. "Miss Stafford has been recovering from a rather terrifying accident."

"Yes, yes. I've heard," Mr. Haskins said.

Lizzy's eyes narrowed, and she pinned the man with a stare.

Mr. Haskins smiled broadly. "My wife, you know. She wrote all about the violent storm and the dashing rescue. I believe you have a brother, Miss . . . er . . . you said, Stafford?"

Instead of replying, Lizzy watched the man, and Mr. Everly responded in her stead. "Yes, Miss Stafford's half-brother, Thomas, is quite smitten with Bethany. You may have to call him out to regain your wife's attentions."

Mr. Haskins laughed. "Speaking of Bethany's attentions, she's waiting for us in the drawing room. Shall we?"

After Mrs. Haskins poured out, Lizzy sat quietly and observed the family. Mr. Everly and his brother teased their sister until Mr. Haskins valiantly intervened and turned the jest back on the men. Mrs. Everly watched the banter, inserting a motherly reprimand when necessary.

Sorrow descended over Lizzy's heart. Amid the teasing and taunts lay a solid foundation of love. The Everlys understood and embraced the concept of family. It was a concept that was lost to Lizzy. With her parents gone, only Thomas remained, and she swore once again that she would protect him, provide for him, love him, until her dying breath. The sacrifice would be great. Becoming Thomas's guardian in this furtive way, Lizzy would forgo society. She would not be included in invitations to dinners or balls, even if she became a governess. As a governess she would walk a thin line between servant and gentry, but Lizzy's only desire was to keep Thomas safe.

"Have you visited London, Miss Stafford?" Mr. Haskins's question pulled her from her thoughts.

Lizzy steadied her teacup in her lap. "Not recently. My father took me several years ago, and I've never cared to return."

"Hmm," Mr. Haskins mused. "I only ask because, well"—he turned his attention to the entire group—"I attended a card party last week." He slid a finger under his cravat and looked sheepishly at his wife. "Sorry, dear. But word about the place was that a man named Simpkin was looking for a lady and her brother. Bethany's letters mentioned your arrival at Everly Manor, and at first I thought there might be a connection, because of the younger lad. But then I recalled that Bethany said your name was Grey, so naturally I dismissed the notion and went about my business."

The mention of Mr. Simpkin paralyzed Lizzy. She sat as still as a statue while Mr. Haskins whispered to his wife that he only played cards for an hour and had lost nothing more than a few guineas.

Once Mrs. Haskins seemed soothed, her husband spoke more audibly again. "I only just realized that Simpkin was looking for a Miss Stafford. 'Tis you, then?" He pointed a hand towards Lizzy.

The blood drained from Lizzy's face, and dread swirled through her stomach. The teacup she held rattled against the saucer, and as she reached to set it on the table, the cup slipped from her fingers.

"Dash it, Haskins!" Mr. Everly moved to Lizzy's side and took her shaking hands in his own. Lizzy could not move; she could not breathe. Fear coagulated every emotion within her.

Mrs. Everly fixed hawkish eyes on Lizzy. "What did Mr. Simpkin want with our Miss Stafford?" she asked.

Mr. Haskins tugged at his cravat once more. His eyes swept over the group before he answered. "He was looking for his fiancée."

Chapter 27

BARTON DID NOT THINK MISS Stafford could blanch any more than she had, but at Haskins's declaration, she swooned. Her consciousness returned quickly, however, and before anyone could object, Barton lifted her into his arms and carried her to her bedchamber.

Fiancée?

What an absurd notion. Surely Haskins had misunderstood the inquiry. Barton did not know if his brother-in-law had even met the man Simpkin. The fact that someone was looking for Miss Stafford in London was indeed a concern. But the city provided an ideal place to disappear. Simpkin was probably working under the direction of Cline Stafford, trying to gather whatever information he could. Referring to Miss Stafford as his fiancée likely served to garner sympathy. Barton assured himself it was only a ruse.

Once he settled Miss Stafford and left Bastian to sit with her, he sought out his brother-in-law. Haskins had retired to his room. Barton knocked once and did not wait for a call to enter.

Haskins stood unbuttoning his waistcoat. His eyes met Barton's while his fingers finished his task. "Sorry about that. I didn't realize the situation was so sensitive."

"Sensitive?" Barton stood near the wardrobe and planted his hands on his hips. "You mean the exact opposite of your approach?"

Haskins grunted and ran a hand across his brow. "I didn't consider that the information would be so shocking. A woman should know her own fiancé, should she not?" Haskins walked to Barton and placed a hand on his shoulder. "At least you know so you can avoid a situation similar to—"

Barton hit Haskins's hand away. He stepped backwards, evaluating his brother-in-law. "Miss Stafford is not Miss Newhall. Besides, she has always insisted her stay is temporary."

"Bethany said you'd be irritable. Miss Stafford is a beauty, but I say good riddance to her." Haskins tossed his crumpled cravat to the side. "I'm sorry I didn't write sooner. Perhaps before you fell for the girl. Bethany just talked of the brother, and I assumed you knew." Haskins sighed heavily before he continued. "Bethany's told me all now, and I will say that if you tossed your hat in with Simpkin, you'd have a fair shot. The man's a right dour sort, old enough to be her father."

"You met him?" Barton narrowed his eyes.

"Like I said, at the card party." Haskins grimaced. "Though that admission got me into a bit of trouble with your sister."

With two large steps Barton stood before his brother-in-law. "Did you tell him about Miss Stafford?"

Haskins raised a hand in defense. "No, man. I told you—I didn't realize they were one and the same 'til an hour ago."

Barton loomed over Haskins, trying to sift through the information.

"Now, step back, Barton." Haskins lifted his chin and pulled his shoulders square. Barton ran a hand through his hair and retreated a step or two. "She really has got you in a dither."

Fire flashed through Barton. He clenched his jaw and took a long breath. Then he harassed Haskins for information until the latter threw his hands in the air and asked Barton to let him be. Barton's inquisition left him with a description of Simpkin, down to the details of Simpkin's jeweled neck pin. It also left him with a plethora of questions.

Barton knew Miss Stafford had intended to attend dinner that evening, but Henderson informed Barton that she would not be joining the family after all and she'd requested a tray in her room. Bethany reported that when she arrived to return Thomas to the nursery, Miss Stafford appeared to be in improved health. Pestering Bethany for more information about Miss Stafford's disposition only garnered Barton a stern rebuke from his sister and the concern of his mother.

He spent the next three days attempting to reconcile his emotions. If Miss Stafford were truly engaged, why did she not turn to her fiancé for protection for herself and Thomas? Barton knew if he were Miss Stafford's intended and she went missing, he would search hill and dale to discover her whereabouts. 'Twould be worth every moment of effort to secure the affection of a woman like Miss Stafford.

Barton avoided contact with the lady. He knew not what to think, how to interpret Haskins's revelation. He'd been so certain of the connection he felt with Miss Stafford. Had a convincing pair of eyes and a smile that brought sunshine to his day duped him again?

On the morning of the fourth day, Barton returned from an early ride to find Mr. Grimes visiting with the groom outside the stables. The men completed their salutations as Thomas came running around the corner, with a little brown pup nipping at his heels. Brutus's ears tweaked at the yapping.

"Ah, Mr. Everly. I've brought your pointer." Grimes bounced in excitement. "Four weeks old, exactly like you asked."

Thomas ran up to Barton. "Isn't he smart, Mr. Barton? He will follow me without even having to call him." Before Barton could reply, Thomas took off running again, and sure enough the brown-and-white puppy followed behind.

Barton chuckled and turned to Mr. Grimes. "Have you settled the expenses with my steward?"

"Yes, I just left Mr. Blaine and came to see how the pup is faring."

Thomas circled around the men again, and Barton smiled as widely as Thomas did.

"Looks like this lad will keep him out of mischief." Grimes nodded at the boy. "What are you going to name him?"

Thomas's ears perked at the question. He ran directly to Barton and tugged on his sleeve. "Brownbeard! Can his name be Brownbeard? Pleeease?"

"Brownbeard? Wherever did that come from?" Barton asked.

"Mrs. Haskins tells me stories about Blackbeard. He's fierce and brave. Your dog is going to be fierce and brave too."

"Blackbeard was a pirate," Barton added with a chuckle.

Thomas spoke with wide, convincing eyes. "But we know the puppy won't be a pirate, and since he's got brown spots instead of black, we can call him Brownbeard. Please, Mr. Barton?"

One look at Thomas, and Barton could not deny his wish. "Very well." Barton reached over and mussed Thomas's hair as he'd seen Miss Stafford do. "Brownbeard it is."

Thomas whooped and jumped high with both fists in the air. Barton laughed despite the ridiculousness of the name.

Mr. Grimes took his leave, and Thomas called the dog to him. "Brownbeard. Come here, boy." Thomas clapped his hands on his thighs, and when the puppy jumped against his legs, Thomas dropped to the ground and allowed Brownbeard to lick him senseless. The boy's giggles warmed Barton's soul.

"You are going to break his heart." Miss Stafford tightened a wool shawl around her shoulders as she stepped beside Barton.

Barton noticed the vibrant color in Miss Stafford's cheeks. "You look refreshed," he said. She granted him a sad smile, and Barton pondered her comment. "What do you mean I will break his heart?"

Miss Stafford turned her attention to her brother. "We will leave soon, and the dog will remain here. Thomas has lost so much already, and now you've added another goodbye. He will regret our departure most acutely."

Barton studied her for a moment. Cook's talents had lifted the sunken pallor from Miss Stafford's cheeks, but the lady's eyes still searched for something beyond the scene before them. On the cusp of a breath, Barton asked, "Will he be the only one?"

Miss Stafford stiffened, her brows lifting quickly before she attempted to appear unaffected. Barton pressed, "What about you, Miss Stafford? Are you anxious to be on your way, or will you perhaps miss Everly Manor?" He held his breath and waited for her answer.

"As I've told you, we can't remain," she replied quickly. Too quickly.

"Because of your fiancé?" Miss Stafford's profile turned to stone. Barton did not mean to cause her discomfort, but he had to know. "Is Mr. Simpkin your fiancé, Miss Stafford?"

Her brows scrunched together, and the pleasing color drained from her cheeks. "I . . . I'm not sure."

Despite Thomas's laughter ringing in the background, Barton's joviality fled. He'd considered Simpkin's claim for days, mulling over Haskins's report of the man and what he knew of Miss Stafford. He needed the truth. "Miss Stafford, it is a simple question. You've promised me no more secrets, so I will ask again. Is Mr. Simpkin your fiancé, or is he not?"

Miss Stafford flinched and pressed her eyes closed. Her bottom lip began to quiver, but only for a moment. She straightened her stance and returned Barton's glower with a scowl of her own. "I've answered your inquiry, sir. I apologize if you do not like my response, but I have spoken true. Now, if you'll excuse me, I came out to enjoy a walk in the garden."

Barton's mouth fell open, and before he could gather his wits, Miss Stafford had turned on her heel and nearly reached the stone path that marked the garden entrance. Huffing at Miss Stafford's indignation, he jogged to catch up to her. "So, you refuse to answer me, then?"

"I answered your inquiry; you refused to accept it." Miss Stafford marched on.

"It is a simple yes-or-no question. You only responded with uncertainty." Barton increased his strides and stepped in front of Miss Stafford, halting her escape.

Miss Stafford raised her chin in defiance. "Then, perhaps it is not as simple as you imply." Her shoulders rose with each angry breath. "I demand you let me pass."

"And I must point out that I have asked nothing unreasonable." Frustration burned through Barton's chest. Why could she not clarify her relationship with Simpkin? "Would you not agree that I have been generous in providing for your recovery and I have shown abundant patience tolerating your secrets and your deception?"

Miss Stafford wilted. Hurt emanated through her features. Barton's words stung, just as he'd intended them too, but he just as quickly wished he could reel them back.

Miss Stafford clenched her fists in her shawl and stepped a bit closer. She lowered her voice and bit out an explanation. "My deception, *Mr. Everly*, is not what you imagine it to be. If you must know, Uncle Cline accepted Mr. Simpkin's suit on my behalf and informed me after it was all arranged. I would have vehemently refused, but when Uncle decided to send Thomas away, I agreed to the engagement because it was the only way Uncle would allow me to leave with Thomas. I never fathomed Mr. Simpkin would search me out."

Barton rubbed a hand over his eyes. "It seems you were mistaken, for it appears he's searching for you quite intently."

Miss Stafford's determination did not falter. Her mouth pinched in a tight line, and she responded quietly. "Not at my request or desire. I want nothing to do with the man. Now, let me pass."

Barton had hurdled his curt words because he wanted her to deny any attachment to Simpkin. As he pondered on the cause of his vehemence, empathy pierced his soul. Barton squared his shoulders, trying to look calm despite the turmoil coursing through his limbs. "I can't do that, Miss Stafford. At least, not until I apologize for my gruffness. It was uncalled for."

"It certainly was," Miss Stafford agreed. She tucked a loose lock of hair behind her ear and took a breath. The tension in her shoulders softened with her exhale.

Barton loved her candor. His fingers itched to reach out and pull the wayward lock of hair free again. He'd enjoyed watching it flutter against her cheek. How he wanted to help this woman, to wipe the worry from her brow. He wanted to know what emotion lay hidden, buried in the defenses she'd erected.

"There is one more question we have not addressed," Barton said. Miss Stafford pouted, and Barton found her look of agitation rather endearing.

He stared at her until she blinked and then huffed in frustration. "What is your question, Mr. Everly?"

Barton swallowed past the lump that now lodged in his throat. "You said leaving Everly Manor would break Thomas's heart. What about yours?"

Lizzy did not immediately answer Mr. Everly. What could she say? Despite her tenuous introduction to Mr. Everly, friendship had blossomed. She cherished everything Mr. Everly had done for her, for Thomas, and she admired the man standing before her. His goodness, his sincerity, his ability to forgive her mistakes, and his efforts to earn her trust had unified her soul to his. She'd been welcomed into his home and could not deny that the thought of leaving caused a giant pit to open inside her. She did not look forward to running away with Thomas or leaving Mr. Everly and the security he provided, but knowing Mr. Simpkin pursued them, she had little choice.

She slowly offered her response. "Since my parents' passing, the comfort of family has been elusive at best. Everly Manor has provided an unexpected respite from the world. And that I will miss."

Mr. Everly took a step forward. His blue eyes swept over Lizzy's face, causing her heartbeat to quicken. "Is that all you will miss? My family? Your respite?"

Lizzy pinched her lips tight and nodded. She could not admit he'd claimed a piece of her heart. It would hurt too much, and Lizzy did not want to hurt anymore.

Mr. Everly moved closer, leaving only the space of a breath between them. "Are you certain?"

His nearness churned havoc through Lizzy's body. Her legs wobbled, her mind muddled, and her breaths quickened. She raised her hands, intent to demand he cease his advance, but before she could utter a word, her shawl slipped from her shoulders and her palms came to rest on Mr.

Everly's sturdy chest. His heartbeat raced beneath her fingers. The rhythmic palpitations beat directly to her core.

Mr. Everly covered one of her hands with his own, pressing her cold fingers into a solid cocoon of warmth. "I must confess that should you leave, I would miss you, Miss Stafford. I would miss your determination, your candor, and even the indecorous squeal you emitted when we first met." Mr. Everly lifted her hand, his warm lips brushing against her skin. "I hope it is not only my family you are loath to leave."

She looked at Mr. Everly's lapels, his starched cravat, and his fingers holding her own. She could not meet his searching gaze.

"There is no need to run," he whispered. "You and Thomas are welcome here for as long as you like. Let me be your escape."

"Mr. Everly, I—" Lizzy began.

He pressed a warm finger to her lips. "Barton. Please, call me Barton."

Lizzy cherished the invitation and repeated his name softly before making the mistake of raising her eyes to his. "I can't . . . ," she whispered.

The intensity of his magnetic gaze caused Lizzy to lean forward the tiniest bit. Barton must have interpreted her movement as an invitation, for in the next moment his fingers tightened their hold on her hand. His other arm wrapped around her back, and he pressed his mouth to hers.

Lizzy's initial shock fell away as she yearned to feel more of the peace Barton's kiss supplied. She leaned in to him, the gentle caress of his lips pulling a sigh from her soul.

Barton lingered for a moment, his soft lips resting against her own before he drew back. "Do you not know I will protect you?" Barton's blue eyes assured Lizzy of the truth of his words. He looked at her as if she were sunshine.

Lizzy wanted to believe. She wanted to continue swimming in the beautiful current, but Uncle's fury rose up in her memory and crashed over her like a bitter wind. "You don't know what Uncle Cline is capable of," she whispered.

Barton moved his hand from her back and fingered the wayward strand of hair she'd tucked behind her ear. "Perhaps if you returned the jewels?" Barton's words hit stronger than a physical slap, and Lizzy took a step back, freeing herself from the hypnotic cocoon his presence created.

"You would have me relinquish the one token that binds me to my mother?"

"No . . . I . . ." Barton sighed and shifted to hold both of Lizzy's hands in his own. "I'm trying to help."

His sincerity pricked Lizzy's defenses. She looked at their clasped hands, an anchor of hope, of a future better than she could imagine. "Perhaps you're right. It's selfish of me to keep the jewels if giving them up means Thomas will be safe. Do you truly think if I return the sapphires, Uncle will let us be?"

"What more could he want?" Barton asked.

Lizzy stiffened. She could only imagine. Uncle sought money and power and indulged in women. There were a great many things he could want beyond the gemstones.

Barton released one of Lizzy's hands and ran his fingers along her temple. "The memories of your mother are here. No one can take those away." Lizzy pressed her eyes closed and then felt Barton's breath near her ear. "Please don't run from me."

Lizzy wanted to comply. She wanted to wrap her arms around Barton's neck and never let go, but she'd given her heart away, promised it to Thomas. "Don't you see, Mr. Everly—"

"Barton," he corrected her.

Lizzy blinked rapidly in a vain effort to keep her tears from falling. "I will sacrifice anything for Thomas."

"Even if it means forfeiting a future at Everly Manor?" he asked.

Lizzy's emotions nearly strangled her. "Even then."

Lizzy heard a high-pitched yip and looked around Mr. Everly to see Thomas's large blue eyes staring at her. She called his name, but before she could reach him, he turned around and ran from the garden with Brownbeard chasing the shadow at his heels.

"Thomas!" Lizzy called. "Come back!" Lizzy pulled her hand free from Barton's grasp to follow her brother, but her stiff body could not move quickly enough.

Barton bent down and retrieved Lizzy's shawl. He handed it to her. "Allow me." Barton turned and ran to the corner where Thomas had disappeared.

Lizzy chastised herself for speaking so freely. How did Barton so easily uncover her secrets and fears? She had been able to shelve them away since her father's accident, carefully selecting any emotion she revealed. Yet Barton continually managed to remove the mask she'd worked so hard to perfect.

Lizzy focused on the path before her, determined to catch Thomas and assure him all would be well. When she rounded the final corner, a polished black boot entered her line of sight, and Lizzy looked up to see the broad figure of Mr. Rudyard Simpkin right before colliding with his chest. Another unladylike squeal escaped her lips as she bounced off his large frame and landed on her derriere, in the dirt.

"Miss Stafford?" Mr. Simpkin began. "Is it really you?" he asked with exuberance.

Lizzy shook her head clear as a gloved hand reached down to assist her. Pain pulsed through Lizzy's ribs, and it took a moment for her to catch her breath. She accepted Mr. Simpkin's help but cried out in pain as he pulled her to her feet. She immediately pulled her hand from his and tried to take long slow breaths in an effort to temper her abounding agony.

Barton joined her a moment later, huffing from his sprint after Thomas. He looked briefly at Mr. Simpkin before addressing Lizzy. "Miss Stafford, have you hurt yourself?"

"'Tis nothing greater than my previous injuries, sir." Lizzy glanced briefly between the two men.

She watched the rise and fall of Barton's chest for a moment. When she dared meet his gaze, she was struck by the intensity she saw there. He seemed to plead for her trust while simultaneously questioning her intent. "Are you certain you're all right?" he asked.

Lizzy's heart sped, and her answer slipped out quietly. "I'm not quite sure."

"I cannot tell you, Miss Stafford, how happy I am to find you at long last," Mr. Simpkin interjected.

Barton looked down at Mr. Simpkin. What Simpkin lacked in height he made up for in girth. The man adjusted the tall hat on his head to further cover his shock of thick-grey hair and puffed out his ample chest.

"I don't believe we've met." Barton clasped his hands behind his back and tilted his head. "I'm Harrison Everly, and you are?"

The larger man reset his walking stick at his side, twisted his lips in a misshapen smile, and offered a partial bow. "Mr. Rudyard Simpkin, at your service."

"And what brings you to Everly Manor?" Barton's tone remained cool.

"Miss Stafford, of course." Mr. Simpkin's smile never faltered as he continued his charade of innocence. "You can't imagine the worry I've felt over the disappearance of my fiancée."

Chapter 28

FIANCÉE—THERE WAS THAT DEUCED WORD again. It seemed no matter how hard Barton tried to push it from his mind, the moniker kept being thrust at him.

Miss Stafford held herself erect, her hands still at her side, but trepidation remained evident in her features. Her eyes altered between translucent amber and a rich liquid gold. Barton considered her apprehension a testament to her words. She truly had not thought Simpkin would seek her out.

"You can imagine my utter joy at finding you, my dear." Simpkin reached for Miss Stafford's hand, but she quickly stepped back and thrust her fingers behind her.

"I was never lost, sir." Miss Stafford said, and Barton silently applauded her strength.

"Hmm." Simpkin's lips pressed downward, and his eyes darkened as he perused Miss Stafford's figure. He turned to Barton. "Might you provide a room for Miss Stafford and me to discuss arrangements for her return to Leicestershire?"

Barton's greatest wish was to oust Simpkin from his property and never see or hear from him again.

"Perhaps we could use the front parlor?" Miss Stafford's voice snapped Barton's thoughts back within the bounds of propriety.

"Of course. The parlor is at your disposal." He waved a hand towards the front door of the manor.

Simpkin turned and extended an arm to Miss Stafford. "Shall we, my dear?"

Miss Stafford's fists clenched, and she sucked in a long breath. Then she turned to Barton, her eyes shifting to golden sunlight. "Thomas?" she asked on a breath.

"He's with Murray, brushing the horses." Barton sensed his answer was not quite enough. "Let's conclude this business. Then I'll bring him to you." Barton shifted his attention to Simpkin, who observed them keenly. Simpkin once again offered his arm to Miss Stafford, and Barton's ire returned.

Miss Stafford pressed her lips together, the lips he'd recently kissed, and placed her arm on Simpkin's. Barton needed a moment to collect himself, to formulate a strategy to dismiss Simpkin once and for all. "I'll request a tray and join you shortly," he said.

Simpkin's grating laugh shattered all thought. "A chaperone is hardly necessary, Everly. As I explained, Miss Stafford and I are to be wed. In fact, it is at her uncle's request and due to my own concern for her well-being that I have assumed responsibility for returning Miss Stafford home." Simpkin tilted his head and eyed Miss Stafford before turning back to Barton. "So you see, it is all on the up and up."

Miss Stafford's hand shifted on Simpkin's arm. He immediately drew her nearer, and Miss Stafford released a small squeal. A match touched the tinder in Barton's chest, setting his anger aflame. "Miss Stafford is now under my protection," Barton said.

"Protection?" Simpkin laughed again. "Why would she need protection from her betrothed?" His brow furrowed, and he stepped closer, dragging poor Miss Stafford forward with his movements. "What game are you playing, Everly?"

Barton met Simpkin's sneer with a warning. "'Tis no game, Simpkin. Miss Stafford is welcome to remain at Everly Manor for as long as she desires. The choice of whether or not to leave will be hers and hers alone."

Simpkin pulled back and puffed out his chest once again. "Mah, but of course it will. I trust Miss Stafford will choose to honor her word and protect her family."

Miss Stafford stood slightly behind Simpkin, and therefore the pompous man did not see her press her eyes closed. But Barton did. He knew Simpkin's threat had hit its mark. Summoning great restraint, he said, "Then, my presence in your tête-à-tête will be of no moment." Determined to not leave Miss Stafford alone with the man, Barton led the small group to the house.

"Stay near, Henderson. Our uninvited guest will not be staying long," Barton said quietly as he handed his things to the butler. Henderson nodded.

Without preface Simpkin handed over his hat and gloves and took Miss Stafford's arm again. "Shall we?" he asked with a smug smile.

Miss Stafford did not say a word.

Upon entering the parlor, Barton noted they were not alone. His mother sat at the desk penning a letter. Barton cleared his throat, and his mother turned, quickly evaluating the scene. She focused for an extra moment on Mr. Simpkin but said nothing. The matriarch rose from her chair and walked towards the stranger.

"Mother, this is Mr. Simpkin. He is here to . . . inquire after Miss Stafford," Barton said.

Mrs. Everly extended her hand, and Simpkin bowed politely. "How do you do, madam? Thank you for inviting me into your humble home."

"'Tis my son's home now, Mr. Simpkin, so your gratitude may be directed towards him." Mrs. Everly led the group to a cluster of couches and chairs, sat herself down, and wasted not a moment. "How are you acquainted with Miss Stafford?" she asked as the others also sat.

Simpkin grinned stupidly, reminding Barton of the puppy frolicking in the yard. "We are to be married."

"Oh. So the rumors are true." Barton's mother turned her attention to Miss Stafford. Her look of caustic disappointment echoed the sentiment roiling through Barton's gut. Miss Stafford paled under the scathing glare but still said nothing.

Simpkin's eyes narrowed. "Rumors?"

"'Tis nothing." Barton's mother fluttered her hand as if she could wave the tension away. "I believe you know my son-in-law, Marcus Haskins?"

At the mention of Marcus, Simpkin resumed his smile. "Yes, yes. Met him last week in London. Friendly chap. He's got a keen eye for blackjack." Simpkin winked then sat back and sobered. "Although, I didn't realize the relation, until now."

"Did you not?" Barton's mother asked. "I assumed that was how you came to know where to find Miss Stafford."

"No, no. That bit of information came from an acquaintance I'm sure we're both familiar with." Simpkin turned his chin and leaned towards Barton's mother as if they were coconspirators. Noticing the blank expression he received, his eyes widened. "No! You really are unaware? I thought perhaps he would arrive before me."

Barton's mother rolled her eyes, and Barton could sense her patience was wearing thin. "Do tell us, Mr. Simpkin, to whom do you refer?" she asked.

"Why, your son, of course. Mr. Franklin Everly." A smirk spread across Mr. Simpkin's lips.

Barton's jaw tensed. "Franklin?"

"Indeed. A mutual acquaintance made the connection." Simpkin chuckled and ignored the shock on Miss Stafford's face. "Mr. Franklin and I were both asking about the same thing." He turned towards Miss Stafford. "You, my dear." He laughed and patted her hand. "Quite a lucky break, don't you think?" Simpkin looked Barton over. "Your brother looks a lot like you, Everly. A smidge shorter, of course. And his temperament is decidedly good-natured." Barton ignored the insinuation and instead turned to evaluate Miss Stafford.

Miss Stafford donned a blank mask, but her pallor marked her distress. Barton suppressed a growl, determined to clarify Simpkin's story. "I was under the impression Franklin's trip to London was due to some business on your behalf, Mother."

Barton's mother glanced briefly down at her lap. "Business was the purpose of his trip . . . initially."

Barton's stomach plunged. "What are you implying?"

His mother lifted her chin a notch. "You know I've your best interest at heart, Harrison." Barton clenched his jaw, but with a light laugh and wave of her hand, his mother swept away his unspoken chastisement. "It hardly matters now. Mr. Simpkin has come. Let's hear what he has to say."

"Thank you once again, madam." Simpkin's smile widened, and he inclined his head. "I'm grateful for your care of Miss Stafford. You can imagine my worry, and that of her uncle, when shortly after accepting my suit, she went missing." He turned his attention to Miss Stafford. "What happened, my dear?"

"There was an accident," Barton interjected.

Simpkin's bushy eyebrows jumped nearly to his hairline. "Really?"

Miss Stafford remained silent, so Barton continued. "A terrible series of storms passed through. I found Miss Stafford pinned beneath an uprooted tree."

"Unfortunate indeed!" Simpkin echoed. Barton found the man's dramatics rather impressive. "Were you severely injured, my dear?" Simpkin asked.

Miss Stafford pressed a hand to her midsection and answered slowly. "Some bruises, scratches, and several cracked ribs."

Simpkin reached for Miss Stafford's free hand. "My darling." Miss Stafford flinched at the endearment and abruptly pulled her fingers free.

Simpkin's words stalled for only a moment, his gaze trained solely on his fiancée. "Why did you not send word? Your uncle or I would have come at once, had we known."

Which Barton knew was the precise reason they were not sent for. "She has been well cared for. My physician has been tending her injuries and has not yet cleared Miss Stafford for travel." Barton hoped to buy some time, thus the stretching of facts came easily.

Simpkin's brown eyes darkened. "But to not notify the family? It's most unusual and raises . . . questions." Simpkin's attention moved to Barton. "When Miss Stafford agreed to be my wife, I agreed to be her protector."

Barton leaned back in his seat with the hope of dismissing Simpkin in a somewhat civilized manner. "And therein lies the quandary. Did Miss Stafford agree to become Mrs. Simpkin?"

A chortle jumped from Simpkin's mouth. "So, that is your game, is it?" He reached inside his jacket and removed a folded piece of paper and held the document up for display. "I've the marriage contract here."

Barton reached an open palm across the space. Without hesitation Simpkin handed it over. Barton's heart constricted further with each line he read.

"Mr. Everly?" Miss Stafford's plea floated to his ears.

Barton finished reading but continued to stare at the document while he gathered his thoughts. From the corner of his eye, he could see Simpkin's grin. "There is no jointure or dowry. But otherwise the contract appears legitimate," Barton said. He inhaled deeply, skimmed the document one more time, and then slowly lowered the paper. Miss Stafford sat still, her eyes empty of emotion.

Simpkin retook the contract. "Her dowry is but a trifle. Perhaps you noted that Stafford and I have negotiated an exchange of land rather than funds. And, as we've both signed the document, everything is proper. I have money enough for the both of us, so Miss Stafford need not worry. She will live comfortably for the rest of her life." Simpkin tucked the document back into his jacket pocket. "Now that we've verified the situation, may I please have a private word with my intended?"

Before Barton had a chance to dispute, Miss Stafford dipped her head, agreeing to Simpkin's request.

Barton rose. "Mother." Barton's mother eyed Mr. Simpkin and Miss Stafford and gave her son a weak smile before he followed her from the room.

His mother ignored the frustration pulsing from Barton and placed a hand on his sleeve. "I was only trying to help."

Barton pulled his arm free. "You've overstepped your boundaries, Mother. Perhaps I'll forgive you in time, but for now, I have more pressing concerns." Without waiting for a reply, Barton walked away.

Chapter 29

LIZZY PRESSED HER FINGERS AGAINST her tender ribs. She longed to feel the physical pain, the sharp opposition of broken bones to a healthy body. Anything was better than the torment washing through her soul. She'd failed. Mr. Simpkin had come. Now she was destined to marry the man.

Yet, there had been no mention of Thomas. Perhaps Lizzy could still ensure his future away from her uncle and the high seas.

"Miss Stafford," Mr. Simpkin began. "Your uncle and I have been quite worried."

"I did not mean to cause concern."

"Yet, you did." Mr. Simpkin stood and moved in front Lizzy. He clasped his hands behind his back and looked over his portly stomach, searing her with a look of chastisement. "Are you going to tell me where you've been these past four weeks?"

Mr. Simpkin's girth and his beady eyes did not intimidate Lizzy; it was his relationship with Uncle Cline that she feared most. "It hardly matters." Lizzy felt the unfortunate truth of her words.

Mr. Simpkin growled. "As your intended I have a right to know where you have been. To make sure your virtue remains intact."

"I assume responsibility for myself, sir. We are not married yet." Lizzy bit back the remainder of the tirade building in her chest.

"Ha! I've your uncle's blessing. You know 'tis only a matter of time until you are my bride. My wife will honor her husband." Mr. Simpkin grinned and looked Lizzy over. She shuddered at his intimate perusal. With a tilt of his head, Mr. Simpkin began anew. "Now, I'll ask again. Where have you been?"

Time was limited. Lizzy had to find a way to save Thomas. She had to ensure he would be safe, no matter the cost. She donned her theatrical cap on behalf of Thomas's future. "As Mr. Everly explained, I was hit by a tree."

"Do you care to elaborate?"

"A tree fell on me, Mr. Simpkin; it is quite simple. There were multiple witnesses, if you should not believe me." Lizzy primly folded her hands in her lap.

Mr. Simpkin's face flushed to an unbecoming shade of red. "Very well. You will learn your place, in time." He marched to the fireplace, took a deep breath, and when he turned around, a feral grin spread across his lips. "Your uncle has given me charge to escort you and young master Stafford to Downey Place. While in London I procured a special license. We will depart at once and marry immediately upon our return to Leicestershire."

Lizzy's breath rattled in her chest. "But I am still in mourning, and . . . and . . ."

"And there is nothing more to discuss." Mr. Simpkin spat as he pulled the marriage contract from his jacket pocket. With a shaky fist he thrust it towards Lizzy. "'Tis all agreed. You are to be my wife! Your uncle has made the arrangements. Your mourning is but a trifle."

"A trifle?" Lizzy jumped to her feet, allowing her anger to build with the pain that shot through her. "Sir, you trivialize my pain! You have no right to make such demands."

Mr. Simpkin smirked. "I have every right. As this document verifies." He held up the paper once again. "However, two points may be negotiable." He stepped closer to Lizzy, and a shiver of foreboding ran the length of her spine. "The brat need not come with us; I'm only to bring him if you refuse to return the jewels to your uncle."

"They belong to me." Lizzy's heart raced.

"Not my rules, dear." Mr. Simpkin waved the contract once more in front of her face before stuffing it back into his pocket. Then his eyes raked over her figure again, and a wave of nausea washed over Lizzy. "The second issue is when exactly I claim you as mine."

"You are no gentleman," Lizzy said on a shaky breath.

Simpkin winked. "I'm simply delivering a message." He rocked back on his heels like a giddy schoolboy.

Lizzy's knees knocked together. She lowered herself back onto the sofa, clutching the armrest in a vain attempt to ground herself. The decision, it seemed, had been made for her. There was but one choice—Thomas. His freedom would be easily purchased with the sapphires, but where would he go? What would become of him? Would the sparse funds Lizzy had remaining be enough to guarantee his future? Perhaps Barton would accept him as her ward. Surely he would do this for Thomas, for her. And if not, Mrs. Haskins. Her fondness for Thomas mirrored that of a mother.

Mr. Simpkin snapped his pocket watch closed. "Come, Miss Stafford, we must be on our way."

"One day." Lizzy dropped the theatrics and looked up at him with raw pleading. "Please, sir. Give me one day to make arrangements for my brother. Then, tomorrow, I will come with you."

"Ha!" Simpkin threw his head back. "You mistake me for a fool. Your uncle fell for your tricks, but I will not be so easily thwarted. I have searched long and hard to discover your whereabouts, and I refuse to leave and allow you to run away again."

Lizzy pushed to her feet and begged. "Please, sir. I give you my word, I will not run."

Mr. Simpkin rubbed his jaw in consideration. Lizzy stepped forward and placed a hand on his sleeve. "I will give you the jewels now, and you can lodge at the Hilly Crest Inn. I will settle Thomas and say my goodbyes to him. Then you may return tomorrow, and we can be on our way." Lizzy swallowed the bile rising in her throat. "Allow this to be . . . your wedding gift . . . to me."

His eyes narrowed, and a savage grin spilled across his face. Mr. Simpkin covered Lizzy's hand with his own. "Very well. We wouldn't get far before nightfall. But I *will* return at sunrise. Prepare yourself, Miss Stafford, and know that if you cross me again, you will consider your uncle's threats a tender mercy compared to my temper."

Chapter 30

BARTON SEETHED AS MISS STAFFORD handed over the velvet-wrapped gemstones. Her face remained solid and stonelike, but he sensed her breaking heart. He could feel it within his own chest.

When he'd left his mother, Barton had paced in the hall, unable to decipher the muted words Simpkin and Miss Stafford exchanged. And while Barton did not know the details of the arrangement, he knew parting with the family heirloom was only a portion of it.

Simpkin unequivocally proclaimed that he would return in the morning with a hired carriage to transport Miss Stafford to Downey Place. Barton unequivocally disagreed, but he held his tongue and quelled his numerous questions until Simpkin had ridden out of sight.

Miss Stafford stood beside him, projecting a brave countenance, but Barton recognized the façade. Miss Stafford's eyes were dull, and the color was gone from her cheeks. Her shoulders, though straight, were tense and taut. He wanted to pull her close, to rub circles on her back and erase the events of the last hour.

Miss Stafford stared down the lane. Her lips pressed close together, her hands fisted at her side. Tension crackled in the air—tension, dread, and determination. "He will return. In the morning," Miss Stafford said. "Uncle is controlling him, using him as he does everyone else to get his way."

"What does he want?" Barton asked.

"Uncle wants the jewels. Mr. Simpkin wants a bride." Miss Stafford turned her eyes to Barton.

"They cannot force you in this." Barton found it difficult to temper his voice. He wanted to shout, to insist Lizzy fight harder.

"I'm afraid they can." Her eyes fell to the ground. Defeat marred her features.

"No." Barton's jaw tensed. "If you are not in agreement, there are options."

"Perhaps." Miss Stafford offered a broken sigh. "But they've found a way to ensure my agreement. I've vowed to protect Thomas. I plan to keep that vow." She turned towards Barton. "Please excuse me. I must make my preparations."

Barton watched Miss Stafford ascend the stairs and then went in search of his mother. He found her staring out the window in her private sitting room. "Why did you do it?" Barton asked.

"Harrison." Barton's mother acknowledged his presence in word only. She did not relinquish her position at the window. Her shoulders lifted and fell with a slow breath. "I see Mr. Simpkin has left."

Barton's stomach churned with impatience. "Why, Mother? Why did you send Franklin to London?"

His mother turned then and lifted her chin. "Because I care for you, Harrison, and I could not stand to see you hurt again." She bustled over to a table set with a pitcher and crystal glasses. She poured herself a glass of water and took a deliberately long drink before clinking the crystal back down on the tray.

"'Tis not Miss Stafford who has violated my trust, Mother."

She bristled. "I certainly did not expect for that man to show up on our doorstep."

"Yet he did," Barton replied dryly.

"Mr. Simpkin is Miss Stafford's fiancé. 'Tis little wonder he sought her out. Why would she not send word or tell him of her whereabouts?"

Barton narrowed his eyes. "Because he is a vile man, whom she is being forced to marry against her will."

With a tilt of her head, his mother pouted. "Really, Harrison. Mr. Simpkin may be Miss Stafford's senior by several years, but that hardly makes him vile."

"So you would be content for Bethany to marry him?"

Barton's mother grimaced and waved his question away. "Nonsense. Bethany is already married." She took a seat and returned her gaze to her son.

Barton balked at his mother's flippancy. "To a man of her choosing. Should not Miss Stafford be granted the same opportunity?" Barton ran a hand through his hair and paced behind his mother's chair and back again. He stood before her, intent to make his point. "Mother, Miss Stafford's uncle is forcing the union. I don't know what benefit he derives other than ridding himself of his ward. He does not care for Miss Stafford, nor does he care for Thomas. The boy has now become a pawn. Mr. Simpkin will return in the morning to collect them both. If Miss Stafford refuses, Thomas will be sent to sea."

"His Majesty's Navy is worthy employ." His mother straightened her shoulders.

"Thomas would not receive a commission, Mother. His uncle has indentured him to a merchant vessel." Barton's mother pressed her eyes closed and hung her head. "That is why they were hiding in Doyle's cabin." Anger thrummed through Barton's veins. "Miss Stafford is determined to keep Thomas safe. You claim your love for me motivated your actions. Is it so hard to believe the same sentiment guided Miss Stafford in her journey here? She did not intend to get caught in the rain. Nor did she intend to become injured. But she has every intention of not sending Thomas to sea, even if it means her own happiness is forfeit."

"I'm sorry, Harrison." His mother stood, her hands straight at her side. "Truly I am. I did not send Franklin to recruit her fiancé. I only asked him to inquire about Miss Stafford. I could see you were developing feelings for her, and . . . I knew she was keeping secrets."

"I appreciate your concern, Mother, I do. But please remember whom Miss Newhall jilted. I acutely remember the circumstances, and I am not wont to repeat them. I've learned my lesson and do not share my heart carelessly. You must trust me to decipher which emotions are real and which are not. It is, after all, my heart at risk."

A tear trailed down his mother's face. "It is a mother's right to look out for her son."

Barton stepped forward and clasped his mother's hands. "I know." He guided her back to her seat. "But, despite your intentions, Miss Stafford and Thomas need our help. Please, tell me what you know of Franklin's journey."

After wiping her eyes Barton's mother shook her head. "Not much, I'm afraid. I certainly did not know he crossed paths with Mr. Simpkin."

"But you did send him to inquire after Miss Stafford?"

After a quick glance at Barton, she nodded affirmation.

"What did you wish to discover?"

"I only wanted to know a bit about her. Who are her parents? With whom does she associate? What is her reputation?"

Barton ran a hand through his hair. "Could you not simply have asked Miss Stafford herself? Why involve Franklin?"

"I only asked Franklin to meet with Mr. Mullins and ask a few questions." She reached forward and grabbed Barton's arm. "When I attempted to ask Miss Stafford, she artfully avoided any personal questions I posed." Barton's mother squeezed his arm then let go. "Is it any wonder I became suspicious?"

Barton sighed. "I admit I, too, became curious. But now Simpkin is here, and I haven't a clue what to do about it."

"Perhaps Miss Stafford may open up to you more now."

"Only hours ago I might have believed you. She was beginning to trust me." Barton shook his head. "But once Miss Stafford learned of Franklin's involvement, she retreated once again. Now she trusts no one."

His mother straightened in her seat. "Harrison, you are a fine man. Explain to Miss Stafford my part in this. I will do it myself, if you would like. But seeing as time is limited, I suggest you go to her directly and make her talk to you. Make her see she can trust you. You will find a solution. I know you will."

"I hope you are right." Barton stepped forward and kissed his mother's cheek. Then he marched directly to Miss Stafford's bedchamber.

Chapter 31

A BRISK KNOCK SOUNDED AT the door only moments before Barton walked into the room. Lizzy jumped at the intrusion and stashed the letter she'd been writing beneath another piece of paper. "Mr. Everly!" She stood quickly, her cheeks reddening as she turned to meet him.

"Miss Stafford, if I may have a moment of your time?" Barton asked. "I hoped to discuss the particulars of your arrangement with Simpkin." In lieu of a response, Lizzy stared at him. She pinched her lips closed and tears burned, threatening to fall. Barton opened his arms and took a tentative step towards her. "Miss Stafford. Elizabeth. Please. Let me help."

Sorrow engulfed Lizzy. She longed to run into Barton's embrace and allow him to whisper words of comfort. But even in the sanctuary of Everly Manor, he could not protect her. Mr. Simpkin had the marriage contract. Uncle had made his decision, and Lizzy knew he would not be swayed.

She drew a long, slow breath and willed the tears away. "I appreciate the offer Mr. Everly—"

"Barton," he interrupted.

Using his Christian name only further hollowed her heart, but knowing she could not give him everything he asked for, Lizzy wanted to please him in any way she could. "Barton," she began. "I cannot stay."

Barton took another step towards her.

"Stop!" she cried out. "Please." Lizzy held up one hand, and Barton did as she asked, halting his advance. Her voice trembled along with her fingers. "I have to go with him. It's the only way."

Barton planted his hands on his hips and evaluated Lizzy. "Is that really what you want?"

The pleading in his eyes pierced her defenses, and a single tear fell.

Barton tightened his jaw and inhaled deeply. "I don't trust him."

"I have to go. For Thomas." Lizzy could no longer meet his gaze. His eyes held too much hope. Too much hurt.

The moment she looked away Barton closed the distance between them. Her eyes flashed back to his, and he placed his hand on her cheek. "We could leave together. The three of us. We could go now, this very instant. Head to the coast and catch a boat to France. Or we could travel north. Somewhere far away from your uncle and Simpkin."

Lizzy closed her eyes and leaned into his touch. She allowed herself to envision a future with Barton. Her feelings for him were beyond friendship and admiration. He'd stolen a piece of her heart. Then Thomas's face flashed into her mind, followed by Uncle's smug grin marring the beautiful scene and leaving only feelings of despair. Running away would put them all at risk. She could not condemn Barton to a life in hiding. His family loved him, needed him. Lizzy could not ask him to make that sacrifice.

Marrying Simpkin was the only way to guarantee Thomas's safety. Lizzy could not chance Thomas's future. She refused to swap his happiness for her own. Despite her desire to run away with Barton, she simply could not.

She slowly shook her head. "Your place is here." She wrapped her hand around Barton's fingers and slowly lowered them from her face. "I gave my word, and I intend to keep it."

Barton reared back, as though she'd slapped him. "Am I not enough? You'd choose Simpkin over me?"

"That's not fair," she whispered. Pain radiated through Lizzy's chest, and it had nothing to do with her broken ribs. Her heart ached as though it were truly splintering apart.

"Isn't it though? I stand here offering to give up everything for you. To leave this very moment."

"Which is exactly why I can't let you!" Lizzy cried out, desperately wishing he would understand. She backed up one step and then another.

Barton shook his head. "This isn't over, Elizabeth. I will find a way to save you from him." And with that Barton stormed from the room.

Lizzy wept. Could Barton not see how he affected her? His plea for her to stay nearly broke her in two. His devotion, his determination, his protection, meant everything to her. His mother had spoken true. Barton was the best of men, and during Lizzy's convalescence at Everly Manor, he had stolen Lizzy's heart.

She completed the letter she'd been writing when Barton entered her room and ignored the teardrops splotching the page. Her headache grew while she tossed her meager belongings into her tattered bag. Then she sobbed some more while counting out her remaining funds and folding them into a square of paper that she stashed in her pocket to give to Thomas. Only then did she use the sleeve of her grey gown to wipe away the moisture from her eyes. And only because she needed to see her brother and she didn't want to have to explain her tears.

Lizzy dipped a cloth into the washbasin in her room and pressed the cool fabric against her eyelids. The water offered only a slight reprieve. Lizzy would have to offer some pitiful excuse for her red-rimmed eyes; something about needing to rest or her impending migraine. She could claim her injury still pained her. Although, in truth, the pain in her ribs had improved greatly. Her discomfort radiated solely from her heart.

In order to avoid Barton, Lizzy used the servants' staircase to access the nursery, where she found Thomas happily constructing a tower of blocks. She quietly observed him, noting how he narrowed his eyes until he'd placed the block in perfect position. Then his small fingers would slowly release their hold, and he would nod, as if telling the new addition to his tower that it was acceptable. Lizzy longed to hold on to the memory, for it was happy and complete—Thomas enjoying the freedom of youth in a home where he was adored. It was everything Lizzy wished for him. Everything she could give him if she kept her word to Mr. Simpkin.

Thomas ignored her while he maneuvered a triangular piece on top of his creation. When the placement was complete, he slowly crawled backwards, careful not to topple his tower.

"Very impressive." Lizzy walked to her brother.

"It's my biggest one yet," Thomas bragged. "I would make it even taller if there were more blocks."

Lizzy reached down and mussed his hair.

"Mr. Barton said he would have one of the stable hands cut some more wood for me, so tomorrow I will build an even bigger one."

"That's very kind of Mr. Barton." Lizzy's voice caught, and Thomas looked up at his sister.

"Why are you sad, Lizzy?" Thomas stood up with a frown and grabbed Lizzy's hand. His eyes scrunched together. "Did you mean what you said in the garden? That we could not stay?"

She grasped his fingers and swung his arm back and forth, blinking desperately to keep her tears away. Lizzy avoided Thomas's questions and asked one of her own. "Are you happy here?"

A smile spread across Thomas's face, and he nodded vigorously. "Mr. Barton said you were wrong. He said we could stay at Everly Manor. Can we, Lizzy? Can we?"

"You like Mr. Barton and Mrs. Haskins?" she asked.

"And Mr. Franklin too." Thomas looked up at his sister, and his eyes grew wide. "Don't be mad, Lizzy, but I enjoy his lessons more than yours. He tells me the funniest stories when we are practicing our equations."

"Really? I didn't realize mathematics were amusing." A smile touched Lizzy's lips. She appreciated Mr. Franklin's efforts to make learning enjoyable for Thomas.

"Oh, it is. Last time Mr. Franklin told me all about the elephants that needed to get to the festival, but there was only a small boat to transport them. We figured out how to fit them all in and make sure their heads didn't hit the ceiling."

"That does sound diverting."

"It was." Thomas tugged on Lizzy's hand and pulled her down to sit on the floor with him. "And Mr. Franklin said next time we would have to figure out if they'd all fit in the queen's sitting room, but Mr. Franklin had to leave for a few days, so I don't know when we will do that problem."

Lizzy's heart clenched at the reminder of Mr. Franklin's absence and his contribution to her current situation. Perhaps if she'd left the jewels behind, Uncle would have left her and Thomas alone. Maybe taking them had been selfish, but she so desperately wanted the one thing she had left of her mother. Now she would lose both the sapphires and Thomas. At least she'd saved him from a life at sea.

Lizzy withdrew the folded paper square from her pocket. "Do you remember our grand adventure?" she asked.

"Yes." Thomas's eyes lit.

"I want to give you something very important." Lizzy placed the paper into Thomas's small hands. "You must keep this secret, like a hidden treasure."

With careful precision Thomas unwrapped the coins. He picked up a few and enjoyed the clinking sound of them falling back into his paper. "Why are you giving me the treasure?" Thomas asked.

"You have proven you are a very brave adventurer. I want you to watch over the treasure for a while."

Thomas shook his head and tried to hand the coins back to his sister. "No, Lizzy. You keep them."

Lizzy placed her hand over Thomas's and pressed his fingers to secure the coins between his palms. She kept hold of his hands and pulled his attention to her. "Thomas, I trust you with this. You must find a hiding place for the treasure. Perhaps under your pillow or behind your favorite book."

"But why, Lizzy?"

"Because you are now keeper of the treasure. You must keep it hidden and safe until the time is right."

"What if I forget? What if I don't know when the time is right?" Thomas grasped the money in his hand, and his face scrunched in consternation. "You'll tell me, won't you, Lizzy? When to use the treasure?"

Emotion flooded Lizzy, and she waited for a moment before she responded. "Don't worry, sweet boy. You'll know." She choked on the last word but covered her mouth, hoping Thomas wouldn't notice.

"I know where to put it!" He jumped up from the floor and ran into his room, returning a moment later with empty hands. He leaned over and whispered near Lizzy's ear, "Do you want to know where I hid the treasure?"

Lizzy's arms wrapped around his thin frame, and she pulled him close. Thomas laughed as he fell into her lap. Oh, how Lizzy needed the sound of his laughter. It radiated innocence and trust, and Lizzy wished she could bottle up the emotion it held and carry it with her back to Leicestershire. Her heart ached, and she held on to Thomas long after his giggling stopped. She lifted her shoulder to wipe the tears falling down her face, determined that Thomas not know of her sorrow. There was to be no guilt attached to her gift. She wanted to give her brother a life of happiness, comfort, and love.

The siblings enjoyed dinner together in the nursery. Thomas told Lizzy all the tricks he planned to teach Brownbeard, and she acted appropriately impressed. Lizzy dressed Thomas as a pirate, wrapping a cloth napkin around his head and using one of Thomas's stockings to secure a toy sword to his side. She played the part of damsel in distress, begging Thomas not to make her walk the plank. In the end, his soft heart prevailed, and he allowed Lizzy to live on a deserted island with plentiful fish so she wouldn't be hungry.

Then Lizzy read Thomas his favorite story and lay by his side long after he'd drifted off to sleep. She stared at his angelic face, taking solace in the fact that he would sleep contentedly here for many nights to come. At least, she hoped he would. Barton would make the final decision, but she'd come to know the innate goodness he embodied. She only hoped his frustration with her would not transfer to her brother and that somehow, someway, Thomas might call Everly Manor home for a long time to come.

Chapter 32

BARTON MARCHED OUT OF MISS Stafford's room wanting to throttle someone. Anyone. But particularly Simpkin. What had Simpkin done to ensure her compliance? Barton knew the answer. He knew that through Simpkin, Mr. Stafford had threatened Thomas for leverage. He also knew Miss Stafford would defend Thomas until her dying breath. But why did Cline Stafford insist on his niece's return to Leicestershire? Why couldn't he let Elizabeth be?

"Henderson!" Barton shouted as he hurried down the grand staircase to the ground floor. Henderson rushed into the hall, and Barton jerked his head, indicating the butler should follow him. "Locate the two fastest riders among my staff and have them mount at once." He walked into his study. "I will have two letters ready momentarily, and they must be delivered forthwith."

"Very well, sir." Henderson bowed and left to do as requested.

Barton addressed the first letter to his solicitor in London, Mr. Mullins. He asked Mr. Mullins to investigate Mr. Rudyard Simpkin and Cline Stafford. Then he asked for specific directions on how to nullify the marriage contract between Miss Stafford and Simpkin, explaining that all parties had not agreed upon the stipulations of the contract.

The second letter was for Franklin. The rider carrying this missive would have a more difficult time, as Franklin's precise location was unknown. Barton wished his brother were at Everly Manor so he could ask him about his interaction with Simpkin. Recalling Simpkin's perusal of Miss Stafford's figure, Barton clenched his fists and acknowledged the wisdom in Franklin staying away. The brothers shared a close rapport, but knowing Franklin had disclosed Miss Stafford's whereabouts made Barton want to pummel him senseless. He quickly sealed the letters and bellowed for Henderson once more.

The riders departed, and Barton dragged a hand through his hair. His heart beat rapidly, like pounding horse hooves. The day was slipping away, and morning would arrive too soon. If he could not change Miss Stafford's mind, convince her to leave, what more could he do?

Simpkin.

The thought came to him like a fist to his gut. Barton loathed the man, but perhaps Simpkin could be persuaded to break the contract. Calling again for his faithful butler, Barton ordered Starfly to be saddled.

While Starfly's speed was exhilarating, the ride to Hillcrest was not long enough for Barton to cool his temper. He dismounted and handed Starfly to the familiar stableboy. Barton paused at the door to the inn, inhaling deeply in an effort to coherently form the argument he would present to Simpkin, and then he pulled the door wide and stepped inside.

It didn't take long for him to find the obtuse man. The thick grey hair on Simpkin's head resembled a grey squirrel nesting atop his scalp. Barton stood unnoticed near the entrance and decided he needed a few more minutes before raging his battle.

Simpkin's beefy fingers wrapped around a mug of ale, and he took a long deliberate drink. The man slammed the glass down then signaled for the servant girl to bring him another. Barton's stomach clenched as he watched the lusty look in Simpkin's eyes as he appraised the girl's figure. If Barton were a violent man, the solution would be much simpler.

The servant girl set a full mug in front of Simpkin and quickly scurried away. Simpkin chuckled to himself and then reached inside his coat pocket. Barton only caught a flash of the blue gemstones, but he knew they were Miss Stafford's sapphires.

Anger and a determination to keep Miss Stafford safe propelled Barton forward. Without asking permission, he sat across from Simpkin. The lofty man looked him over with a smug grin.

"Everly. Come to drink away your frustrations?" Simpkin asked.

Barton clenched his teeth and said nothing.

Simpkin raised a single bushy-grey eyebrow. "Perhaps celebrating, then? Eager to be done with the chit?"

Barton clung to every bit of self-control he possessed. He clasped his hands and set his elbows on the table. "Actually, I've come to negotiate."

"Ha!" Simpkin's boisterous laugh echoed through the room, and fire seared through Barton's veins. "You assume I'm open for negotiation?"

"With the right motivation, everything's negotiable."

Simpkin smirked. "Not in this case."

The innkeeper walked over to Barton. "Can I get ya anything, Mr. Everly?"

Barton did not take his eyes off Simpkin. "No, thank you." The innkeeper evaluated both men then walked away.

"What do you get out of this?" Barton asked.

"I should think that's rather obvious. I get what you want—Miss Stafford. That is why you're here, is it not?" Simpkin lifted his chubby finger and casually wiped a drop of condensation from his glass.

Barton tensed with restraint. "What about the sapphires?"

Simpkin took a swig of his drink then leaned back in his chair. "They don't belong to me."

"That's one thing we can agree on."

Simpkin chuckled. "The sapphires will be returned to Stafford, but I don't really think you're here to reclaim the gems. What is it you want, Everly?"

"Void your marriage contract. Leave Hillcrest and Miss Stafford, and never return."

Simpkin pushed out a breath. "I can't do that."

Barton leaned closer. "Why not?"

Simpkin answered with a tilt of his head. "Because I'm in need of a wife and an heir. Miss Stafford's father refused to entertain my suit. Fortunately her uncle can see the wisdom of our alignment, and we have come to an agreement."

"You must know he is forcing her hand. All Stafford wants is to be rid of his ward, I am willing to support her living. Surely you can find another bride."

A nefarious grin spread across Simpkin's face. "I've paid my dues. She'll be coming with me."

"What do you mean?"

"What I mean, Mr. Everly, is that you cannot take what I've previously paid for." Simpkin ran a finger over a large ring on his opposite hand. "I've shown you the contract. Miss Stafford belongs to me now."

"She belongs to no one," Barton growled.

Simpkin sighed dramatically and spread his arms wide. "And only a moment ago we were in agreement."

Barton's jaw ached. He could not allow Miss Stafford's marriage to proceed. But what recourse did he have? "You are vile," Barton said.

Simpkin sobered and leaned across the space between them. "No, I'm a businessman."

Without hesitation Barton took the opportunity presented. "I'll pay you double."

Simpkin pulled back and laughed long and hard. "She's worked her charms on you, I see. Unfortunately you've come to negotiate too late."

Barton's muscles tensed. "You fool. I'm not paying for her. I'm paying for her freedom. Name your price, Simpkin."

"Tempting, I admit, but I've never been seduced by lucre. No, that's Stafford's vice. I have plentiful funds. My weakness lies with an enticing woman who currently resides at your estate." Simpkin's eyes turned black. "I've admired her for a long time, and I will not give her up now or ever. Her uncle and I have reached an agreement, and I always keep my word. Miss Stafford will be my bride." A long moment passed, and then the hard lines in Simpkin's face softened. He leaned back in his chair. "I've heard good things about you, Everly. Honorable. Esteemed. You wouldn't want your reputation marred. Nor would we want any harm to come to the boy."

Barton seethed.

"Good." Simpkin pulled some coins from his pocket and clapped them down on the table. "Then, we are in agreement. You'll stay out of my way when I arrive to collect Miss Stafford. And then you will forget about her and return to your valiant, charitable life."

Barton stood. "This isn't over, Simpkin."

Simpkin rose and matched Barton's stance. In a blink Simpkin's face hardened once again. "Actually, Everly . . . it is."

Starfly seemed to understand Barton's urgency. Barton had to get Miss Stafford and Thomas away from Everly Manor. Away from Simpkin. Far away.

If he'd ever questioned Miss Stafford's reasons for running, he understood now. Aside from her fears for Thomas, her life was in danger. Simpkin may not physically strike her as her uncle had, but he would leave scars much deeper, the kind that would not heal with balms or the passage of time.

Forget Elizabeth's deuced promise to Simpkin. Barton would take her away tonight. Even if he had to haul her over his shoulder and strap her into the carriage, he refused to watch her leave with that man.

The moment Starfly reached the steps, a boy ran out from the stables to care for the horse. Barton dismounted and did not look back as he rushed into the house. Henderson stood in the entryway and silently watched him, but Barton did not pause. He ascended the stairs two at a time and moved quickly past the first floor and up to the second, where he turned down the hallway to Miss Stafford's room. He could not reach her quickly enough. Barton's breaths came fast, his chest heaving as he knocked then threw the door open.

"We are leaving at once." Barton barged in and headed for the fire. "I cannot stand by and allow you to marry that abhorrent man." Barton picked up the candle sitting on the mantel and lit the wick from the dying coals. He stirred the embers to life and turned around to face the bed.

"Miss Stafford, please," Barton begged. "We must get as far away as possible. I give you my word that I am not freeing you from this forced marriage only to bind you to another. I will behave as a perfect gentleman and guarantee you and Thomas every happiness and freedom."

The mound of blankets lay still, and dread sank like a stone in Barton's gut.

"Miss Stafford?" In four long strides Barton stood beside the bed. He touched the coverlet and watched it wilt beneath his fingers. He cursed and bellowed for Henderson.

Barton's butler stepped through the doorway, followed shortly thereafter by his mother. "Whatever is the matter?" his mother asked as she tied the sash on her dressing robe.

"She's gone." Barton's heart ached with the words. "Miss Stafford is gone."

Chapter 33

LIZZY HOPED MR. SIMPKIN FOUND the note she had enclosed with the sapphires. When Barton had held her close and asked her to run away with him, it had almost been her undoing. But Barton did not understand men like Mr. Simpkin and her uncle. Men who stopped at nothing to get what they wanted. Barton grew under the influence of his father, an ideal role model, similar to that of her own father. If only Lizzy's father remained alive. Lizzy's view of the world had changed the moment Uncle Cline claimed his inheritance at Downey Place. Uncle and Mr. Simpkin thrived on her hopelessness, brewing it to their advantage to force their will upon her. Lizzy had to accede, for Thomas.

She hurried along the gravel path, running until her ribs ached and forced her feet to slow. Clouds scurried over the moon, muting its hollow light. A rider had passed only minutes before. When Lizzy heard the pounding horse hooves, she had pulled her cloak around her and ducked behind a thick tree trunk. She held her breath and did not get a glimpse of the rider before hurrying on her way. She'd brought nothing with her beyond the clothing on her person. Lizzy had been wearing borrowed clothing from Mrs. Haskins and had very little to call her own. It seemed simpler to leave it all behind, especially since Mr. Simpkin had promised wealth, clothing, comfort. Lizzy cringed at the other promises he'd made.

She passed the large willow tree that marked the turnoff to the tenant cottages and ran to the intersection of the main road. She turned right and walked about fifty yards before ducking back into the trees to wait.

The next minutes passed slowly. The quiet blackness of the night closed in around Lizzy, pressing her fears and her bleak future upon her. The whinny of a horse made her jump. Lizzy's heart ricocheted in her chest, and she clamped her hands over her mouth to keep herself from screaming in fright. She looked out to the road and recognized Mr. Simpkin. He sat on his horse and held the reins of a dark mare. Lizzy stepped out from her hiding place.

"There you are." Mr. Simpkin cocked his head. "I wasn't sure you'd show."

Lizzy squared her shoulders and walked to the riderless horse. Without a word Mr. Simpkin dismounted and offered his knee. Lizzy stepped up and settled into the saddle. "I gave you my word." Lizzy anchored her boots in the stirrups.

"Your besotted knight did not seem to think much of your word." Simpkin mounted his own horse beside her.

Lizzy hated herself for not being able to ignore his bait. "What do you mean?"

"Truly, you don't know?" Mr. Simpkin laughed loudly. "Everly foolishly thought he could stop our marriage. Came to see me, hoping I would cry off."

Lizzy's breath stuck. Barton had tried to help her once again. Even after she'd treated him so terribly. She clenched the reins in her hands, unable to speak for the sorrow engulfing her heart. A brisk breeze rustled the branches overhead.

Mr. Simpkin turned his horse to face her. "I hope you didn't waste all of your wiles on him, because I am quite looking forward to our union."

Bile churned through Lizzy's stomach. She could not think about tomorrow or the next day. She could think only of Thomas. This moment was the one that would set him free. "I'm ready, Mr. Simpkin. Let us depart."

"Anxious to be away, are you?" Simpkin chuckled. "Lead the way, my dear."

Lizzy kicked hard at the horse's side, and the animal responded. Shadows danced across the dirt road, fluctuating with the peekaboo moon. Lizzy flew down the road, her skirts billowing around her. The cold night air swept past, pulling the tears from her cheeks. Lizzy's pace in the darkness was dangerous, reckless. The moment she'd left Everly Manor, her life was forfeit; at least on horseback she felt a pull of excitement, a bit of daring. And if her head ended up smashed to pieces, it hardly mattered anymore. So Lizzy pushed harder, determined to outrun the sun, hopeful that tomorrow might never arrive.

Chapter 34

HENDERSON QUICKLY LIT SEVERAL MORE candles in Miss Stafford's room. Barton's mother pointed to the letter on the writing desk. "Go on. It's addressed to you."

Barton crossed the room, wishing he were walking towards Elizabeth rather than the improbable consolation of a letter. He slipped his finger beneath the seal, and his chest ached while he unfolded the page.

> *Mr. Everly,*
> *Your generosity to Thomas and me has been a godsend. And while I still remain in your debt, I must ask one thing further. Uncle does not care for Thomas. Upon our return my brother would be sent away. Knowing your gracious heart, I beg for your forgiveness and charity once more. Will you please accept Thomas as your ward? I will send payment for his expenses as I am able. I promise to infringe upon you no further. Please let me go and share your heart with my brother—'tis the only way to ensure his safety.*
> *Sincerely,*
> *Miss Elizabeth Stafford*

Barton lowered the paper to the desk and buried his head in his hands. His mother walked near and touched his shoulder. "Harrison?"

He scrubbed a hand over his face. "It's done. She's gone." Barton straightened his shoulders and tried to ignore the thrumming of his heart.

"Oh dear." Barton's mother pressed her fingers to her chest. "Poor, poor, Miss Stafford."

Barton's restraint snapped. "What did you think would happen, Mother? You wished for her to be gone. Now she is."

Tears pooled in his mother's eyes. "This is not what I wanted. Not like this. What will become of her? And little Thomas?" Her tears spilled over, and she grabbed her son's arm. "Harrison, we must help them."

"She's asked that Thomas remain here." Barton thrust the letter forward. "Read it yourself."

Barton's mother took the missive and quickly read the words. Her head shook, and more tears fell. Barton sat his mother in the chair near the desk and then looked to his stalwart butler still standing near the door. "Henderson, please locate Drew and have her come sit with Mother." Henderson offered a prompt bow and disappeared.

Barton passed his handkerchief to his mother, and she dried her eyes. "You must go after her, Harrison."

"You read the letter, Mother. She's asked I let her be."

"Nonsense." She grabbed Barton's hands and gripped them tightly. "She's sacrificing herself for her brother. I respect her willingness to play the part of a martyr, but there has to be another way. You are a good man. You have a good heart. Surely you can see that she loves you."

"If she loved me, she would have stayed." Even as the words left Barton's mouth, he questioned their veracity. He had felt something more and believed Miss Stafford had as well.

His mother squeezed his hands again then released them and stood. "Your heart is muddling your brain. Miss Stafford loves you, but she loves her brother too. You would make the same sacrifice for Bethany, Franklin, or for myself if it were required of you."

Barton thought on his mother's words. He would do anything to protect his family. And he was certain Miss Stafford did not care for Simpkin. Her heart did belong to Thomas, but could he hold a place there as well? Did Elizabeth love him? Could it be possible?

"You know it, don't you?" His mother asked. "That feeling burning deep in your chest. The desire to see her smile and hold her close." Her eyes began to tear up again. "I loved your father. You deserve the same. You love her, and the least you can do is find out if she loves you in return. Go after her. Give her the chance to share what truly lies in her heart before she marries that awful man and it is too late."

Drew and Henderson returned to the room. Barton looked from them to his mother.

"Go," she whispered. "Bethany and I will look after the boy."

Barton strode to the door. "Henderson, have Starfly saddled again at once. I will depart immediately."

"Barton!"

At the sound of Franklin's voice, Barton's frustration shifted to anger. His fingers curled into fists as Franklin looked up at him from the entryway.

"Has he come?" Franklin asked, his chest heaving. "Simpkin?"

Barton did not slow his advance, nor did he notice his sister descending the staircase behind him. He stepped off the final step, marched up to his brother, and swung his fist into Franklin's face.

"Barton!" Bethany hurried down the remaining stairs to Franklin's side. "Have you gone mad?"

Franklin raised his hand to his nose and acknowledged the blood on his fingers. "I deserved that." With his clean hand Franklin pulled a handkerchief from his pocket and held it to his nose. "So I take it Simpkin has been here?"

"How did you know that?" Bethany asked.

"Because he's the one who sent him." Barton wanted to punch something else.

"Oh dear." Bethany covered her mouth.

Franklin held up his free hand. "That was not my intention, Barton."

Barton's mother joined the fracas, and Haskins emerged from the library.

Barton worked a muscle in his jaw.

"What happened, Franklin?" the matron asked.

Franklin dabbed at his nose with his handkerchief and took a deep breath. "I went to London to find out more about Miss Stafford. I didn't discover much until Simpkin approached me. Said he'd heard I was looking for information on the girl. He agreed to tell me what he knew if I did the same. I suppose I should have recognized him from Marcus's description, but I didn't realize."

"You didn't ask his name?" Bethany asked.

Franklin sighed. "When you're looking for information in disreputable places, you tend to ask only the most pertinent questions. Beyond that, he claimed to be a relative of her late mother's. Once I realized his true intent, it was too late." He dabbed at his nose.

Henderson approached Barton and cleared his throat. "Your horse is ready, sir."

Barton turned from the group, resolved to leave.

"Barton, wait." Franklin caught his brother's arm. Barton turned on him, ready to strike again. Franklin took a step back and raised both hands. "Just hear me out. Once Simpkin revealed himself, I went to Mullins, hoping we could find a flaw in the marriage contract. Something Simpkin said didn't feel right. It took some digging and quite a few bribes, but the old solicitor, Mr. Palmer, kept a copy of the will." Franklin pulled a roll of paper from his jacket and handed it to Barton. "Mr. Stafford's *unaltered* will."

Barton skimmed the page, his heartbeat echoing through his head. "You mean . . . ?"

Franklin nodded. "It all belongs to her."

Chapter 35

LIZZY'S HEAD BOBBED FORWARD, JOLTING her awake. Her anger and resolve had melted away, leaving a puddle of exhaustion. She didn't know how far they had ridden, but Lizzy knew she could not remain atop her horse much longer.

"May we stop at the next inn, Mr. Simpkin?" Lizzy hated the defeat in her voice. Her ribs ached fiercely, and pain radiated through every breath she took.

Simpkin's smile reminded Lizzy of the devil himself. "Certainly, Miss Stafford. You should get a proper night's sleep, for tomorrow will be our wedding night."

LIZZY's stomach lurched. It took every bit of energy she possessed to pull on her theatrical cloak once more. She hoped he fell for her charade. "Now, Mr. Simpkin, there's no need to rush things. We will be wed soon enough. I would like my uncle to be at the ceremony, and surely you want my injuries to heal." Lizzy knew she could only deflect him for so long, but she hoped to utilize every moment possible.

A chuckle rumbled through Mr. Simpkin's chest. "Your injuries seem quite recovered, and I've waited long enough, my dear." He turned back to the road. "Ah. There appears to be an inn just ahead."

They rode to the Dandy Prince, and Mr. Simpkin hollered for a stableboy. Lizzy slid from her horse and clung to Simpkin's arm as she stumbled towards the door. Only two guests remained in the main room, and Lizzy was grateful her lack of a chaperone would go unnoticed, at least until morning. Thankfully, Simpkin requested two rooms, and the proprietress led Lizzy up at once. Simpkin bid her good night and remained in the taproom to order a drink and some food.

The simple bedchamber looked clean enough. Lizzy shed her cloak but remained in her dress. She dropped onto the bed without bothering to unpin her hair for the night and immediately fell asleep. Her dreams were scattered with visions of Mr. Simpkin standing at the front of a church and Lizzy slowly walked towards him, remembering her pledge, her purpose—to keep her brother safe. Her stomach turned and clenched, but she kept marching forward, until a feral smile spread across Mr. Simpkin's lips, his face taking on the expression of a wild boar, and Lizzy panicked. She turned to run away, only to find the church door sealed shut. She pounded on the door in desperation, hitting the solid wood again and again and again.

As the pounding grew louder, Lizzy woke with a start. She sat up and groaned against the pain pulsing through her midsection. Perspiration beaded her forehead, and her fingers clutched the bedsheets.

Lizzy jolted as the pounding began again. Light had not yet touched the horizon, and Lizzy feared to open her door. Perhaps Mr. Simpkin had changed his mind and wished to claim her now. Trembling with fear, she pulled the sheets to her chin and pushed her back against the wall.

The pounding continued, and Lizzy's heart jumped in sync with the rhythm. Muffled voices sounded through the wooden door, and then a key rattled in the lock. Tears trailed down Lizzy's cheeks. She pressed her eyes closed and turned her face away.

A moment later a warm hand touched her cheek. "Elizabeth?"

Lizzy turned to find Barton sitting beside her. He brushed back her hair and then trailed his fingers down her arms, grasping and gently squeezing her upper arm then her elbows and wrists.

The innkeeper stood just inside the doorway, holding a candle. The single flame splashed varied light across Barton's pulled brow. "Are you harmed? Has he hurt you?" Barton asked softly.

Lizzy's chest burned. Elation mixed with confusion. Barton sat before her. The words she wanted to say, the questions she wanted to ask, remained buried inside.

Barton's hands moved back to her face, his thumbs brushed away her tears, and then he held her head and met her eyes. "Elizabeth. Did he hurt you?"

Lizzy pinched her lips closed and shook her head.

"Thank heavens," Barton said on a breath. He pulled her head to his chest and wrapped his arms around her. His breath stirred her hair, and Lizzy could not quell her tears. Her hands moved to his jacket, and she pulled tight, desperate to never leave the security of his embrace. Barton ran a hand over her head. "Why? Why did you run away?" he whispered.

"Get your hands off my bride!" Mr. Simpkin's voice filled the small room.

Barton pressed a kiss to Lizzy's forehead. Then he stood and faced Mr. Simpkin. "As I told you before, Simpkin, she does not belong to you."

The innkeeper looked between the two men; uncertainty filled his face.

Lizzy pushed back into the corner and pulled her knees up to her chest.

"She will be my wife!" Simpkin bellowed and pointed a thick finger at Lizzy.

"No. She won't." Barton's hands hung fisted at his side. "Stafford forged the will. He has no right to Downey Place, Thomas, or Miss Stafford. Your marriage contract is invalid."

Lizzy could not breathe. Could it be?

"You're lying." Simpkin stepped farther into the room, and Lizzy couldn't stop the whimper that escaped her lips. She pressed her hands over her mouth. "And even if you're not, Stafford is her uncle. He can speak on her behalf."

Barton clenched his jaw. "Miss Stafford's father disavowed his brother. He named her as his sole heir, until Thomas comes of age."

Lizzy's hands shook. *Sole heir? Her?*

Simpkin narrowed his eyes. "I don't believe you."

"Franklin should be arriving shortly. He's obtained a copy of the original will, and you can see for yourself." Barton's eyes remained fixed on Mr. Simpkin, and he inhaled deeply. "Now." Barton extended his hand to Lizzy. "Miss Stafford will be leaving with me."

Lizzy could not bring herself to look at Mr. Simpkin, so she focused on Barton.

"I've paid for the trollop, and I'm not leaving without her." Simpkin pushed past the innkeeper and took another step into the room.

Barton swung his fist into the man's face. The innkeeper jumped out of the way as Simpkin staggered backwards and fell against the doorframe. Simpkin cursed and held a hand to his nose.

Barton resumed a fighting stance, holding both fists near his chin. "It's time for you to leave," Barton ground out.

Mr. Simpkin regained his footing, spat on the floor, and then he was gone.

Barton claimed the candle from the innkeeper. "Thank you. If you have an extra room, my brother will be arriving shortly."

The man mumbled something then bobbed his head and left, leaving the door ajar.

Barton set the candle on a side table and turned to Lizzy. He extended his hand and gave a single nod. Lizzy leaned forward to place her hand in his, and when she did he gently wrapped his fingers around hers and gave a soft tug to pull her to her feet.

"Is it true?" Lizzy whispered. "About the will?"

A smile spread across Barton's face. "Yes."

Lizzy gasped in delight. "Father did not abandon us to Uncle."

"No. I saw the will myself. All is right now," Barton said.

Lizzy leaned in to the solid comfort of his chest. Their clasped hands rested between them, and Barton ran his fingers along Lizzy's temple. She closed her eyes until Barton pressed a kiss to her brow. Despite the shadows, Lizzy noticed the angry bruises and discolored skin across Barton's knuckles. "You've hurt yourself." She pulled his hand to her lips and kissed his knuckles once and then again.

Warmth and peace flowed through Lizzy. She traced each of his fingers up and down. When she'd covered all five fingers, she raised her gaze to his. The look in Barton's eyes reflected her own intense longing. He leaned forward and pressed his lips to the side of her mouth. Then he placed another kiss on her lips and a final one on her forehead before pulling her closer, tighter, a promise of something more.

Lizzy shivered, breaking the long silence. "I can't believe you came."

Barton's hand cradled the back of her neck. He pulled slightly back so she could see his eyes. "I will always come for you."

Chapter 36

Barton relished the feeling of holding Elizabeth in his arms. She was safe and whole, and Barton planned to ensure Simpkin would never come close enough to hurt her again.

A cough sounded from the doorway. Franklin stood leaning against the wooden frame with raised brows and a knowing grin.

Elizabeth tried to pull her fingers free and step back, but Barton held on tight. "You've terrible timing," Barton told his brother.

"Or perhaps I have ideal timing," Franklin said. "You are, after all, alone—"

"And most pleasantly passing the time after a horrid night," Barton cut in. He finally stepped away from Elizabeth, missing her warmth immediately. "Besides"—Barton motioned to his brother—"you're here now, so everything is proper." Barton squeezed Elizabeth's hand before releasing it. "Is Simpkin still around?"

"No. The innkeeper said he left quite suddenly." Franklin pushed off the doorway. He reached into his jacket and withdrew a piece of parchment. "Miss Stafford, I apologize for my part in this. I hope this will make amends."

Barton looked at Elizabeth. "Would you like to see it for yourself?"

Elizabeth nodded.

"Very well, we've kept the innkeeper up the majority of the night anyway. Perhaps he may provide a private room and something warm to drink. Join us, Franklin." Barton reached his hand towards Elizabeth once more, and when she placed her fingers in his, he pulled her forward and tucked her arm through his own before escorting her downstairs.

It was nearly three o'clock in the morning. The innkeeper grumbled only until Franklin handed him ample compensation. A warm pot of tea, a slab of cheese, and day-old bread was laid out on the table, and then the innkeeper bid his patrons goodnight. Franklin circled the room then joined Barton and Elizabeth at the table.

"Are you sure you don't want anything more than tea?" Barton asked Elizabeth as Franklin sat down.

"No, I . . ." Elizabeth began but halted and placed a hand on her stomach.

Barton tried to read her expression. He leaned forward and touched her shoulder. "Are you sure you wish to proceed?"

"If what you said is true . . ." Elizabeth's lips pressed together, and she nodded.

Franklin laid the document flat on the table and ran his hand over the corners to flatten them. "Shall I read it to you?"

Elizabeth nodded.

After clearing his throat, Franklin began. "Let it be known from this, the eighteenth day of May, in the year of our Lord eighteen hundred ten, that upon my death, I, Reginald Eugene Stafford, do bequeath all of my land, holdings, possessions, and so on and so forth, to my wife, Esther Gale Stafford. In addition, she is the sole benefactor and guardian of our son, Thomas Eugene Stafford and my daughter, Elizabeth Stafford. In the unfortunate circumstance that my aforementioned wife, Esther Gale Stafford, passes before me or that we leave this earthly life together, I leave sole possession of the before-mentioned assets, including guardianship of Thomas Eugene Stafford, to my daughter, Elizabeth Stafford, until Thomas reaches the age of eighteen, at which time all property, investments, and benefits of the estate shall be divided equally between Elizabeth Stafford and Thomas Eugene Stafford, allocating said inheritance as they both deem appropriate, with the exception of the Stafford family sapphires, which shall belong solely to Elizabeth Stafford."

Barton turned to see tears trailing down Elizabeth's cheeks. He'd not replaced his handkerchief since loaning it to his mother, so he lifted a cloth napkin from the table and handed it to her.

"Father kept his promise. He never wanted Uncle in our lives." Elizabeth wiped her eyes with the napkin. "Forgive me."

Barton laughed lightly. "There's nothing to forgive, my sweet." The endearment fell easily from Barton's lips, and he did not regret allowing Elizabeth to know how he felt. Tears continued to well in her eyes, reflecting the crackling fire and radiating like glistening pools of liquid amber.

Until Franklin shattered the tender moment. "There's more: a detailed listing of your late father's assets, a record of investments, and there's a provision at the end that I think may be of special interest to you. Would you like me to continue?"

Elizabeth turned away from Barton to look at his brother. "Yes, please," she said and wiped her eyes again.

Barton could not resist reaching across the space between them and taking her hand.

Franklin quickly read off an accounting of Mr. Stafford's holdings. He took a deep breath and looked up from the paper in his hands. "Here's the portion I believe you will be particularly interested in." Franklin traced the words with his finger. "In addition, let it be known that due to knowledge of his illicit behavior, I sever all ties to my brother, Cline William Stafford, and renounce any previous claim he has, or may have, on my estate, Downey Place, including but not limited to additional holdings and rights in regards to my property, my wife, my children, and my assets. Signed, Reginald Eugene Stafford." Franklin looked up from the paper. "He signed and dated it here."

"May I see?" Elizabeth asked, and Franklin handed the document across the table. Barton released Elizabeth's hand, and with trembling fingers she reached for the will. "This is Father's signature. However did you discover this?"

"Your father's solicitor, Mr. Palmer," Franklin said. "Your uncle threatened Mr. Palmer and forced him to destroy the original will. Stafford believed Palmer had done it, but Palmer had the foresight to advise your father to make a duplicate, which Mr. Palmer kept in his possession."

Elizabeth shook her head, disbelieving. "He let me think Father had abandoned us to my uncle."

"I don't condone Palmer's actions, but your uncle threatened his family. It seems Stafford has a reputation for working with a man who goes by the name of Hayman, to carry out his threats. Palmer feared for his safety and felt he had no choice. Initially he did not admit his part, but his story did not add up. I pushed until he confessed. In the end, once I promised we would bring Simpkin to justice, Palmer was anxious to correct his error."

Elizabeth skimmed the will. "Thomas is safe. Forever."

Relief flooded Barton's senses. "And so are you."

"And what of the sapphires?" Elizabeth asked.

"I will work with the magistrate in Tolford to have them returned." Franklin sighed. "'Tis the least I can do."

"Thank you, Mr. Franklin." A smile twitched on Elizabeth's lips. She reverently brushed her hands over her father's signature. "Oh, Papa," she whispered. "I can't wait to tell Thomas."

Franklin stood. "I don't know about the two of you, but I will be needing a few hours of sleep before I make the trip."

"Would you mind keeping this safe until we return to Everly Manor?" Elizabeth handed the document back to Franklin. He took the will, bowed, and quit the room. "I-I'm not certain I could sleep now." She glanced at Barton.

Barton motioned to the couch near the wall. "There's a small sofa here. Why don't you lay down, and I will sit outside the door and make sure you are undisturbed." Barton did not miss the exhaustion pulling at her features.

"But you need to rest as well," Elizabeth said.

Barton stood and moved to assist Elizabeth with her chair. She rose to her feet and searched his face. A surge of emotion swelled within Barton's chest. "I won't leave you."

"You would sacrifice your sleep for me?" Elizabeth asked.

Barton took her hand and brushed his lips against the back of it, his eyes never leaving hers. "And so much more—if you'll allow me."

Elizabeth's cheeks colored. She dipped her head the slightest bit, and her lips turned up in a smile.

It was the perfect answer.

Chapter 37

WITHIN MOMENTS OF LYING DOWN, Lizzy had fallen into a quiet sleep. Barton had remained true to his word and sat sentry outside the door. A soft knock sounded as sunlight crested the horizon.

Lizzy opened her eyes to see Barton stepping inside the room. He left the door slightly ajar. He stared at her, and she unabashedly observed him in return, wondering how fortune had seen to bless her with the protection of such a stalwart man. Emotion bubbled within, threatening to choke her words before she could get them out.

Lizzy carefully shifted her legs from the couch to the floor and then stood. "Thank you for coming last night." Lizzy ran her palms down her wrinkled skirt. Why did Barton still stare? She reached a hand to her hair, realizing she must look a fright.

Lizzy took a breath and pressed her eyes closed. When she opened them again, she gasped. Barton stood not a foot away. He turned his head, evaluating her tousled hair.

Lizzy raised her hands to her cheeks, certain they were on fire. She opened her mouth, intent to say something, anything, to excuse her untidy state, but Barton reached forward and began to pull the remaining pins from her hair. The words she meant to say died on her lips, and air slipped from her lungs. Barton tugged the last pin free, and Lizzy's hair tumbled in tangles down her back. Barton took another step forward, closing the distance between them. He again reached around Lizzy, pulling a strand of hair forward and playing with it between his fingers.

Barton released Lizzy's hair and turned his eyes to hers. "Did you have pleasant dreams?"

Pleasant was only one of the words Lizzy would choose to describe the feelings rolling through her. "Yes. Thanks to you."

Barton's grin turned mischievous. "Does that mean you dreamt of me?"

Lizzy was certain her cheeks burned as red as the coals in the fireplace. She could not hold Barton's gaze and dropped her eyes to stare at her twisting hands. Barton slid his fingers around hers and rubbed his thumbs across the backs of Lizzy's hands. A warm tingle spread through her body, mixing with the soreness thrumming through her ribs.

"Elizabeth?" Barton's voice cut the silent breaths between them.

"Yes?"

"Promise me you'll never run away again?"

The burning in Lizzy's chest shifted to a pleasant ache, a longing to remain with him. "I promise."

"I could not bear to lose you." Barton leaned forward and stole a slow, intoxicating kiss.

The door flew open, and Lizzy jumped back in fright, shielding herself behind Barton's body. He heaved a long sigh. "That was uncalled for."

Mr. Franklin stood shaking his head with an unrepentant grin. "I've procured a carriage. We will be ready to depart shortly." He looked at his brother. "And I will be riding with the two of you, so Barton, you might want to cool off a bit."

Lizzy gasped, and Barton chuckled. "Thank you, Franklin," he said.

Embarrassment heated Lizzy's cheeks once again, until Barton smiled at her. In that moment she knew he would stand as her protector—always.

The carriage arrived at Everly Manor in the early afternoon hours. It seemed the entire staff poured from the house to receive the party, but Lizzy longed to see one face in particular.

Mr. Franklin and Barton stepped down from the carriage, and then Barton turned to assist Lizzy. He gave her fingers a gentle squeeze and then let her go. Lizzy lifted her skirts and walked forward, searching the smiling faces: Drew, Bastian, Henderson, and Mrs. Brown. Mrs. Everly stood at the forefront. And while Lizzy appreciated the welcome, she could not quell her frantic desire to see her brother.

"Thomas?" she asked Mrs. Everly.

"He's here." Mrs. Haskins stepped around one of the footmen, holding Thomas's hand in her own.

Lizzy ran to him and dropped onto her knees in the dirt. She whispered his name through happy tears and ran her hands over his shoulders and arms.

"Lizzy!" Thomas shrugged out of her grasp. "What are you doing?"

"It's all going to be all right, Thomas." Lizzy reached for him again and pulled her brother into her arms.

"Then, why are you crying?" Thomas asked, wiggling to break free.

Lizzy laughed.

"That sounds funny." Thomas pressed his head against Lizzy's chest. Then he began to giggle. "Now you're laughing and crying."

Joy diffused through Lizzy. She squeezed Thomas until he begged to be released. Even then she held him at arm's length to breathe in the sight of him.

Thomas cocked his head. "Did you go on a trip?"

Lizzy stood up and mussed his hair. "Why don't we go inside, and I'll tell you all about my latest adventure."

Thomas's eyes had nearly popped out of his head when Lizzy explained that the two of them were the new owners of Downey Place. She told Thomas how Mr. Everly and Mr. Franklin had discovered Uncle's lies. She did not elaborate on the adventure in its entirety.

Lizzy sat at the edge of Thomas's bed, running her fingers through his hair, long after he'd fallen asleep.

"I can see why you don't want to leave his side." Barton leaned against the doorframe. "He emanates peace."

Lizzy could scarce believe such abundant joy was possible, and she touched a hand to Thomas's cheek. "While he is sleeping, yes. He's very peaceful. Your siblings could probably testify that his waking hours can be an entirely different story. Thomas can be quite the negotiator when he chooses."

Barton chuckled. "Franklin and Bethany adore him."

The words stuck in Lizzy's throat, but she forced them out. "I know."

"Was he pleased with your news?" Barton walked forward and stood next to the bed.

Lizzy nodded, remembering how Thomas had questioned her again and again. The particulars of the will were difficult for a nine-year-old to grasp, so Lizzy tried to keep it simple. In the end, Thomas knew the most important thing—Uncle could not send him to sea. But Thomas also spoke of the adventures he would have with Brownbeard and how he and Mrs. Haskins had begun writing a story of their own. Lizzy had not told him they would soon be leaving Everly Manor.

"And what about his sister?" Barton asked. "Is she pleased?"

How could she answer? Mr. Franklin's discovery was more than Lizzy had hoped for. Downey Place belonged to her and Thomas. The staff would no longer have to suffer Uncle's berating temper. Barton had sent an express to the constable in Leicestershire. Uncle would be removed and lightness, joy, and tranquility could once again nestle comfortably throughout the estate. For Thomas's sake, Lizzy could ensure Downey Place would serve as a refuge from the ugliness in the world. But Barton had shown Lizzy that more than one refuge could exist. Everly Manor itself had become a refuge. Barton had become a refuge.

While Thomas had clapped his hands at the prospect of owning the great treasure Downey Place, he showed little inclination to return to his childhood home. Lizzy admitted to herself that she too was loath to return.

"Elizabeth?" Barton's voice soothed Lizzy like a warm caress.

She wanted to tell him, to exclaim, that *yes* she was pleased—but she was also scared. Scared of returning to Downey Place alone with Thomas. Scared of trying to manage an entire estate without her father or mother to guide her. Scared of how her heart pulsed when Barton looked at her.

But what could she say? Lizzy stood. She stared into Barton's solid blue eyes and forced herself to push aside the theatrics, to put away the mask and speak to him from her heart. "I'm very pleased."

Barton's lips pushed up in a smile, and Lizzy ran a hand over her midsection, a reminder of fresh wounds and the possibility to heal, to start again. She walked from Thomas's room into the nursery, and Barton followed. Emotion pulsed through Lizzy, unable to be contained. If only she could somehow transform her feelings to words.

She turned to face Barton. "You have been so very gracious and kind . . . it's more than I deserve. What if you hadn't come into the apothecary that day? There was no reason for you to allow Thomas and me to stay at the cabin, but you did." She took a breath and blinked back the hot tears in her eyes. "I don't know why Providence sent you to us, but I will forever be grateful. And now . . . now, what will we do? I must care for Thomas. He needs to go to school, and I haven't the slightest idea how to run an estate—"

Barton stepped forward and set a single finger against Lizzy's lips. She stopped talking and enjoyed the cool touch of his skin. "None of that matters." Barton took Lizzy's hands in his own.

"Yes, yes, it does." Lizzy's voice broke. "Because despite my hurtful words, my lies, you came . . . you came for me."

"I told you, I will always come for you," Barton whispered.

Lizzy dropped her head. Her chest tightened, and she willfully forced her lungs to inhale the next breath. "I must return to Downey Place."

Barton's smile fell away. "What do you mean? You have a place here. I will care for you." Lizzy did not miss the catch of Barton's breath.

"That's precisely why I need to go."

"I don't understand."

"It's been you. It's all been you," Lizzy said. A single tear fell from her eyes.

"So, let it continue."

Lizzy shook her head and tried to blink the moisture away. "I can't. Don't you see?"

"No. I don't. You're happy here. Thomas is happy here. I can take care of you here." Barton bent his head low so he could look into Lizzy's eyes. "I thought you trusted me."

"I do." Lizzy choked on the two small words.

"Then, what is this about? You've promised not to run away, remember?" Barton's smile was stilted. He released Lizzy's hand and ran his fingers over her cheeks to wipe the tears away.

Lizzy leaned in to his touch, longing for more than she had a right to claim. "You don't understand what Uncle was like. What he did. I must return to Downey Place and set things right." Barton's hand fell away. If only she could make him understand. "Uncle Cline ruined my home. My staff valiantly served me, even disobeying his orders to shield Thomas and me from his violence. I cannot remain here knowing the gloom they have endured. They need to know I have not forgotten them."

"Your uncle will be removed in a matter of days."

"Removing him does not remove the despair about the place. The evil he ushered into Downey Place came quickly, in a matter of days, and it suffocated everyone. Everything." Various faces—Clarke, Marlow, Henry Buford—flooded Lizzy's mind. She steadied her breath and tried to ground her emotions. "I cannot desert my home when I have the opportunity to make it right. The servants were loyal to me to the end. I tried to keep them unaware of my plans, but I shudder to think of the punishment Uncle inflicted when he found out I had taken the jewels. Things may never return to where they were, but I have to try."

Barton's jaw tensed, and he lifted his chin a notch. "So, you are going to run. You're leaving me . . . again?"

"I . . ." Lizzy opened her mouth, ready to explain, but Barton's face turned hard, effectively suffocating any words she meant to share. He took a step back.

Warm tears continued to fill Lizzy's eyes, and she could not stop them from falling. Barton stood stoically, and Lizzy recognized his mask for what it was. She was practiced at artifice, and while she'd hoped to leave her theatrics behind, Barton had perfected his own.

"I told you I would not release you from one engagement to force you into another," he said with an eerie calm.

Lizzy raised her hands to try to explain, but Barton continued, every word slicing through Lizzy's fragile resolve. "I am a man of my word, and I will respect your decision, Miss Stafford. I will have Henderson arrange for a carriage to transport you home first thing Wednesday morning. Three days should be adequate time for your uncle to be removed from the estate."

"So soon?" Lizzy said on a whisper. Barton gave an abrupt nod, turned on his heel, and left. Lizzy's breath hitched, and her heart splintered once again.

Chapter 38

BARTON HAD BEEN A FOOL to think the kisses they'd shared meant something to Elizabeth. She'd been distressed, and he'd comforted her in a selfish way. He couldn't help himself. She'd always told him Thomas held her heart. But Barton had remained an optimistic fool, hoping her desires had changed, evolved into something more. He'd hoped he might hold a place in her heart as well. Now he was just a plain fool, and it was better that he let her go.

Despite Elizabeth's rejection, his heart remained hers. He did not attempt to sleep, for he knew his efforts would be in vain. Instead he racked the billiard balls and wandered around the table, taking aim until the table was cleared, only to start over again. Over the next two days he avoided Miss Stafford, although his days were filled entirely with thoughts of her. Of their unorthodox greeting and her fabricated story of her cousin. He reflected on her fondness for Thomas, her skepticism with himself, her witty words, her bravery, her kiss. Every memory pelted his fragile heart. He loved Elizabeth Stafford, yet she refused to stay with him.

Come Wednesday morning, Barton did not see Miss Stafford or her brother off. She'd made it clear her future was not with him. Watching her step into the carriage would only make Barton grovel for her to stay. And Barton refused to grovel. In the early-morning hours he left instructions with his staff. Brownbeard would be his gift to Thomas, a tangible memory of Everly Manor. Then he saddled Brutus and rode away before the first light of dawn touched the sky.

Barton urged Brutus forward with no destination in mind, content to recuse himself from the emotions of goodbye.

His mother vacillated between pathetic remorse for her part in alerting Mr. Simpkin to Elizabeth's location and overbearing interference, insisting

Barton spill his heart at Elizabeth's feet and refuse to let her leave. Barton could not take another look of pity or any more observations made by his mother. She may have been party to the events surrounding Mr. Simpkin, but Elizabeth had made her desires known, and Barton would not ask her again to remain. He could not. His heart could not face another rejection.

Barton found himself staring at the crooked door of Doyle's cabin. A blanket of clouds stretched across the sky, muting the sun's efforts to provide warmth and light. Brutus snuffed and tossed his head. Barton heaved a sigh and slid off the horse. He tied the reins around a nearby bush, walked to the door, and pushed it wide. Memories of Doyle sitting near the fire and weaving great tales of adventure mixed with his memories of Elizabeth and engulfed him. He recalled the smiles she granted her brother and the way she mussed his hair. She was determined, brave, and selfless in a way Barton reluctantly admired. But in the end, Elizabeth's selflessness had driven her away from him.

Elizabeth's grand adventure had been a mission to save Thomas. Barton, Everly Manor, and tangled emotions had never been on the docket. Elizabeth had always intended to devote herself to her brother. Barton's interference had only ensured she could do that from the comfort of Downey Place rather than on the run. And that he could not, he would not, regret.

Barton's feelings for Miss Newhall had been nothing like the aching, the yearning he felt now. Refusing to see Elizabeth off did not lessen the fissures in his heart. They spread deep. They spread wide, twining through Barton's insides like the sticky tendrils of a spider's web. He was wounded, and he doubted his heart would ever heal.

Doyle's tales had always ended with the same admonition: making the right choice could be hard, but that didn't make it any less correct. Doyle had left behind the disparity of his homeland. He fled to England, searching for truth, for freedom, for a right to life. Barton wanted to succeed; he had tried to make the right choice and follow his heart. Why, then, did he find the battle for love to be marked by one defeat after another?

Lizzy knew her departure from Everly Manor would be difficult. She had rehearsed it in her mind: Mrs. Haskins's quiet tears, Mrs. Everly's continued profuse apologies, and Mr. Franklin's easy smile. She imagined the warm squeeze she would give Drew, Bastian, and Mrs. Brown, and Lizzy even considered kissing Henderson's cheek. They had all been so good to her, but none more than Barton. And he'd chosen to stay away.

For the past three days Lizzy had mustered every ounce of strength she possessed to not ask after him. She suppressed her disappointment as she expressed her gratitude to each member of the staff. Lizzy spouted false cheeriness about their next adventure while she pulled Thomas away from Mrs. Haskins's skirts, his eyes brimming with moisture. His quiet tears fell only once the carriage pulled away. Lizzy heard his sniffles and felt the splatter of several teardrops against her hand as she held him close.

Thomas clung to Brownbeard. Even the pup settled quiet and somber as the carriage rocked back and forth, taking them away from Everly Manor. Only once Thomas's tears exhausted him and his head lulled against Lizzy's arm did she allow her own tears to fall.

Late afternoon light dusted Downey Place in a hazy glow when they arrived the following day. Lizzy stroked Thomas's head. "We are home," she said.

Before the footman had a chance to lower the step, Thomas opened the door and jumped down behind Brownbeard. The dog pushed his nose to the ground and began an inspection of his new home. Thomas called after Brownbeard and tried to keep up as the dog raced after a scattering of blackbirds.

The staff hurried out to welcome Lizzy, standing with wide eyes and hesitant smiles. She was grateful that upon perusal, all the servants, except Henry, seemed to be accounted for. It gave her a sliver of hope that she might be able to restore all Uncle had tarnished.

"Miss Stafford," Mr. Clarke stepped forward and greeted her. "Welcome home." His sincerity soothed Lizzy's nerves.

"Thank you, Clarke. Has . . . is Uncle . . . ?"

"The constable escorted him off the property this morning, ma'am."

Lizzy winced. "I don't imagine that was a pretty sight."

"Pardon me for saying so, Miss Stafford, but the staff and I agree it was a rather beautiful sight," Clarke said.

"Indeed." Lizzy smiled.

Lizzy's beloved staff embraced her return. Cook prepared her favorite dishes and made Thomas extra sweets. Clarke deferred to Lizzy for decisions regarding the estate, guiding her through the issues she knew nothing about and giving gentle direction. She wrote to Mr. Palmer and rehired him as solicitor. She also made plans to visit all of the tenants. Marlow took extra care in the selection of Lizzy's gowns and in the styling of her hair. Lizzy should have felt happy and complete. Instead hollowness consumed her.

Several days after Lizzy's return she wandered down the east corridor and realized one of her favorite tapestries no longer hung in the hall. She looked up and down the length of the wall to verify she correctly remembered the position of the piece. A small portrait of a trio of apples hung where a vibrant scene of fairies and woodland creatures ought to have been.

Lizzy found Clarke in his private office. He stood at her entrance. "Clarke, where is the tapestry of the fairyland creatures? The one that used to hang in the upstairs corridor?"

Clarke's mouth dipped in a frown. "Mr. Stafford sold it, ma'am."

"Why would he do that?" Lizzy's question was rhetorical, and she stood musing over possible reasons when Clarke cleared his throat. "Yes?" Lizzy looked up and waited for him to speak.

"I overheard Mr. Stafford speaking to his new man of business. I can't say for sure, ma'am, but I heard them discussing the estate coffers. I believe your uncle had several outstanding debts. Large ones. The solicitor warned him not to take any more from the estate because the tenants were growing restless, as many of the tenant accounts remain unsettled." Clarke's voice dropped. "Mr. Stafford sold that tapestry as well as the one in the ballroom."

Sadness and anger pulsed through Lizzy, clashing together until she became numb.

After a silent moment Clarke spoke again. "He also sold the silver candlesticks and your stepmother's vases."

"The entire collection?" Lizzy asked.

Clarke nodded. "Mrs. Hull was quite upset."

"Thank you, Clarke. Is there anything else?"

"We've discovered the silverware is missing, and beyond that I can't say for sure, ma'am."

"Please work with Mrs. Hull and make an accounting of the household items, particularly anything of value."

"Yes, ma'am."

Despite Lizzy's work to dispel any reminder of Uncle Cline, the scars continued to appear. While the majority of the staff was grateful they'd known nothing about Lizzy's disappearance, Marlow confessed that Lizzy's deception had hurt.

"I was trying to protect you," Lizzy explained. "How could Uncle punish you for something you did not know?"

"That didn't stop him." Marlow's tears fell freely.

Late into the night Marlow wept as she told Lizzy of Uncle Cline's unwanted advances. He'd started with pretend politeness, and the more Marlow avoided him, the more he sought her out. Uncle's frustrations had turned to anger. One day he'd cornered Marlow in the hallway and forcefully kissed her. When Marlow tried to cry for help, Uncle had cursed and knocked her head against the wall. Thankfully, Clarke had appeared and since that day had taken extra care to be aware of Marlow's whereabouts. He had stepped in several times and used his imposing stature to rescue Marlow from Uncle's pursuit.

Lizzy's heart broke, and she begged for Marlow's forgiveness. Lizzy may not have been able to prevent the gloom Uncle spread, but she might have been able to do something. Lizzy settled Marlow in her room, and long after the girl had fallen asleep, Lizzy lay awake feeling small and insignificant. How could she have saved them all? She'd focused on Thomas. He was safe, but lately he'd been despondent and withdrawn.

Yesterday Lizzy had watched Thomas slowly circle the stables while Brownbeard nipped at his heels for attention. Thomas had picked up a stick and thrown it for the dog with no sign of enthusiasm. Daily he asked Lizzy when they might return to Everly Manor, and daily her heart broke as she explained how they were needed at Downey Place.

"But I miss Mr. Barton and Mrs. Bethany," Thomas whined.

"As do I." It was all Lizzy could manage. She mussed Thomas's hair and tried to appease him with one of Cook's treats.

Lizzy had asked Marlow to assist with Thomas's care until a tutor could be found. It was an additional duty, but Lizzy wanted Marlow to know she trusted her. The scars Uncle had left could not be removed, but perhaps Lizzy could help heal some of the pain.

Lizzy often found herself wandering to the kitchen, searching for comfort through the familiarity of her staff. After confirming the menu with Mrs. Hull, Lizzy sought Marlow out and asked after Thomas.

"He seems especially distraught today," Marlow said.

"Perhaps an adventure in the woods will cheer him up." Lizzy asked Marlow to get Thomas ready and changed into her boots.

Once they were outside Thomas walked quietly beside Lizzy. The clouds overhead hindered the sun's efforts to provide light, and the air sat heavily. "I'm up for a new adventure today. What do you think?" Lizzy asked Thomas, determined to make him smile.

Thomas shrugged. "I don't know that I like adventures anymore."

"Why ever not?" Thomas's response surprised Lizzy. She swung their clasped hands between them, trying to force some joviality into the dismal morning.

"I like happy endings." Thomas pulled free from his sister's grasp. "I used to think all adventures had a happy ending. I don't believe that anymore."

She understood the sentiment precisely and sucked in a quick breath. "Well, if it's our adventure, I think we get to choose the ending, and I declare it will be happy."

Thomas looked up at her and pressed his lips together. "Can we be explorers today?"

"On a daring adventure." Lizzy twirled in a circle then crouched low. "Shall we set sail to discover a new land or brave the wild animals in the jungle in search of the lost princess?"

Thomas grinned. "The jungle." He sprinted ahead of Lizzy, Brownbeard at his heels.

"Brownbeard can be a ferocious jaguar." Lizzy laughed and chased Thomas into the trees.

They played make-believe until the sun set. Cook served a warm stew, and only once Lizzy had settled into the quiet of her room did she stop and think about Barton. His face lingered at the edges of her mind; he was always smiling and reaching for her, asking for her trust. She had sent a letter to Everly Manor to let Barton know of their safe arrival. She'd thanked him for gifting Brownbeard to Thomas and told Barton of her brother's high opinion of him and his siblings. Lizzy hoped Barton would realize Thomas's praise was only a sliver of her own admiration for the man. Barton never replied to her letter, and Lizzy mourned that she would never see him again, even if it was only to say goodbye.

Chapter 39

BARTON AVOIDED HIS MOTHER FOR an entire week. When he had visited Doyle's cabin on the day of Elizabeth's departure, he decided to make the necessary repairs himself. Every morning he employed the same routine: dress, eat, patch the walls in Doyle's cabin, return home, eat, push away the painful memories, and then fall into bed. He devoured his nightly meal, exhausted from his work, but Barton enjoyed the feeling of accomplishment, of having tangible proof of his exertion.

The moment he satisfied his stomach and Mrs. Brown removed his tray, images of Elizabeth returned. He'd stare at the fire, remembering the feel of Elizabeth's lips and the golden hue in her eyes. Then he wondered where things had gone wrong. Securing her trust had been as difficult as any physical task he'd completed. The effort had taken time and patience . . . it had taken love. And in the end it hadn't been enough. There remained no validation beyond her words that she trusted him. Her actions declared the opposite and left Barton with nothing permanent to grasp.

New straw was ordered for the roof of Doyle's cabin, and Barton asked his groundskeeper to acquire the necessary tools. At the end of the week, the supplies arrived. Barton walked around the perimeter of the cabin, admiring the newly patched walls when Murray pulled up in his wagon.

Murray moved slowly, stepping down from the bench and walking to where Barton joined him, and together they silently unloaded the materials. When the wagon bed was empty, Barton stood with his hands on his hips and evaluated the pile of straw and the ladder and tools sitting beside it.

"'Tis a bit of work to rethatch the roof. You sure you don't want help?" Murray asked.

Barton clapped a hand on the old man's back. "You've helped more than you know."

Murray grunted.

Barton looked through the trees to the clouds racing overhead. "I'd better get started if I hope to beat the rain."

Murray turned and walked back towards his wagon. He climbed up the step and settled onto the bench. He took the reins in hand, but before he urged Rose forward, he stared at Barton with a frown. "The rain's coming whether you want it to or not. You can try to run away, but yer bound to get wet."

Barton shook his head. "You're being cryptic, old man. Why don't you simply tell me what it is you're trying to say."

Murray flicked the reins and clicked his tongue. "You'll figure it out. Yer a smart lad, even if yer a bit thickheaded."

Barton watched Murray slowly disappear down the overgrown path, pondering his obscure admonishment. Then he leaned the ladder against the side of the house and got to work. Barton adjusted his work gloves and then tossed a pile of straw to the edge of the roof. He climbed the ladder with the set pin and a handful of spars.

Barton prodded the roof with the set pin, looking for obvious holes to patch. He continued the process and thought on Murray's words. Barton did not wish to outrun the rain; he only wanted it to hold off for an hour or so to allow him some time to work. Then he realized if the rain fell, he could more easily determine where repairs were needed.

Poke, stick, gather a small bundle of straw, and attach with the spar. The repetitious work allowed Barton's thoughts to wander. Again and again he thought on Murray's insinuation that he was running. Barton knew he'd been avoiding his mother; the entire household knew that. After Bethany sent him a note chastising him for his behavior and reminding him she and her husband would return home in less than a week, guilt settled in and Barton had joined the family for dinner. But Murray cared little for the goings-on within Everly Manor, and Barton knew the old man referred to something more.

Barton climbed down the ladder and looked over the small section he had completed. Pleased with his work, he hefted another bundle of straw to the roof as the first raindrop fell. The trees filtered a portion of the rain, and Barton continued his work. After thirty minutes his shirt was soaked through and Brutus snorted his complaints from where he stood hitched at the side of the cabin. Barton gathered his tools and climbed down from the roof once again. When lightning flashed overhead, Barton decided to take refuge inside and wait for the storm to pass.

A drop of rain fell onto the crown of his head. Barton looked up and acknowledged the additional leak in the roof at the same time Murray's words returned to his thoughts. He could not outrun the rain. He missed Elizabeth. He wanted to be by her side. He missed her strength and her loyalty—the same loyalty that ensured she returned home. Her valor, her sense of right and wrong, had allowed no other alternative. She needed to look after her servants. She needed to look after Thomas, and Barton conceded she would sacrifice her own wants and needs to do exactly that.

While he wished she didn't always put others first, it was one of the qualities he loved about her. She freely gave of herself. Barton wanted only a small portion of her. He wanted her to stay, he needed her to stay—would she not sacrifice for him as well? Then Barton realized he'd never asked her to. He had never told her his undiluted feelings. He'd asked her to remain, insisting he could take care of her, but all the while he needed her to care for him.

Another raindrop hit his head, and enlightenment dawned. Barton ran outside into the rain. Barton needed to tell Elizabeth why he'd asked her to stay. He'd never told her he loved her, he needed her, and he meant to correct the error as soon as possible.

Chapter 40

EVERY DAY LIZZY MADE A concerted effort to compliment one of the servants, to meet with Mr. Palmer to learn about one of the tenants, and to spend time with Thomas. If she could do a bit of good, she counted the day well spent. She tried to emulate Barton's charity. Thoughts of him came often, and if she did not quickly push them away, they consumed her. Thus, she made a practice of dismissing any thought, memory, or reference to Barton or her time at Everly Manor.

Thomas, however, was not so easily appeased. He talked frequently about how proud Mr. Barton would be with Thomas's training of Brownbeard. He asked Lizzy when he might resume riding lessons and whether Mr. Murray might be willing to come teach him.

These discussions with Thomas required patience from Lizzy. Yes, Mr. Barton would be proud of Thomas. He would praise his efforts and smile at Thomas's persistent training of the dog. And Lizzy had no doubt that if Thomas asked Mr. Barton to secure Mr. Murray as a riding teacher, Barton would find a way to do so. Barton's natural inclination was to help.

But since Lizzy's departure from Everly Manor, Barton had remained a ghost, a far-off memory. When Lizzy refused to stay, he had dismissed her. The only exception was a letter from Mr. Franklin that had arrived one week after Lizzy had returned home. The missive simply relayed that Mr. Franklin had met with the family solicitor, and together the two were working with the local magistrate to retrieve Lizzy's jewels from Mr. Simpkin. Mr. Franklin made no mention of Barton. In fact, it seemed Barton had passed all association with Lizzy off to his brother.

Barton's absence seared painfully and deeply. Lizzy missed him. She could not deny it. The calm mask Lizzy had projected when leaving Everly

Manor marked her best theatrical performance to date. But Lizzy grew tired of wearing masks, tired of pretending, and tired of denying the constant pain roiling through her.

She sat with Clarke and Mr. Palmer in the day room, listening while Mr. Palmer read the list of missing items. For every object Mr. Palmer listed, Clarke gave a single nod. Lizzy stopped listening. Clarke's head bobbed too many times to keep track of it all.

Mr. Palmer and Clarke finished their report, and Lizzy rose while Clarke escorted Mr. Palmer out. She crossed the length of the room once and then once again, her thoughts crossing between frustration for Uncle's imprudence and gratitude that she now assumed the position to make things right. Uncle had amassed enormous debts on the estate in only a matter of months. Mr. Palmer assured her he would try to locate a handful of the items Lizzy treasured most, but he could not guarantee their recovery.

Reality proved a difficult place to exist. The following day Lizzy ate breakfast with Thomas then pulled him outside, intent on spending some time out of doors in a make-believe world. The overcast sky mirrored Lizzy's frustrations, but she tried to focus on the beauty the subdued light cast on the trees. She walked next to her brother, once again feigning a levity she did not feel.

"What shall we play today?" she asked. "Pirates? Knights? Or perhaps you'd rather explore a dragon's lair?"

"Hmm." Thomas's step slowed, and his face scrunched in concentration. Lizzy watched him with a smile then started in surprise as Thomas suddenly jumped and turned his excited eyes to hers. "Let's go on an expedition to find a dragon egg!"

"Very well. Dragons it is."

Thomas took off for the trees and called over his shoulder. "I'm the leader, and you can be my assistant."

Lizzy's heart lifted. If only she could embrace the simplicity her brother saw in life. Being an adult, shouldering responsibility, tested her mettle. She grasped her skirts and ran after Thomas.

He disappeared into the forest before Lizzy could catch him. "Thomas?" she called in a singsong voice. "Oh, leader extraordinaire! Where are you?"

"Here, Lizzy!" Thomas's voice rang through the trees.

Lizzy turned right. "Wait for me, silly boy. I can't be your assistant if you keep dashing away."

"Come on, Lizzy. Come on. I'm sure the dragon's nest is over here." Lizzy saw a flash of Thomas's brown coat through the shadows.

"Thomas, wait," Lizzy called after him.

Thomas came running back through the trees with an enormous grin spread across his face. "I'm the best explorer ever! You have to come see what I've found." He grabbed Lizzy's hand and turned back in the direction he had come from.

Thomas's quick pace caused Lizzy to stumble, but she righted herself quickly and followed after him.

They moved deeper into the trees. Thomas's contagious excitement drew laughter from Lizzy. "Where are you taking me?"

"Right here." Thomas stopped in a small clearing, his chest heaving from the exertion.

Lizzy stepped around him, and her joviality fled. Warm, smoking ashes, the remains of a fire, lay in the center of the clearing. Lizzy's stomach plummeted as she took in the scene. A single blanket spread across a patch of barren ground, and two or three more blankets lay wadded up in a pile. A tin plate scraped almost clean and a bladder of water sat near a rock. An empty flask, with the lid cast aside, sat in the dirt next to a rectangular box Lizzy recognized. She stepped forward and unclasped the latches on either side of the box, lifting the lid to see the maroon satin lining inside. Only half of the silverware remained.

Lizzy sucked in a breath and stood. "We must return to the house." Lizzy held out her hand, expecting Thomas to take hold, but her hand remained empty, cold. She spun around. "Thomas!" she shouted. "Thomas!" He had vanished.

Chapter 41

BARTON SHRUGGED INTO HIS DINNER coat and thanked his valet just as Franklin bounded into the room. Barton raised his brow. "Don't bother to knock, Brother." Barton smiled and adjusted his cuffs.

Franklin stepped forward, undeterred by Barton's sarcasm. "An express just arrived from Downey Place."

Barton froze, and his smile fell.

"Read it." Franklin thrust the letter forward, but Barton stood in place, stalling for a long minute, before he took the paper in hand.

His eyes skimmed the words quickly. The short missive sliced like a dagger through his chest.

> *Thomas has been taken by my uncle. I fear for his life. I've nowhere else to turn.*
> *Elizabeth Stafford*

"Are you coming?" Barton asked Franklin.

"I've already instructed Henderson to have my horse saddled, along with Starfly. I shall meet you downstairs, post haste." The moment Franklin left the room Barton called again for his valet and quickly changed into his riding attire.

Bethany and Barton's mother met the brothers in the front hall. Tears filled Bethany's eyes. "You must save him."

Barton nodded and walked directly to the door. Franklin reached out and squeezed Bethany's hand as he passed. "We will," Franklin said.

Three horses were led from the stables in the dimming evening light. "What is this?" Barton asked motioning to the third horse.

"Thought I might join you," Haskins said as he jogged from the house to catch them. Barton gave a single nod. Franklin clapped Haskins on the back, and then all three men mounted their horses.

"I'm warning you now, Starfly can run. If you can't keep up, I'll see you at Downey Place." Barton turned his horse down the lane.

"Understood," Franklin said.

"Let's go." Barton kicked Starfly into a gallop and began counting down the moments until he reached Elizabeth's side.

Due to Barton's epiphany at the cottage, he had planned to travel to Downey Place the following morning. Elizabeth's express simply propelled his timeline forward and guaranteed the company of Haskins and Franklin.

The men rode through the night, stopping only to rest their horses when absolutely necessary. They reached the village of Tolford at noon the following day. Barton verified directions and pushed the horses forward again after only a brief reprieve until the dominant façade of Downey Place rose into view.

The trio reached the estate entrance and reined in their mounts. A large man, immaculate in his servant's dress and stoic expression, immediately descended the front stairs and stiffly examined Barton and his companions.

Barton quickly made introductions. "Harrison Barton Everly of Everly Manor, Mr. Franklin Everly, my brother, and Mr. Marcus Haskins, my brother-in-law. We've come at the request of Miss Stafford." Two stableboys arrived, and the men handed off their horses.

The butler nodded decisively. "Miss Stafford will be glad you've come. Right this way." He led them into the house, and the men handed over their things.

"How is she?" Barton asked.

The butler froze and thoroughly evaluated him. "Not well, sir. She's not slept and has been pacing the kitchen for hours now." Clarke led them to the drawing room. "I shall let Miss Stafford know you've arrived."

"Nonsense," Barton said. "Take us to the kitchen."

The butler straightened his shoulders and looked at Barton with a single raised brow.

Barton dropped his authoritative tone. "If that is where she is most comfortable, it would be best to talk with her there."

The butler remained silent.

"We don't mind." Barton motioned to his companions. "We've come to help however we can, and right now it seems our help is needed in the kitchen." Barton walked to the doorway. "If you would kindly lead the way, Mr. . . . ?"

The man's expression did not change, but his eyes softened. "Clarke. This way," the butler said. Barton nodded as Clarke passed, and the three men followed him to the kitchen.

A blazing fire rendered the room sticky and hot. A small woman, whom Barton assumed was the cook, stood in the corner, wringing her hands as she stared across the open space. She turned her weary eyes to the men as they entered the room, and the butler asked her to prepare some refreshment.

Barton went directly to Elizabeth. She paced away from them. Her hair hung loosely down her back, as tangled as Barton's emotions. When she spun on her heel and faced them, she stumbled to a stop. Her red cheeks shone with tears. Dark circles lined her eyes, and her frame shook with every breath she took.

Barton could not help himself. He crossed the room and pulled her into his arms. She cried out in surprise and then sobbed into his chest. Barton held her close, keeping her secure against his body. He bent his head and whispered into her ear, "I'm so sorry, my darling."

His hold did not waver as Elizabeth continued to cry. Eventually her sobs turned to stuttered breaths. Barton rubbed her back in steady, even circles. He trailed his hands down her arms and took one hand in his. She looked at him, and Barton's words caught in his throat. He pressed a kiss to the back of her hand and managed one word. "Come."

Barton led Elizabeth to the table, where the other men sat, and insisted she take a place beside them. Cook set out tea, bread, and apples, and Clarke stood nearby, monitoring every interaction.

Elizabeth offered Haskins and Franklin a shaky nod. Franklin's eyes conveyed his sympathies. "Miss Stafford, let me offer our deepest apologies. Now, please tell us what happened—from the beginning."

Elizabeth took a moment to collect herself and then told the gentlemen all she had discovered upon her return to Downey Place. "I suppose Uncle became desperate. This arrived after Thomas went missing." She pulled a note from her sleeve and held it forward.

Barton snatched it up and read aloud. *"Miss Stafford, Thomas is unharmed—for now. Do not notify the authorities. If you wish to negotiate your brother's release, bring the sapphires Friday at dawn to the clearing in the woods. Come alone. Only then will I release the boy. —C. Stafford."*

"Tomorrow morning? That doesn't give us much time, and his terms are clear." Haskins set his elbows on the table. "We don't have many options."

Barton cursed under his breath. "I don't like it. You don't even have the sapphires to bargain with."

Elizabeth's voice was soft. "Perhaps he would take me in place of my brother."

And therein lay the problem. Barton knew she would trade circumstances if she could. She'd unequivocally claimed she would sacrifice anything for Thomas. He'd witnessed it firsthand.

Clarke cleared his throat. "If I may?" He stood in rigid perfection as all attention turned to him. "While you were absent, Miss Stafford, I overheard your uncle and his new man of business talking."

Barton jumped from his seat. "Go on," he said.

Clarke lifted his chin. "They were discussing who would inherit if Thomas and yourself were . . ." He paused. "Removed entirely."

Elizabeth's bottom lip began to tremble. "Uncle Cline is Father's only relative."

"Thus, despite the exclusion in the original will, Downey Place would belong to him," Franklin finished.

Haskins stood and moved to the end of the table, near Barton. "That was obviously his plan from the beginning. He hoped to send Thomas to his death at sea and have Miss Stafford married off to secure his place." He paced to the kitchen door and back, tapping his hand against his leg.

"Before, he was willing to let others do the dirty work. Now, it seems, he has taken matters into his own hands," Franklin said.

"We need more time." Haskins planted his hands on his hips.

"Which we don't have." Barton's mind reeled, and his chest ached. He'd promised to protect Elizabeth, and despite his determination, he felt helpless.

"You musn't go meet him, Miss Stafford," Franklin said.

"I must," Elizabeth cried. "I have to save my brother."

She wobbled in her seat, and Cook rushed forward to aid her. "You've been up all night, Miss Stafford. It'd be best if you rested a bit."

Elizabeth nodded consent. She stood, and Cook helped her move towards the back stairs. Elizabeth gripped the woman for support. Without a word Barton stepped forward and lifted Elizabeth into his arms. Elizabeth rested her head against his shoulder and closed her eyes. He turned to Cook. "Lead the way."

Barton delivered Miss Stafford to her room but did not linger. He returned to the kitchen and found Franklin and Haskins eating the fare Cook had set out.

Franklin spied Barton and pushed another plate forward. "I doubt any of us will be sleeping. But we will need our energy."

Barton sat but did not touch the food. "I haven't an appetite."

Franklin pushed his empty plate aside. "Then start talking."

"Where's Clarke?" Barton asked.

"Here." The butler stepped out of a room located just off the hallway.

"Have the authorities been notified?" Barton asked.

"I made the recommendation to Miss Stafford, but she refused to contradict Mr. Stafford's demands. She asked that I only send the express to you." Clarke looked over the three men at the table. "I'm sorry to say on this I agree with her. I've witnessed Mr. Stafford's temper."

Barton motioned to a place on the bench next to him. Clarke hesitated for only a moment before he sat down. "What else can you tell us about Mr. Cline Stafford?" Barton asked.

Clarke quickly updated Barton on Mr. Stafford's impropriety and filled in multiple things Elizabeth had left out. The men decided to confront Simpkin, as he still possessed the jewels Stafford demanded in exchange for Thomas. Barton, Franklin, and Haskins rode to Simpkin's home, while Clarke remained at Downey Place.

Barton planned to offer Simpkin money in exchange for Elizabeth's sapphires, but if negotiation did not work, he was prepared to take them with physical force.

Simpkin did not receive them warmly, but after explaining their plight, Barton's visit with Simpkin proved invaluable. Simpkin may have not cared for money, but it turned out he despised being double-crossed. He eagerly volunteered his knowledge and assistance, explaining that upon his return to Tolford he'd begun looking into Mr. Stafford's affairs.

Simpkin's associates extended from the aristocracy to a slew of unsavory acquaintances. His inquiries had uncovered a connection between Stafford and the death of Elizabeth's father. Simpkin also elaborated on Stafford's mounting debts, his gambling vice, and a host of other crimes. The man revealed all, including the fact that in addition to negotiating a prime parcel of Downey Place as Elizabeth's dowry, Simpkin had actually paid Stafford an exorbitant amount of money for the land, in essence buying it at an inflated price and paying for Elizabeth to be his bride. And while Stafford had signed the marriage contract and taken Simpkin's money, he had never deeded the land, forcing Simpkin to keep the sapphires as collateral. Simpkin revealed that Miss Stafford had written to him, explaining her dire need for the gemstones and pleading that he return them to her.

The man welcomed the opportunity to confront Stafford, and prior to Barton's arrival Simpkin had planned to do so himself. His confidence that he could blackmail Stafford and discover Thomas's whereabouts worried Barton. Stafford was desperate and unpredictable, but confronting him now was likely the only opportunity they would have to retrieve the boy. While Barton wanted to be by Elizabeth's side, it made more sense for Simpkin to meet Stafford while the other three men searched for Thomas. The men talked late into the night, and an hour before sunrise, they finally agreed upon a plan.

Chapter 42

WHEN MARLOW SHOOK LIZZY'S SHOULDER, Lizzy shrugged her away and turned in to her covers.

"Come, miss. Mr. Clarke said I must wake you. Dawn is approaching." Marlow lit the candle near Lizzy's bed.

Dawn. The single word shattered Lizzy's peaceful rest. Why couldn't she disappear into her dreams and remain there forever? She knew the answer, of course—Thomas. She raised herself in her bed, recalling the relief that filled her when Barton had lifted her into his arms and carried her to her room.

"Did our guests get settled?" Lizzy asked. She hadn't hesitated to send the express to Everly Manor, even while she knew Barton's presence did not change the course of what she must do. She'd known they would come, that he would come, and the arrival of the three men provided a fraction of peace. Lizzy was not foolish enough to believe that once she met Uncle in the woods she would return to Downey Place. She only hoped Thomas could. Perhaps she had summoned Barton for that purpose, in the hope that she might once again ask Barton to look after him. She knew Thomas would be taken care of; Barton would make sure of it. She also knew she had asked Barton to come for one selfish reason. She needed him. She needed to see him one last time, to know he did not hate her. With that assurance, she could face her dawning fate.

Marlow made her way around the room, lighting every candle. "I heard the gentlemen were up all night. But I haven't seen them this morning, so they must be sleeping now."

Lizzy slid from the bed and moved to a chair, where Marlow began to run a comb through her hair. Once Lizzy had received Uncle's letter, she knew she would enter the forest alone. She only hoped . . . Lizzy shook her head. Her hopes had ceased to matter the moment her parents died.

Marlow quickly worked her fingers through Lizzy's hair, plaiting and pinning it up. "Has anyone else arrived?" Lizzy asked.

Marlow's fingers slowed. "Were you expecting someone else?"

"Never mind." Lizzy watched Marlow insert the final pin and thought of the second express she had sent. It didn't have to go far, as the recipient was Mr. Rudyard Simpkin. She needed the jewels, and he had them. She knew Clarke would protest, so she'd sent the letter on her own, asking a stableboy to deliver it and paying him an absurd amount to keep quiet. If she could precisely follow Uncle's demands, maybe she could bring Thomas home and normalcy would return. If she did not have the gemstones, her only hope was to try to persuade Uncle some other way.

Marlow lifted Lizzy's plain grey day dress over her head and adjusted the buttons. Lizzy pulled on her gloves and slipped her arms into her pelisse.

Marlow stood back, shifting her weight between her feet. "Are you sure you should go, miss?"

"I don't have a choice," Lizzy said quietly.

"Oh!" Marlow ran to Lizzy and wrapped her arms around her shoulders. She sniffled near Lizzy's ear before she pulled away and wiped the tears from her eyes. "Be careful, miss. He's a terrible man."

Cold dread filled the hollow place in Lizzy's heart. "I know, Marlow. Pray for Thomas."

"I'll pray for both of you, miss."

Lizzy picked up a nearby candle and walked into the darkened hallway. Shadows flickered off the wall, dancing and teasing, mocking the uncertainty echoing through Lizzy's mind.

Clarke stood at the bottom of the staircase. A portable lantern glowed near his feet. He lifted it as Lizzy neared. "I think you can manage this one." He traded the lantern for the candle in her hand. "The lamps throughout the gardens have also been lit. I shall remain near the house, as you've requested, but if you shout, I will come."

"Thank you, Clarke." Lizzy placed her hand on his arm. "You've been an anchor through this storm."

Clarke nodded and covered Lizzy's hand with his own. "Hurry back."

Lizzy followed Clarke to the back door and stepped into the chilly morning. The cold air burned her lungs, and Lizzy welcomed the pain of the elements, hoping they would mask the pains of her heart. She held the lantern aloft, looking for any sign of life, and was rewarded with only a collection of dewdrops on the tips of the leaves in the hedge.

"Are you sure about this, Miss Stafford?" Clarke asked from beside her.

"Not at all." Lizzy thought about Thomas, alone and afraid. "But I have to try."

Clarke looked east. "The sun is coming."

Lizzy blew out a puff of frosty air and turned towards the forest.

Chapter 43

BARTON HATED THAT SIMPKIN WOULD be the one to accompany Elizabeth; he wanted to be there himself to guarantee her safety. But the others agreed Simpkin was the logical choice, as his possession of the sapphires granted an excuse for his appearance. Simpkin separated from the other three men, who each concealed themselves and maintained a vantage point of the woods. They hoped to spy Stafford and gain some clue as to Thomas's location.

Haskins and Franklin were both positioned within view of Downey Place. Haskins kept watch on the north, and Franklin concealed himself behind a felled tree, where he had a view of both the house and the entrance from the main road. Barton opted for the more remote vantage point, assuming this to be Stafford's most likely path. A small trail had been cut from the main road into the woods for the purpose of clearing trees. Bushes grew into the pathway, but it was not so overgrown that a horse could not negotiate the terrain. Barton left Starfly at the Downey Place stables and hid himself behind the thick trunk of a yew. He could see movement from the road and also monitor the trail.

Barton's heart pumped steady and loud. He took slow, even breaths to calm himself and clear his mind. He could not vanquish the unease pulsing through him.

The minutes before sunrise passed long and cold, yet Barton's fatigue proved no match for his anxiety and determination. As the sky turned from black to inky grey, a whistle sounded from a rider passing on the main road. Barton's heart ricocheted faster as he acknowledged Simpkin's signal. Stafford had yet to appear.

Barton wondered if he should scout farther back along the main road and had made up his mind to do so when he heard hoofbeats. He peered through the dull morning light to see a small open wagon pulled by a single horse. Another horse was tied behind the wagon. The vehicle stopped, and Stafford jumped down.

"Don't be late, or they won't pay," Stafford said.

"The sooner the better, in my opinion. I'm ready to be done with the scamp," a female answered.

"Stick to the plan. The constable granted my freedom only until the magistrate arrives for the trial. We get the money, and we get out of here." Stafford untied the horse from the back of the wagon. He led the animal down the trail, only feet from Barton's perch.

Barton's head swiveled from side to side as he tried to keep track of both the wagon and Stafford. Stafford tied his horse twenty yards down the trail then continued on foot. Meanwhile, the woman snapped the reins across the horse's back, and the wagon lurched into motion. While Barton's heart pulled one way, his mind pulled the other. Indecision coiled in his gut, building as the wagon wheels picked up speed and rolled farther and farther away. Stafford was in the woods, waiting for Elizabeth to appear. And while Barton wanted to go and ensure her safety, he could not. The conversation he'd just overheard had referenced Thomas, and Barton knew his best chance of finding the boy had just driven away.

He grunted in frustration and snapped into action. "Hey there," Barton softly whispered as he approached the horse Stafford had left on the trail. He gently stroked the animal's neck while purposely breathing into its face. "Shall we go for a ride?"

Barton glanced again down the trail. Sunlight began to push against the milky darkness, and the shadows of the trees played havoc with illusions of movement and motion. He shook his head clear and led the horse back towards the main road.

He mounted the chestnut mare and then turned as a flock of birds scattered upwards into the sky. The air stilled through the trees. Barton's desire to go to Elizabeth weighed heavily in his chest, but he had to follow the lead to Thomas. That is what Elizabeth would want him to do. Barton would have to trust Elizabeth's safety to Franklin, Haskins, and unfortunately, Simpkin.

Barton clenched his jaw and moved the horse into a quick trot. The feeble mare was far from the finest horse Barton had ridden, but the nag obeyed Barton's commands. Within fifteen minutes the wagon came into view. Barton could see the bonnet of the woman at the reins, but she took no notice of him.

He followed at a distance for another minute before he moved in for closer inspection. A pile of blankets and a crate of supplies filled the bed of the wagon. The woman looked over her shoulder. Sections of red hair fell around her face, and Barton offered a friendly wave, indicating his desire to pass.

The woman's features pulled tight, but she turned her eyes forward and guided the wagon to the left side of the road. Barton had moved alongside the cart when something shifted in his peripheral vision. His heart jumped—could it be? Barton glanced into the wagon bed, and one of the blankets fell away, revealing Thomas's large blue eyes and the gag tied around his mouth. Barton raised a finger to his lips, and the boy nodded.

The woman looked back to see if he was passing. She looked from Barton to the horse he rode, and recognition filled her face. Barton kicked the horse into a canter, the staccato beat of his heart outpacing the hoofbeats of the horse. He passed the black horse pulling the wagon then turned suddenly, startling the animal. The black horse skittered to the side, jerking the reins from the woman's hands.

She shrieked and reached for the reins as Barton jumped off the mare. Fury propelled him forward, and the woman's eyes widened at his approach. She abandoned her search for the reins and scrambled to the far right side of the bench, where a wooden box was wedged under the seat.

The woman pulled the box free and reached for the clasp. Barton leapt over the wagon shaft and snatched the box away. "I'll take that." Barton tucked the small box against his side.

"Give it back!" the woman demanded. She pushed her skirts aside and jumped off the wagon. She tried to grab the box, but Barton stepped back and turned away from her. With a grunt the woman attempted again to reach around Barton.

He tsked and shifted away. "I don't believe I've had the pleasure, ma'am." Barton gave a mocking half-bow. "Harrison Barton Everly."

The woman stopped cold. She straightened her shoulders and glanced quickly at the wagon before returning her gaze to Barton.

"And you are?" Barton asked.

"No one you need concern yourself with," the woman said curtly.

"Ah, Miss Masterson, is it?" Barton recalled hearing the name from Simpkin. The woman's pinched lips told Barton he'd guessed right. Miss

Masterson took another swipe for the box. "Come now. Whatever Stafford's grudges may be, the boy hardly deserves to be traded away like a sack of flour."

Miss Masterson huffed and planted her hands on her hips.

"I suggest a trade of our own. Your box in exchange for young Mr. Stafford." Barton extended the box towards Miss Masterson.

She snatched it from his hands and fumbled with the latch. The box fell to the ground, and she pulled out a small gun. With shaky hands she pointed it at Barton.

Barton raised his hands. "Come now, Miss Masterson, shooting me won't solve your problems."

With her free hand, Miss Masterson tore off her bonnet. "You know nothing about it."

Barton took a step forward. "Stafford will be going to trial for fraud, kidnapping, and being an accessory to murder." In the blink of an eye, Miss Masterson's harsh façade slipped, and Barton took another step forward. "You can decide if you want to testify against him or hang beside him." Barton slowly extended his hand. "Hand me the gun, Miss Masterson."

"I . . ."

"Simply hand it over. I give you my word I will tell the magistrate of your willingness to cooperate." Barton reached Miss Masterson in the next step. He reached forward and began to peel her fingers from the gun. She finally released her hold, and Barton breathed his relief as another rider approached.

Haskins pulled in his mount, his chest heaving. He glanced at the wagon and then at Barton standing with Miss Masterson. "You found him!"

"Miss Masterson and I were just concluding our negotiations." Barton handed the gun up to Haskins.

Miss Masterson raised a hand to her head. "He's going to kill me." She leaned against the side of the wagon and closed her eyes.

Barton jerked his head. "You might want to have her sit down." Haskins dismounted, and Barton quickly moved around the wagon.

Thomas smiled around the gag in his mouth. Barton jumped into the wagon bed and removed first the gag then the restraints from his wrists and ankles.

Thomas began talking at once. "Wait until I tell Lizzy about this adventure!"

Barton shook his head and allowed a smile. "She's very concerned about you." Barton examined Thomas's arms, legs, and face. "Are you hurt?"

"I'm hungry." Thomas absentmindedly rubbed his ankles where he'd been bound. "And my head hurts. Uncle talked an awful lot. He said Lizzy would pay for taking Downey Place from him, but I knew she'd be safe." Barton sobered, and Thomas's smile fell. "She is safe, isn't she, Mr. Barton?" Thomas asked. "He can't hurt her like he wanted?"

Thomas said it so matter-of-factly, and Barton wished he could answer affirmatively, that he could mask his trepidation. "I came for you. Franklin and Mr. Simpkin are helping your sister."

"Mr. Simpkin! Where is she?" Thomas demanded.

Haskins walked into view. "That one's a bit feisty." He motioned towards Miss Masterson.

"Where is Lizzy?" Thomas shouted louder.

Haskins glanced at Barton. "I'm not sure," Haskins said. "Once she followed Simpkin into the forest, Franklin and I decided one of us should see if you'd discovered anything. You weren't at the trail, and I saw the fresh hoofprints." Haskins shrugged. "I followed my hunch and, well . . ." he motioned to Thomas sitting in the wagon.

Thomas turned to Barton. "We have to go help her! Uncle will hurt her!" The boy scrambled to his feet and grabbed Barton's hand. "Come on, Mr. Barton. Lizzy needs you."

"Take my horse. I'll wait until Miss Masterson settles, and then we'll bring the wagon," Haskins said.

Thomas scurried to the ground and stumbled. He caught himself and then ran to Haskins's horse.

Barton's feelings matched the boy's. He needed Elizabeth to be safe. He quickly followed Thomas and lifted him away from Haskins's horse. "That one's mine." Barton set Thomas in the saddle of the old mare. "Make her mind you. The stirrups won't fit, so do the best you can."

With a nod of determination, Thomas kicked the horse and pulled on the reins to turn the mare's head down the road. Barton swatted the animal's backside, and she moved into a quick trot. He mounted Haskins's horse and kicked him forward.

Barton's gut twisted into a jumbled knot. Elizabeth had to be safe. Simpkin and Franklin would protect her. They'd all discussed the plan, agreed it was the best course of action. Simpkin would lure Stafford away from Elizabeth, Barton would secure her safety, and the others would find Thomas. Only, Barton had followed his hunch, tailed the wagon, and left Elizabeth alone.

He had to trust Simpkin would uphold his part of the agreement, that Franklin would ensure Elizabeth's safety, and that his own decision to follow the wagon would not jeopardize her. Because Barton needed Elizabeth. He needed her well and whole. And once she stood tucked close beside him, he had no intention of allowing her to leave him again.

It didn't take long for the two horses to cover the distance back. They neared the small forest trail where Barton had concealed himself only an hour before. Tension, uncertainty, and worry pulled tight through Barton's chest. Thomas rode beside him, his features drawn tight with determination as he prodded his horse forward. A gunshot sounded through the trees, startling the old mare. Thomas jerked the reins hard, stopping the nag completely.

"Lizzy!" Thomas cried out. "Go, Mr. Barton. Go save her!"

Barton turned from the woods to look at Thomas; then he looked back to the trees.

"Please," Thomas said softly, tears running down his face. "You saved her before. You must do it again."

Barton's horse skittered beneath him. He turned back to Thomas. "Ride directly to the house. Tell Clarke what has happened, and then wait inside. I am going to get your sister and bring her home." Barton kicked his horse hard and ducked into the trees.

Chapter 44

THE TEMPERATURE DROPPED FURTHER WITH every step. Lizzy's thoughts centered on putting one foot in front of the other. She let the cold seep in, let it carry her to her fate. As she neared the forest, a rider approached. Had Barton come? Her heart leapt until she recognized Mr. Simpkin astride the horse. The tiny spark of hope she'd harbored instantly smothered.

"Miss Stafford." Mr. Simpkin's voice scratched abrasively, like scrubbing the contents from a burned pot. "You sent for me."

"You must have misread my letter, sir. I sent for my sapphires." Lizzy's fingers tingled. The lantern hung heavy in her hand.

Simpkin dismounted. "You mean these?" He pulled the velvet wrapping from his greatcoat.

"Do you intend to give them to me?" Lizzy asked.

"I mean to finish my transaction with your uncle." Simpkin crudely tossed the reins of his horse around a branch and stepped into the forest.

Lizzy scurried after him. "You must go back." She held the lantern in one hand and her skirt in the other. Light began to touch the sky, but the farther they wandered into the woods, the darker the shadows became. "Please, Mr. Simpkin," Lizzy pleaded. "You cannot be here."

The only reply she received was a grunt. Mr. Simpkin moved rather quickly, despite his rotund frame. "Sir!" Lizzy cried out. "Uncle has Thomas. He insisted I come alone."

Simpkin continued forward. "Is it this way?" he asked.

Lizzy's frantic heart thrummed quickly. She couldn't keep up with Mr. Simpkin, and finally she stopped and evaluated her surroundings. Mr. Simpkin had started out towards the clearing, but his course had veered too far north. Lizzy watched him disappear into the trees, and then she changed direction.

The bird chatter increased as the sky lightened. Lizzy's frozen fingers held the lantern high, but now she hardly noticed the cold for the fear flowing through her. She stepped into the open space to find the clearing empty. The embers that previously glowed warm now lay scattered and lifeless.

Lizzy lifted her eyes from the ground to the sky. Night began to fade high above, but the trees remained skirted in shadows and secret hopes. She heard movement to her left and spun around. "Hello?" she called. Her voice tremored, mirroring the rest of her body. "Uncle?"

"I thought I told you to come alone." Uncle's voice sounded from farther left, and Lizzy turned again.

The lantern swung in her hand, and anxiety pulsed through her, heavy like the darkness. "I did. I mean, I tried. But I didn't have the jewels. Mr. Simpkin has them. I asked him to return them, and instead of giving them to me, he came into the woods." A loud crack sounded, like a branch snapping in two. Lizzy startled and turned again. "Please, Uncle, let Thomas go."

"Shut up!" Uncle Cline hissed.

Lizzy pressed her lips together.

"Where is Simpkin now?" Uncle's voice moved again.

Lizzy shook her head, unsure if she should answer. Uncle stepped from the trees on her left and grabbed her shoulder. He pulled her close and pressed his mouth to her ear. "Where is he?"

"I don't know," Lizzy whispered. "He went the wrong way, so I left him and came here."

"Stupid girl!" Uncle spat. He yanked the lantern from her hand and extinguished the flame before setting it in the pile of cold ashes.

"Wh-wh-where's Thomas?" Lizzy asked.

"I told you to shut up," Uncle hissed. His fingers clamped around Lizzy's upper arm, and she muffled her cry the best she could. Uncle walked backward, pulling Lizzy along with him.

"Stafford!" Mr. Simpkin's voice echoed among the shadows. "Show yourself!"

Uncle continued his retreat with Lizzy. Lizzy heard footfalls draw close, and Uncle began to move with more urgency.

"Stafford!" Mr. Simpkin called again and Lizzy saw a flash of movement among the trees.

"Here!" Lizzy called before she registered what she had done.

"Shut up!" Uncle twisted Lizzy's arm, turning her towards him.

Her shoulder pinched in pain, and she whimpered in protest. Uncle released his hold, and his hand flew across her cheek, knocking her to the ground.

"Enough!" Mr. Simpkin said as he stepped into view.

Uncle Cline's lips pushed into a hard line, but he remained quiet. Lizzy raised her free hand to her cheek and tried to blink away the stinging pain.

"We had a deal, Stafford. I've kept my end of the bargain." Mr. Simpkin pulled the sapphires from his coat pocket and tossed them to the dirt at Uncle's feet.

Uncle reached down and clamped Lizzy's arm again. He yanked her to her feet and then pushed her forward in offering. "Here's the trollop. I was bringing her to you like I promised."

"Your promises don't hold much weight anymore. But you're right—the girl belongs to me." Mr. Simpkin grinned, and his voice deepened. "Come, then, Miss Stafford." With a jerk of his head Mr. Simpkin indicated Lizzy should move behind him.

Uncle's fingers tightened around Lizzy's arm, and she could not step away even if she had wanted to. A low growl sounded in Uncle's throat, and he tensed beside her.

Mr. Simpkin pulled a pistol from his belt and took another step forward. He did not point the weapon at anything in particular; instead it sat comfortably in his hand.

The two men exchanged weighted glares. Uncle glanced down at the sapphires then to Mr. Simpkin's gun. Mr. Simpkin extended his empty hand towards Lizzy and motioned for her to take it. Sounds of an animal scurrying nearby sliced through the deafening silence, echoing like the crackle of thunder. Lizzy tried to focus, to concentrate on a single breath, to push past the fear and exhaustion. To think of Thomas. She looked warily at Mr. Simpkin's proffered help, considering which option would lead her to her brother. She leaned forward the tiniest bit to test Uncle's hold. His grip remained firm.

Mr. Simpkin spat in the dirt. "See, Stafford? She wants nothing to do with me." Lizzy looked at her arm then her uncle. The choice was out of her control, and really, what sort of choice was it anyway?

"Since when does it matter what the chit wants?" Uncle spat again. He suddenly shoved Lizzy forward. The shock of the movement stole her breath as she tumbled into the dirt at Mr. Simpkin's feet. Pain shot through her ribs, and the palms of her hands burned where they hit the ground to stop her fall. "She's yours. You were supposed to make certain she disappeared. This time make sure it happens."

Mr. Simpkin stepped slowly, moving between Lizzy and her uncle, as if he meant to protect her. "Just like her parents? Or her brother, when you sent him to sea?" She shook her head, trying to clear it so she could grasp what the men were saying.

"All you had to do was shut her up." Uncle's voice dropped. "What are you playing at, Simpkin? You knew the plan."

Mr. Simpkin chuckled mirthlessly. "Not all of it, it seems." He pulled back the hammer on his pistol, the metallic cock ricocheted through Lizzy's head. She remained seated in the dirt, her mind spinning with Mr. Simpkin's raw revelations. Mr. Simpkin continued, "When Everly exposed you, I did a little digging. I always thought it curious you approached me before your brother died. Does the name Hayman sound familiar?"

Lizzy dared look at her uncle. His face drained of color, and she tried to comprehend what it all meant. Simpkin turned and offered her his hand again. This time Lizzy placed her shaky fingers in his and stood. When her feet were steady, she pulled her hand free.

Simpkin spared her no attention. Rather, he confronted her uncle again. "You hired Hayman to kill your brother."

Lizzy's senses spiked as she digested Mr. Simpkin's words. She stumbled to the nearest tree and leaned against it for support. Every breath became a chore, and Lizzy felt certain her lungs would implode. She pressed her hands into her stomach, willing it to feel something other than emptiness and despair.

"You may have gotten away with murder and forging the will, but I paid a lot of money. I want my bride and my land," Mr. Simpkin said.

Mr. Simpkin's accusations choked every sensibility. Lizzy leaned over and retched. It had been so long since she had eaten that she vomited only bile, but her ribs burned with each heave of her stomach. After a long minute, her stomach surrendered. She closed her eyes against the pain and sucked in the clean, cool air.

When she opened her eyes once more, Uncle Cline raised a shaky finger and pointed at her. "Take her."

Mr. Simpkin clicked his tongue. "Oh, I plan to, but that was only half of our deal. If you can't provide the land, then I demand you return my money."

"I . . . I don't have it." A flash of shame crossed Uncle's face, but it disappeared so quickly Lizzy wondered if she'd seen it at all.

"Where is it?" Mr. Simpkin's voice remained eerily calm.

"Gone." Uncle's jaw tightened, and his eyes darkened.

"That's a shame," Mr. Simpkin said, pointing his weapon towards Uncle. "I understand Hayman is very good at what he does."

"Take the sapphires in trade." Stafford kicked his foot at the bundle, but the velvet-wrapped gems moved only inches.

"I don't believe they're yours to bargain with." Mr. Simpkin called over his shoulder, "Miss Stafford, would you please come retrieve your jewels?"

Lizzy's breaths slowed, though her stomach still churned. She stepped away from the tree and willed her shaky legs forward. Her eyes darted between the two men, and she stalled for a moment before she bent down to collect the sapphires. Lizzy crouched down, her shaky fingers brushing over the surface of the blue-velvet wrappings before picking up the gemstones.

A barbaric yell sliced through the morning air, and Lizzy suddenly flew backwards as Uncle barreled into her, his momentum knocking Lizzy into Mr. Simpkin's legs. The gun Mr. Simpkin held was hurtled into the dirt; the man's girth could not match Uncle's stature, and a melee of arms and legs flashed across Lizzy's vision. Grunts, curses, and the sound of crunching flesh rang in her ears. Lizzy tried to push away, to unravel herself from the fracas, but her body was too weak for her efforts to have any effect.

Suddenly the men rolled away from her, and Lizzy realized her legs were unimpeded. She yanked at her twisted skirt, anxious to right herself and flee from the woods. She ignored the torn, stained fabric and scrambled to her feet. Her hair had been pulled free, and her hands now bled in several places, but Lizzy thought only on getting away.

Before she took her first step, a gunshot shattered the air. Her entire body jolted with the sound, and she looked back to see her uncle standing with a smug grin over Mr. Simpkin's unmoving body.

Lizzy's thoughts became lucid. *Run.* She willed her body to move. A loud curse sounded behind her, and her head whipped back as Uncle yanked her hair and tossed her again to the ground. He moved near, slowly, methodically. Savage revenge framed his darkened eyes. Lizzy felt Uncle's hatred cover her as thoroughly as his shadow. He fiddled with the trigger of the gun at his side, and Lizzy knew he intended to be rid of her once and for all.

"Get away from her!" Barton shouted as he rushed into the clearing. He lowered his shoulder and aimed for Uncle's chest.

Lizzy knew she needed to shout, to send Barton a warning about the gun, but when she opened her mouth, nothing came out. A second shot echoed through the forest. Barton's rescue halted. Blood saturated his left shoulder.

His eyes found Lizzy's. "I'm sorry," he said before his knees buckled and he collapsed to the ground.

Lizzy screamed Barton's name and tried to push past Uncle to reach his side, but Uncle blocked her. His fingers wrapped around her arm, and he pulled her face close to his own. His rancid breath blew across her check. "You will regret crossing me, Elizabeth," he hissed in her ear. He raised the gun, and Lizzy froze. Uncle fiddled with the trigger, cursed, and then tossed the weapon to the dirt. "I don't need bullets to finish you off."

Lizzy tried to shake free, but Uncle's hold did not yield. She looked back at Barton's prostrate form. Emotion swelled within her. Uncle had stripped away everything good in her life. First he'd killed her parents. Then he'd suffocated all joy from her home. He'd kidnapped Thomas. Shot Barton. Anger replaced her fear, pulsing in her bones and extremities like an army answering the call to battle. With the marching cadence, her energy surged. Lizzy twisted her shoulders, pulling Uncle's stance off balance, and with a turn of her hips, she thrust her knee into his groin.

Uncle's hold gave way. He grunted and doubled over, cursing again. "I warned you, girl!" he shouted.

Lizzy grabbed a branch near her feet and held it ready to strike. When Uncle straightened to his full height she began to slowly step backwards, placing distance between herself and the crazed look in the man's eyes. "Stay away from me!" Lizzy shouted.

Uncle's upper lip curled, and he laughed manically. Lizzy swung the branch, and he laughed again. He clenched his fists and began walking towards Lizzy.

"Stafford!" Barton had turned and now faced Lizzy. The sight of his blood-soaked garments turned Lizzy's stomach. "Let her be!" he yelled.

Uncle evaluated Barton then turned his attention back to Lizzy. He bent over and retrieved a branch of his own. He clasped both hands around the base of the branch, positioned it over his right shoulder, and charged Lizzy.

"Elizabeth!" Barton shouted.

The deafening crack of a rifle echoed through the surrounding trees, and Uncle's body arched backwards. The stick was thrown from his hand, and Uncle Cline landed flat on his back.

Lizzy's arms and legs felt like leaden weights. The stick she held fell to her side. Every breath required so much effort.

Clarke moved past her to Uncle Cline's body. He set his rifle aside and knelt and searched for a pulse. Clarke shook his head and then turned towards her. "Are you hurt, Miss Stafford?"

"No. But—" Cognizance returned at once. Lizzy lifted her skirts and ran to Barton's side. "Barton!"

She held her hands over his form, moving as if to touch him then hesitating before ever making contact. "Thomas is safe," Barton rasped before wincing in pain.

"Really?" Lizzy asked.

Clarke answered. "'Tis true. Mr. Franklin is tending him at the estate."

Emotion swelled through Lizzy's chest. Thomas was safe. Mr. Simpkin's words sounded again in her mind. Uncle's intention had been to kill them all. And he would have succeeded if Barton had not arrived. Barton had saved her life again.

Lizzy ran her hand down Barton's cheek. "Stay with me, Barton."

"Stafford's dead. So is Simpkin," Clarke said as he returned to her side. "We must get him to the house." Clarke bent forward and lifted Barton into his arms. Barton's entire body fell limp, and his head lolled to the side.

"Barton!" Lizzy jumped to her feet. "Don't you dare leave me now," she whispered and let her tears fall freely.

Chapter 45

Pain. So much pain. Barton wanted to tear his arm from his torso and rid himself of the piercing agony raging down the left side of his body. Memories, cognizance, slowly returned. Thomas, Cline Stafford, Elizabeth . . .

Barton forced his eyes open and tried to speak, but the words only tumbled through his mind. Then black spots dotted his vision, and he returned to the land of dreams.

"Will Mr. Barton be all right?" Thomas asked Lizzy. They sat in the drawing room on the cream sofa opposite the fireplace. Mr. Haskins stood near the window, and Mr. Franklin paced in front of the mantel.

Lizzy squeezed Thomas's hand. The question was a difficult one, and the possible answers swam through Lizzy's mind. Some she knew were wishes, others nightmares.

"I knew he would save you, Lizzy. I knew it! I told him to save you, and he did," Thomas said.

Lizzy's heart swelled again with gratitude for the sacrifice Barton had made for her. She looked Thomas in the eye. "With all my heart I pray for his recovery, but the truth is—I don't know."

Clarke appeared in the doorway and cleared his throat. "Doctor Goule," he announced.

Dread-laden anticipation filled the room. Doctor Goule reported that the bullet had struck just beneath Barton's left shoulder. It had cleanly entered and exited, but a portion of muscle was shredded and part of the bone was shattered. However, Doctor Goule believed that if Barton allowed for a slow recovery, ample rest, and limited use of his arm, he would be able to heal and recover the majority of his mobility.

"Thank you, Doctor." Mr. Franklin shook the man's hand.

"Cook has prepared something for you to eat," Clarke said from his position near the doorway.

"Very well," the doctor said, following Clarke from the room.

Lizzy stood. "I must see him." She rang the bell and then looked at the gentlemen. "Please ask Marlow to look after Thomas." Mr. Haskins and Mr. Franklin exchanged a look, but neither attempted to keep Lizzy from leaving.

When she reached Barton's sickroom, Mrs. Hull tried to dissuade her from remaining, but Lizzy would not be fazed. "Very well. But you mustn't wake him," the housekeeper said.

Lizzy sat quietly in a chair near the couch that served as a makeshift bed. She watched the rise and fall of Barton's chest for a full ten minutes before Mrs. Hull excused herself to gather more mending.

Lizzy owed so much to this man. He'd saved her brother, and he'd saved her. Lizzy studied Barton's features, his solid jaw and smooth skin, his wavy sun-kissed hair that continually fell into his eyes. She loved him completely.

Lizzy leaned over and brushed his hair back, as she'd wanted to do so many times before. Then she lifted his right hand and caressed the back of it. As she did so, she noticed Barton's lips turn up in a grin.

"Barton?" she whispered softly.

His light lashes fluttered a few times before he opened his eyes completely.

A smile split Lizzy's face. "You're awake."

"Or I'm in heaven," Barton said.

Warmth pulsed in Lizzy's cheeks. "Does it hurt so very badly?"

"No, my darling," Barton said, and he squeezed her fingers. But then he moved to push himself upright, and he winced with the pain.

Lizzy tsked. "No more lies, remember? You've been shot. There is no need to continue playing hero." Lizzy filled a glass and held it to Barton's lips. "There was so much blood," she said.

She returned the glass to the table, and Barton spoke again. "I didn't see the gun." Lizzy turned around to look at him. Barton reached across his body and touched the bandage around his shoulder. "But I would do it all again." Barton planted his right elbow into the couch and pushed himself up.

"What are you doing?" Lizzy extended her hands, waving them over Barton's body as if to force him back down, but she did not touch him. "You must lie back down."

Barton sat up. The sheet fell away from his torso, revealing his bare chest. Lizzy's eyes shot wide as she stared at the exposed skin. Slowly her eyes wandered to the bandage on his shoulder and then to his face. A blush heated her cheeks.

"You saved Thomas," Lizzy said.

"Yes," he murmured. Barton extended his right hand, and Lizzy placed her hand in his. Barton pulled her forward and pressed a kiss to each of Lizzy's knuckles. "Elizabeth. I need you to understand something. I will take a bullet for you. I will always come for you. I will be your protector and your defender, always . . . because I love you. With all of my heart."

Lizzy moved her free hand over her heart. "You love me?" Her pulse thrummed through her entire body, her heart yearning to give Barton her gratitude, to tell him how she needed him, how her feelings mirrored his. His touch was soft and delicate. How could such a gentle touch elicit such fervent ardor?

Barton gave her arm a gentle tug, pulling her near so she sat beside him on the sofa. The space between them felt complex and yet simple. "You've captured my heart, my dearest Elizabeth, from the moment I laid eyes on you. Through your misfortune you have shone brave and bright."

Lizzy shook her head. "No . . . you are mistaken. I've been secretive and kept the truth from you. I don't think things through . . ."

Barton released Lizzy's hand and trailed his fingers down her cheek. She leaned in to his touch. "I love your impulsiveness. Except when it lands you under a tree." Barton winked. Then his countenance sobered. "When I asked you stay at Everly Manor, I didn't give you a reason. I mean to correct that mistake now. I love you, Elizabeth Stafford."

"But I do not deserve you." Elizabeth could not believe her fortune.

"No, my dearest, it is I who do not deserve you. I love you with all my heart. The choice is yours: Downey Place, Everly Manor, or wherever you decide. If you'll have me, I promise to stay by your side for a very long time." Barton pulled Lizzy close and kissed her. She savored the perfection of his lips, the warmth of his breath mixed with her own.

Breathless, Lizzy pulled away. "I love you, Harrison Barton Everly. You are my refuge, and I want only to be with you."

Franklin coughed loudly from the doorway. Barton turned and scowled at his brother.

"Franklin, go away." Barton looked back at Lizzy. "Better yet, would you please write mother and tell her we've a wedding to plan?"

"Tell her yourself," Franklin said with a grin.

"Where is Harrison?"

"He's sleeping, Mother."

"I have traveled all this way to confirm for myself that he is whole. I must see him."

"I promise he is well. Allow him to sleep for a few minutes more."

"Step aside, Franklin. I intend to see my son."

A moment passed before the door creaked open and Barton's mother stepped into the room. She pointed her nose to the rafters, and Barton couldn't help but smile at her poised authority. Thankfully Elizabeth had returned to her seat near the sofa and Clarke had assisted Barton in donning a loose linen shirt.

His mother scoffed. "Sleeping. Ha."

Franklin gave an unrepentant shrug.

"Hello, Mother," Barton said.

Her features softened as she looked him over. "My dear boy." She fell to her knees beside Barton's sickbed and touched a hand to his cheek.

Barton raised his hand and covered his mother's. "All is well."

Barton's mother waved away his comment and turned back to Franklin. "Obviously Harrison is—" She glanced at her son. Barton's grin lit his entire face.

Franklin finished the sentence. "In good spirits."

"Indeed I am," Barton said.

"Mr. Barton! I knew you'd get better." Thomas bounded into the room, holding something behind his back. Haskins and Bethany followed behind him.

"Did you now?" Barton asked Thomas.

"Oh, Barton!" Bethany held a hand to her chest.

Barton reached for Bethany's hand. "Hello, dear sister." When she placed her fingers in his, Barton gave them a gentle squeeze. "Please do not fret. Mother has that covered."

The matron tsked, and Barton chuckled. "Thomas. What do you have there?" Barton asked.

"Mr. Clarke told me to give these to Lizzy. He said he found them in the forest." Thomas handed Elizabeth what appeared to be a swath of white muslin.

Elizabeth unwrapped the fabric to reveal her mother's sapphires. Her eyes lit with joy.

"Mr. Clarke said the clasp got broken," Thomas said.

"'Tis all right, Thomas—" Elizabeth began.

Thomas cut her off. "But, Lizzy, you said I would know what to spend the treasure on. I know now." Thomas reached into his pocket and pulled out a folded square of paper. He opened it to reveal a handful of coins. "You can fix mother's necklace with our secret treasure."

Elizabeth laughed and raised a hand to her mouth. She set the jewels in her lap and pulled Thomas into a hug. "Thank you, Thomas."

"What became of Miss Masterson?" Barton asked.

"Once Thomas arrived and explained what had happened, Clarke headed into the forest, and I met Haskins and Miss Masterson," Franklin said.

"She was certainly a spirited woman," Haskins said, pulling at his cravat.

"Indeed," Franklin agreed. "She continued her protest even as she was escorted off the property by the constable."

"She talked a lot," Thomas said.

Elizabeth kissed his brow. "I'm sorry you had to endure all of this."

Thomas wriggled free of Elizabeth's hold. "It wasn't so bad. We had an adventure, Lizzy, with a real-life hero. But I'm sorry you got shot, Mr. Barton. I wish that part didn't happen."

Barton chuckled. "You're safe. That's all that matters."

Franklin leaned against the doorframe and crossed his arms. He looked at his brother. "The doctor said you'll live. Expect to be sore as the dickens for a week or two." The side of Franklin's mouth turned up in a teasing smile, but Barton noted the weariness in his eyes. "Seems you were close enough when Stafford fired that the bullet went clean through."

His mother blanched. "Oh, Harrison."

"I will be fine, Mother." He glanced at Elizabeth and saw her smile matched his own. "In fact, I consider myself to be among the most blessed of men. Elizabeth has agreed to be my wife."

His mother's eyes widened in shock. She stood, and Franklin moved to her side. "Come now, Mother, 'tis really no surprise," Franklin said. "Clarke, would you be so kind as to have a tea tray sent to Mother's room?" With a smile Clarke left to make the request, and Franklin returned his attention to his mother. "Let's get you settled." She spoke not a word as Franklin led her from the room.

Haskins chuckled and wrapped an arm around Bethany. "Come, Thomas, let us see how Brownbeard fares." Thomas did not need prodding. He jumped up and ran from the room. Bethany and Haskins followed.

"Mother took that rather well," Barton said once he and Elizabeth were left alone.

Elizabeth's smile warmed Barton's heart. He felt that Father Time had paused existence for a tiny moment. Every care and pain he possessed halted and hung in the air. He motioned for Elizabeth to come near, and the moment she did he kissed her again.

"I love you," Barton said.

"And I love you." Elizabeth raised a hand to her colored cheeks.

"Whether a tree falls on you . . . or you collide into me at the apothecary." Elizabeth's eyes widened in mock offense. "You, sir, ran into me."

Barton grinned. "Perhaps. But I cannot apologize for it." Elizabeth playfully swatted Barton's uninjured arm. "I will love you, and I will be your escape"—Barton leaned forward, wrapped his good arm around her waist and pulled her close—"Always." And then he kissed her again.

About the Author

CHALON LINTON WAS FIRST INTRODUCED to the Regency era by a dear friend, and now she can't get enough of handsome men in tailcoats. Chalon's intrigue in the genre stems from a nostalgic longing for manners, wit, and true love.

Fortunately, she found her dashing gentleman, married him, and now lives happily ever after in Southern California.

You can learn more about Chalon's books at https://chalonlinton.com.